RAFFERTY STREET

Lee Lynch

New Victoria Publishers

Published by New Victoria Publishers, Inc., a feminist literary and cultural organization, PO Box 27, Norwich, VT 05055-0027

Cover design Claudia McKay
Back cover photo by Christopher Briscoe

Printed and bound in Canada
First Edition

1 2 3 4 5 2002 2001 2000 1999 1998

Library of Congress Cataloging-in-Publcation Data

Lynch, Lee, 1945–
        Rafferty street / Lee Lynch.
            p.   cm.
        ISBN 0-934678-93-6
        I.   Title.
PS3562. Y426R34   1998
813' .54– – dc21

                                                          98-6890
                                                            CIP

DEDICATED TO THE MEMORIES OF:

Valerie Taylor, a woman of peace, a good friend and mentor.

Terri Jewell, a passionate writer.

Michelle Abdill and Roxy Ellis, may they be forever out and loving.

Linda D'Orio, a devoted friend, and an athlete at anything she did.

Six-pack between us, recovery ahead, we shifted up and down those glorious Valley hills many a sunny Saturday.

MY DEEP GRATITUDE TO:

Akia Woods, my partner, for your unshakable faith in my work.

Anthony Johnson for your language and culture.

Kate Ryan for convincing me I'm a writer.

Jennifer di Marco, Amy Candela, Garbo, Lesléa Newman and Joan Nestle for breathing life back into my spirit.

Suzanne Pharr, Marcy Westerling, Kathleen Saadat and Sky for your courageous and life-changing work.

Mary Byrne, Midge Stocker, Loraine Edwalds—and all the dear women at the National Women's Music Festival.

Robert Collins at the Chelsea Public Library.

Barb Byes for her help with Lorelei and the Herb Farm.

CF & Deb Lovely for indulging my passion for wandering Morton River Valley.

Bobby Jo and the rest of the crew at The Factory.

Spock, my cherished Volvo.

CHAPTER 1

Annie whistled through her bus route. Her team had actually won its first game the night before. That seemed to clinch the rightness of her move to the Valley. Besides, in a spring that had been unusually wet and chilly, this was a glorious daffodil-bright early May day and she was back in shape, just achy enough to know she'd played ball.

"You're happy, Annie," said Lorelei, leaning over her seat, flipping Annie's softball cap around so the brim was backwards. Annie righted it.

Lorelei Simski was her favorite passenger, a high-spirited white twenty-year-old with Down's Syndrome who insisted on hugging Annie on sight. Scrupulously clean though often in mismatched clothing, Lorelei was well under average height and round as a beach ball. She had thick glasses and wore her blonde hair in a Dutch boy cut.

"Sit back down and buckle up, Lor," she said, tempering her ferocious New York cabbie tone. This was Lorelei's most aggravating habit. Once she was out of her seat, the rest of the riders tended to follow.

"Whistle some more, Annie!"

"Yeah, Annie, rock 'n roll!" urged Errol, with slurred words. Errol, her second favorite, was a bright, twenty-eight-year-old, six foot black man with communication disorders and an ability to learn only visually.

"Are you in love?" Lorelei asked.

"Annie's in love!"

A wolf whistle was followed by other teasing.

"Annie's not in love," she told them.

"What's his name, Annie?" someone asked.

"What's her name?" asked Errol, sending most of the riders into giggles.

"Can it," Annie shouted. The silence was total. Had she

overdone it again? In the rearview mirror she saw Lorelei pulling a long face.

She shook her head and pulled into the Old Herb Farm parking lot. The Farm was one of the businesses of New Way, Inc., an agency that worked with developmentally disabled people. Some workers made window boxes, large deck planters and wooden composters, others packaged seeds, dried and batched herbs for teas or worked the gardens, planting, harvesting and preparing flats for sale in local nurseries. Annie contentedly transported workers who weren't on the regular bus routes, delivered products to the surrounding cities and towns and rotated from one department to another, covering for absent trainers and supervisors.

After all those years in New York, where she'd grown an armadillo hide, the job had seemed exactly right. It had never been her intention to be a cab driver all her life. She'd wanted to do some good in the world, but never could figure out what she had to offer. And she'd never found it until she'd left the craziness of New York to move to Morton River Valley where so many of her old friends had been putting down roots.

At the Farm she'd immediately been drawn even to the most recalcitrant of the workers, seeing in them the frustrations and moods she hid. Now, though, Lorelei's behavior was stirring things up and Annie seesawed between squelching her and being the pussycat she'd been in her younger years.

She turned around to face her little gang. "It's softball season. That's all."

Lorelei immediately perked up and boasted, "We're on the same team, Annie and me. We won yesterday. I'm bat girl!" she shouted, swooping at the others.

Errol yelled, "I'm Batman!"

There was a great commotion as some of the riders clamored to come to the next game. "Okay, okay," Annie said. "I'll ask Judy."

Judy Wald was the director of the Farm, a scattered woman of boundless energy. Judy might be able to organize such an after-work outing.

Annie was whistling again during her break as she strolled to Judy's office. She shrugged out of her ancient shit-kicker black leather jacket. Lorelei was right, of course, something more was going on with her than just softball season.

Today was her forty-second birthday. She had a comfortable home, a great roommate, a job she loved, friends. And maybe Jo. She couldn't get over how she was becoming involved with a bank manager—or that she was getting involved at all after Marie-Christine. She'd always had a love-hate relationship with love—afraid of being trapped in a bad marriage, lured by the concept of forever. But the thought of Jo Barker's long upper lip turned up at the corners, of that sultry elfin look, made her smile.

She swaggered to a stop, straightened her blue and green striped rugby shirt, snapped a loose thread from her way-faded loose fit jeans and presented herself in Judy Wald's doorway.

"Annie!" said Judy, jumping, eyes wide, obviously startled.

"Didn't mean to spook you, Judy."

"I was about to come find you, as a matter of fact," said Judy, a look of desperation behind thick glasses.

I'm in for it now, Annie thought. Judy had spoken with her before about being gentler with the workers. It was hard switching from the dregs of humanity she'd sometimes ferried around New York to these innocents.

Judy's long hair, as always, was disheveled, whole corkscrews of grey rebelling from a leather barrette. She wore a faded and slightly frayed tan cardigan that looked as though it had once been expensive. Her button-down shirt was patterned with tiny ducks, its shirttails threatening to escape her khaki slacks. All her clothing looked too big on her. "I don't know what to do. Sit down."

Annie helped herself to a sourball from the dish Judy kept on her desk and unwrapped it as she dropped into a chair. Judy was a comfortable, caring boss. Despite her apparent disorganization, she'd made a success of the Farm and was expert at squeezing funding from every available source—and then finding new resources. Her staff was devoted to her. She'd cut Annie some slack.

"You look worried," Annie told her. She held the unwrapped sourball in her fingers. "Is there a fiscal crisis? A layoff? I knew I shouldn't have let myself get so attached to the workers." She knew she was talking from nervousness, but couldn't stop herself. "Did I ever tell you what it was like, driving a cab, Judy?"

7

Annie said.

Judy looked at her in a confused way. Annie plunged on.

"Dispatch was always giving me a cab with broken air, because I was the white girl driver. So I'm out at JFK, windows wide open, trying to pull around a bus, and this crazy-looking guy—I mean, dirty, scraggly beard, bloodshot eyes—sticks a gun in my window, square against my head." She mimed a pistol with her fingers and jabbed against her cheekbone.

"How awful!" Judy said, staring at Annie.

"He's asking for my cash when I feel this wet stuff on my cheek. Understand, I'm just about peeing my pants and I'm wondering did he already shoot me? Is this blood? Then I get it. The jerk's holding me up with a water pistol! The bus found a place to pull over and I'm out of there."

"Did you report him?"

"I radioed it in. Never heard anything. All in a day's work."

Judy snapped her focus back to her search. "I know I put that note here somewhere. I didn't want anyone else to see it." She shuffled through piles of paper, picked up the phone and peered under it, then looked beneath her desk. She pawed through her waste basket. "I must have hidden it well." Annie's anxiety was building. She put the sourball in her pocket. "Oh! In your file! I hid it in your personnel file."

Annie lay her jacket on her knees and leaned her elbows on it, waiting.

Finally Judy sat behind her desk again, drumming her fingers. "This just doesn't feel right." Judy moved in her wheeled office chair around her desk to face Annie. "I got a phone call this morning. First thing. I don't think my eyes were even open yet. I'm never ready for unpleasantness."

The ducks on Judy's blouse seemed to swim as Judy shifted positions. "Do me a favor, Judy? Just get to the point? You're weirding me out."

"I try not to interfere with the personal lives of the staff, Annie, but I have to deal with this."

Annie's mind raced from one absurdity to another. Something's happened to Marie-Christine. No. Why would she call me—she's probably got half a dozen new lovers. My parents were caught in cross-fire between drug gangs.

"What, Judy, what?"

"Were you out at Division Field last night?" Judy's lips were tight, her eyes troubled.

"Yes. We had a softball game."

"Was Lorelei Simski there with you?"

"Not with me. She's bat girl for the team."

"A Mrs.," Judy consulted the scrap of paper she'd pulled from Annie's file, "Norwood called to say that she saw you kissing Lorelei."

"Bullcrap!"

"And touching her in ways that were what she called not normal."

"No way, José! What kind of a sicko does this woman think I am?"

Judy winced at the onslaught of Annie's anger.

Annie softened her tone. "I know what she saw. That's one reason I'm here. Lorelei did kiss me. On the lips." She tried to keep her nose from wrinkling. "It was too quick for me to stop. Lorelei's always hugging me and she's been getting more and more disruptive."

"Tell me more," Judy urged.

"According to Dusty, Lorelei's been a major fan for years, if sometimes for two opposing teams in the same game."

Judy smiled at that.

"Ever since Lorelei got the bat girl position, she's been off the wall. Last night, as the game was starting, she flung herself at me, which I'm used to, but instead of hugging me, she kissed me. I about fell over. She was gone before I could give her hell."

"Do you spend a great deal of time with Lorelei outside work?"

"Of course not. I hang at Dusty's Diner. Lorelei lives next door to the owner. Dusty sponsors our team and Lorelei's been bugging her for the bat girl job. Dusty and Elly are Special Olympics sponsors partly because they know Lorelei."

Judy crossed her legs. "In other words, it was true."

"That's not what I said! It's not the way you make it sound, Judy. Geez." Her shirt was soaked under her arms.

"That's the other problem. The woman who reported this accused the whole team of being lesbian. That you have no business putting a developmentally disabled woman among lesbians."

She thought of Maddy and her outrageous buttons. Why else would someone label the whole team gay? The other players were closeted. Oh, maybe some people had figured it out, but if the team had been flagrant, they'd probably have been thrown out of the league. Even she, with her loose-limbed walk, the face she'd been told all her life was so open and friendly, her medium height, just-this-side-of-chunky weight—even Annie looked "normal" to most people.

"Judy! I can't believe this is you talking! Do you think, even if there are gay women on the team, that they, I—" She couldn't imagine what a non-gay woman would imagine.

"No. No," Judy answered. "Mrs. Norwood obviously has a problem on this subject, poor woman. And she knows Lorelei's background. You can see how that would make the woman even more upset."

"I can?"

"I suppose I ought to tell you the whole story."

"I'd appreciate it," Annie replied, swallowing her rage, "because I'm getting a little bit insulted here."

"If Lorelei were bat girl for a men's team and this had happened, I'd have to ask these questions."

"But we're not men, for cripes' sake. Do you think we abuse women the way men do? Are you accusing me of molesting Lorelei?"

Judy was quiet for a moment. "It's not simply a matter of what I think. It's the people who give us money I have to be accountable to." She retreated behind her desk. "You know that Lorelei's adoptive parents had a birth daughter who also had Down's Syndrome."

"This is news to me."

"No one reviewed worker files with you? Why didn't you ask?"

"Me? I'm only the driver and the pinch hitter."

"Annie, our workers aren't cab fares. Every Farm employee is a big part of their lives."

"So it's my fault now."

"No, but I wish you'd known Lorelei's story. The parents found out a few years before their birth daughter died that the two young women had a lesbian relationship. They moved the girls into separate rooms, but they'd sneak in together. Finally the parents put Lorelei in a group home. About ten months later the sister died. Lorelei was despondent for two years. It took a lot of counseling to persuade her that her sister didn't die because she left. She was just coming out of it when you arrived. I should have warned you, Annie. She's probably looking for a new 'sister.'"

"So that's why she's so hyped on me."

"Why didn't you tell me?"

"First, I was just about to. Second, I don't know how developmentally disabled people are supposed to act! I wasn't going to make a big thing out of everyday behavior."

"Unfortunately, it is a big thing. Because of same-sex institutionalization and segregation in group homes to avoid pregnancy, because there are some rules—values Mrs. Norwood would call them—that you can't instill in someone with an I.Q. this low, there can be promiscuity." She smoothed out the scrap of paper and seemed to reread it. "I can't afford to have such an accusation made of our staff, Annie. Maybe if you were a married woman—"

"Are you canning me?"

"I'd like to put you on administrative leave until we sort this out. I'm afraid I can't pay you if you're not working."

"But this Norwood woman is way far out in left field."

"I don't know you, Annie. You seem reliable, if sometimes a little rough on the workers."

"I'm working on that, Judy."

"That's all I know about you, Annie. You've only been here a few months—"

Annie was hanging onto her jacket like it could absorb her anger. "If you're doing this to me because I'm a dyke—you want me to resign? Just go away? Why don't you just fire me?"

"I'm not doing this to you, Annie, I'm doing it for the Farm. You don't know this community. This could destroy us. The Farm gives so much to the workers. Do you want me to risk that?" Annie didn't want to admit that almost made sense.

"Why not just talk to Lorelei?"

"I have, over and over through the years. Lorelei's behavior isn't controllable. She'll remember how to act for months at a time and then—something like this. The only reasonable solution I can see is to remove you from the situation. Your good name is as much at stake as the Farm's. I'd think you'd want to get out of this difficult position."

"I don't believe this. Listen, Judy, I dropped out of a community college in Boston when I was a kid. Back then being gay was practically all-consuming. The hiding, trying to meet girls, finding places to go, drinking in the bars. I couldn't juggle school, supporting myself and the gay life. I've been a cab driver, driving in circles, ever since. Then I took all those philosophy courses in New York to figure out my life, but talk about circles! I came to Morton River to change that. I didn't know how exactly, but when I got this job I knew it was right."

Judy smiled, her expression full of regret.

"Am I whistling into the wind here? For the first time I feel like I'm not drifting. Like I can make a difference. The workers—they're important to me. I believe in what the Farm's doing. I've been thinking of taking some night classes in September, starting on a degree in Special Ed. It'd be a long haul, but maybe I can use some old credits. I thought I finally knew where I was going. And now—I just don't believe this. Everyone said you were so fair."

"I like to think I am. You're able-bodied, smart and have some education. These people need my protection—you don't."

Judy's eyes were averted. "I visited a friend, my ex, in Oregon just before the election last fall. The look of exhaustion in Vicky's eyes still haunts me. This is exactly the reason Vicky fought that anti-gay ballot measure out there, so a dyke didn't have to walk away from her dreams without a whimper." Hell if *she* would give up after seeing Vicky fight, Annie told herself.

She stood so forcefully her chair rolled back and smashed against the wall. "This is not okay, Judy. I haven't done a damn thing wrong and I am not interested in being a silent victim. I care about those folks. They've brought me some kind of sunshine I didn't even know I was missing. Maybe this poses a sticky ethical problem for you, but I'm a person, not a dilemma."

Judy opened her mouth, extended a hand, then dropped it and shook her head. "I'm not firing you, Annie."

"No, you're forcing me out, hoping I'll slip through the door, tail between my legs, and take all this trouble with me."

"Only for the sake of our workers."

Annie bit her bottom lip. "Well, I'm out of here before I say too much. You have my number and I'll be back at work the minute I hear from you."

"I can't—" Judy faltered as Annie flung the door open and stalked down the hall, shoving her arms into her jacket sleeves.

Outside, the New England spring seemed absurd, like a travel poster in a famished country. The reek of thriving herbs turned her stomach. She took the sourball from her pocket and threw it as hard as she could across the road.

In her car, she gunned toward town, tires complaining as she leaned into curves where the road hugged the Morton River. She got stuck at the railroad crossing while a never-ending freight train rolled by. It was then that she felt the wetness on her cheeks, like Judy'd held a leaky water pistol to her head—and this time she'd really been robbed. She pulled off to the side and abandoned the car to stalk through the weeds along the tracks.

Between two factories she could see the back of Dusty and Elly's diner. Across the river from it were the narrow backyards of Rafferty Street. Tufts of grass clung tenuously to the river's banks. No wonder this section had flooded so badly in years past, she thought, blotting her tears with a sleeve. Nothing was holding it together. The river could flush the diner, Gussie's house— Annie's home now—out to sea.

Crap, moving to Morton River Valley was supposed to be a solution, not a catastrophe. She'd never been fired for any reason, much less being gay, yet four months in the Valley and here she was out on her ass. What would the workers think when she didn't show up? This could be another trauma for Lorelei.

She picked up a stone and pitched it far out into the river, rehearsing how she'd tell Gussie.

CHAPTER 2

"Uh-oh, you've caught me in the act!"

Red-faced, forehead damp with sweat, overall bib flapping open and hands knotted around a mop handle, Augusta Brennan looked as rickety as the river banks that held up her home.

Annie scolded, "I thought we agreed I'd wash the floor tonight. You're going to have one of your dizzy spells, fall and end up in the hospital."

"You're mother-henning me again, Socrates. This is part of your birthday present. Besides, I have nothing to do but watch the flowers on the wallpaper fade. I used to like to come home and relax after a rough day juggling other people's riches."

"No problem," Annie said, flinging her cap onto the table and herself onto her chair. She was ashamed to meet Gussie's eyes. "I'm not working."

Gussie straightened, carefully leaned the mop against the wall and sat across from Annie. Her eyes, under slackening lids, were grave. "What's happened?"

Annie took off her driving glasses and put them in their case. No more tears. She took a long quivering breath. "You haven't known me very long, Gus. I can only swear to you, dyke's honor, it isn't true. Judy as much as accused me of molesting a worker."

Gussie's face reddened.

With a bitter smile, Annie said. "Happy birthday, Annie Heaphy."

Gussie sputtered, "You? That's impossible!"

"Thanks. I needed to hear that."

"Don't tell me," Gussie said, laying a hand on Annie's, "you thought I'd believe such a thing?"

Annie shrugged, more relieved than she'd expected to be, then gave her details, getting angrier as she watched Gussie's response.

"These arrogant breeders!" growled Gussie.

14

"I thought you liked straights."

"Please! No straight at a women's softball game is going to go bananas over there being gay players. It's common knowledge. Who made this complaint?"

"Some woman named Norwood."

"It sounds familiar. Where do I know that name from?"

Annie picked up her cap and twisted it around and around. "One minute I'm settling right in, the next I'm on the convicted sex offender list."

Toothpick, the stray kitten who had been a going away present from friends in New York, padded into the kitchen and stretched. Annie knelt to stroke her. Toothpick wouldn't care if she were a child molester.

Gussie used the kitchen table to push herself up, then moved stiffly to the sink and gazed out the window. Without her teeth in, Gussie's face had a defeated look. She had retired to the Valley after a lifetime of crisscrossing the country as accountant at one factory, auditor at another, office manager in a sprawling food mill. Her last position had been with Rafferty Brass when the employees bought the company to try, unsuccessfully, to save it. Gussie had plenty of experience with crazy-ass complaints.

"I don't know what to do," Annie said, tugging on her hat. "I don't think Judy really believes this Norwood character, but Judy's stuck between a rock and a hard place. She says this is just temporary. What do I know about small towns? Do you think she'll take me back?"

"You shouldn't even have to be worrying about this," Gussie said, watching the sparrows peck at the window feeder. "I've been through it enough, we've all been through it enough." She faced Annie. "It shouldn't be so terrible today, but this is the consequence. We hid; you pay the piper."

"Gus, it's not your fault."

"Isn't it? What if I'd joined the Daughters of Bilitis in the 1950s? Told the officers at the war plant that I was a little funny? The suppliers and the workers would have gone without pay if I'd been fired, some soldiers without equipment. Even so, back then being homosexual was such a terrible thing we didn't dare say the word aloud."

"Hey, it's not like you're my Mom. You don't have to regret

how you brought me up."

"Maybe I do, Annie. I never had children, never cared about future generations, but you, young Maddy, Paris, Peg, and poor Dusty and Elly with their troubles, you do such a good job sticking up for yourselves. I wish I could say you got your backbone from me." She filled the tea kettle. "Maddy even calls me Gramma Gus. I should have my title revoked."

"The time wasn't right for you back then."

"Does it feel right for you, now? You told me this job could lead to a career for you."

Annie wandered to the window too, her anger replaced by a regret. "Maybe I was moving too fast. But I finally felt like I'd started my real life. What can I do?"

Out the window Rafferty Street seemed cozy and familiar—as it had every weekday since she'd arrived just after Christmas. Traffic droned along Route 83; the butterscotch cat next door cleaned himself in a sunny window. In the vacant lot at the end of the street young men in t-shirts, jeans and boots slouched against cars. Inside, safe from their usual catcalls and guffaws, she was reminded of vultures circling in old westerns, telltale scavengers patiently awaiting the hero's downfall.

Annie felt sweaty. She took her napkin and patted her face dry. "It's never felt real to me before. I always knew we were hated and feared by some people, but when have I had to feel it? Catcalls on the street? Avoiding certain places, not taking someone home for the holidays? It's always been my choice, on the surface, whether to be out or to expose myself. But this—it's funny."

"Funny as a piece of string."

"What happened today was just what I've been expecting all my life. I wonder if it's why I never got serious about anything. I knew some ignorant stranger would come along and pull my covers because I'm gay."

"Annie—"

"Look at Vicky's ballot measure. Maddy's idea about a gay group at the high school getting shot down. The fight's not over by a long shot."

"It's like what they say about child abuse, isn't it?" said Gussie. "All it takes is one generation to end the cycle."

She looked outside again. "Look at the tough guys up the

street. I've seen badder twelve-year-olds on Times Square. And they think they're better than us. They think we're so scared of being knocked down that we won't stand up in the first place."

Gussie attempted at a laugh. "Used to be I always left when people were getting too close. It was better to start new somewhere else than to have a Mrs. Norwood find out about me. But you're not running, Socrates. You're going to stand up to them because it's not over 'til it's over."

"I wish we'd won. I wish Gay Lib had already changed the world," Annie said with a tired sigh. "I sure hope I don't have to make trouble to get reinstated."

"Maybe there's something we can do to make sure you don't have to." Gussie was pensively silent for a moment, then grinned. "Or at least don't have to do it alone."

Annie looked with tenderness at the thoughtful face over the plentiful breasts and paunch. Gussie's hair was a feathery cap of white which she'd mussed in agitation, leaving cowlicks at the crown. Round tinted glasses rested on her ruddy cheeks.

"Judy's a mouthpiece—she told me so. If she wants money for the Farm from big-buck johns she has to follow their rules just like some hooker over by the docks. I didn't let that stuff go on in my cab—why should I put up with it here?"

"We shouldn't."

"We?"

"Don't put me out to pasture yet, dear girl," Gussie said.

"Sorry, Gus. I was doing it again."

"Yes, you are. I still remember the first time you came in out of that blizzard like a lost soul who didn't need an old woman like me in her life."

"Your tone wasn't exactly friendly either," she reminded Gussie.

"I was about as anxious to take on someone new as you were."

"And I suspected you were enjoying being coddled."

"When the new girl in town should have been getting the attention?"

"It didn't take you long to thaw me out."

"And lure you into my den."

That first day, Annie had looked out the chilly kitchen window while Maddy and Gussie talked.

Annie felt cold remembering that winter day. Beyond the railroad tracks, across the river, the diner had been a shadow with a pinkish glow around it. She had imagined the whispery sound of the snow as it hit the river, a split-second wet kiss as it became water and joined the rush to Long Island Sound. A train came inching past the back of the house, its one large bright eye spot-lighting a horizontal column of snowflakes. It hooted over and over through the darkness, calling to her just like the trains of her childhood along the Chelsea River. She'd shivered then, too, missing what had once, happy or not, been home.

It had been hard to swallow her excitement back when when she'd first arrived in the Valley, but she'd come to a community in mourning. Nan Heimer, a woman who'd begun her first lesbian relationship at age seventy-seven, had died just before her ninth anniversary with Augusta Brennan, two years her junior. The funeral had been held the day Annie pulled into town. No one had had time for a newcomer.

Only a few days after her arrival she'd been drawn into the care-taking circle that had sprung up around Gussie Brennan.

Maddy Scala, a seventeen-year-old burly baby butch, backwards New York Mets cap squashed down over rowdy curls, had lofted snowballs into the river below as she led Annie over the bridge from the diner on Railroad Avenue to Rafferty Street. There, emerging from a curtain of snow, had been the strangest row of little houses Annie had ever seen. Some enterprising builder obviously had squeezed all he could onto a narrowing plot of land, a ridge leaning over the river and the railroad tracks. Annie, beguiled, could see that each house was smaller than the one before it.

"This is one of the last streets in town that's still all cobblestone," Maddy had bragged.

Along the silent cobbled street thick maples bore their burdens of snow with stoic dignity. Across the street was a row of brick duplexes, each with an open porch, built for factory workers. Christmas lights glowed in one front window two weeks after the holiday. Rafferty Street officially ended about a hundred yards along at the weed and refuse-filled lot where, Maddy told her, some of the worst troublemakers in Morton River hung out.

Gussie Brennan's side of the street had obviously been the

pride of first generation home owners. Gussie's was the next to last house, built of rough yellowed stone, and looked like an odd fanciful playhouse. The front windows were lined with bric-a-brac. On one sill a luxurious Christmas cactus sported crimson blooms. This had been Nan Heimer's home with her husband. Gussie had inherited it and lived there alone, much to the consternation of the lesbians who fussed over her.

Then Maddy had led her through undisturbed snow around to the back, rapped on the door and they'd gone in from the storm to deliver a good meal to Augusta Brennan. Elly and Dusty might be having their problems, but they weren't letting that get in the way of helping Gussie through her grieving.

Gussie's warm kitchen, with its familiar creature comforts— art deco era appliances and cabinets, a vague scent of burnt toast, the occasional drip from the faucet, even the oilcloth table covering—had felt exactly like home.

Later, she'd asked to use the bathroom primarily to explore the allure of the little house. From outside the building had looked too small to turn around in, but the architect had kept walls to a minimum. The downstairs consisted of two large rooms, the kitchen and the narrower, knickknack-filled living room with laundry and bath at the wide end of the kitchen.

It was a snug, quirkily attractive warehouse of sights and smells from her childhood. She'd been surprised to feel such piercing nostalgia for her early years, filled as they had been with the icy silence of her parents, estranged in the home they shared. Annie had been one terrified little kid, afraid every hour of every day that she'd do something to make them as angry at her as they were at each other.

When Annie had come out of the bathroom Gussie had called tiredly, "Go on upstairs and look around, Annie. I'm not quite up to a nickel tour."

"Thanks!" she'd said into the warm kitchen doorway. "I love your place. This is just the sort of home I'd like someday."

Gussie had sighed. "The house feels terribly big just now. I have my friend Venita looking into the senior apartments on Bank Street where she is. This place may be on the market before long."

Annie dashed upstairs two steps at a time. There wasn't a snowball's chance in hell that she'd ever own a house again. The one she and Vicky had bought had been more of a rambling, falling apart beach shack than a house.

The second story was divided just like the first. One bedroom was filled with mismatched furniture. The other had a four-poster bed smothered in quilts. A decorative pillow radiated the scent of pine. This was a variation on her parents' three-decker house, but without the tension of unsaid angry words, without the atmosphere of impending doom.

A lovely old armoire matched an ornate dresser with an oval mirror. On one side was a photograph of a tall, plain-faced young woman with a gentle look about her eyes and smile. 'Class of '24' was scrawled in white pen across the bottom. On the other side Gussie, capped and gowned, laughed. There were more pictures, stories of two lives that had merged—Gussie and Nan together under the Dusty's Queen of Hearts Diner sign—in another, arm in arm at the edge of a softball field, game in play behind them.

Annie went back downstairs, running her hand lovingly along the banister. In the kitchen Gussie said, "I have a bad time with those stairs. I had a hip problem some years back and the climbing aggravates it. Still, I hate to leave our nest. All the grand memories I have here."

"What about renting out the upstairs, Gramma Gus?" Maddy had asked. Her face still held a child's softness, a breath-taking androgynous beauty.

"Where in the world would I find a congenial, honest soul who'd want to share a kitchen with an old codger like me? Who I could bear to have around watching me suffer the indignities of aging? And who'd be interesting enough to make it worthwhile?" Smiles and mourning flickered across Gussie's lined face.

Listening, Annie began to understand that what she had learned from the philosophy courses she'd dabbled in—trying to figure out what life was all about—paled next to these eighty-three years of lesbian life.

Maddy had introduced Annie as the ex-New York City cab driver who took philosophy courses for fun.

Gussie had turned to her with a dry laugh, "I don't know what to say to a philosopher. I had a friend once who'd explain the mysteries of life after a couple of highballs. We used to call her Socrates."

It had been as if, poking a respectful hole in Annie's persona, Gussie had demystified her own—the old widow woman. Annie hadn't known how to treat her and hadn't liked being introduced to old age and mourning.

Now, in the warmth of May, her memories brought a flush of affection for Gussie. "Okay," she said. "I give up. What do we do?"

"First," said Gussie, "you go down there and demand your job back. What are the laws in this state anyway? I was glad when I saw some law passed, but I didn't think I'd ever need to take advantage of it," confessed Gussie. She poured the tea. "One of the blessings of getting up there in years, Socrates, is that all old women look alike, even funny old women. The world thinks it's safe from us now."

"Ha! Safe from Gussie Brennan?"

"Keep it up, kiddo. You're good for my ego."

"Poor Lorelei."

"Why?"

"What are my riders going to think when I don't take them home this afternoon? Damn it, Gus, maybe I shouldn't make a career of Special Ed, but do you have any idea how good it feels—felt—not to be hustling eight, ten hours a day? Thinking of the minutes of my life as dollars, and measuring people by how much they tipped me? They weren't even people anymore, they were fares.

"The pigs who thought an invitation to their hotel rooms was tip enough. The high-rollers snorting coke in the back seat. The poor families stuffed in together on their way to emergency housing, paying with a welfare chit, some apologetic about having no money for a tip. The thieves who took my whole night's pay—and the next, by the time I got through at the police station. I liked driving a cab until it meant bullet-proof glass and checking the back seat for dirty needles." She whirled on Gussie. "I want this job. I want this life."

"Annie," Gussie said gently from the stove, "believe me. We're not helpless. Just to be sure, we'll call a great gaggle of people and we'll put our heads together."

"Right now all I want to do is go hide in my room. I came here to get my life together. What a downer."

"Do you want to be standing in some kitchen forty years from now knowing the time was right to end the cycle? This town's just the place to take on your demons. We're good at crises in Morton River. Have I told you about the flood?"

"And what about Jo! This'll blow her right out of the water. She can't afford to run around with me now."

Gussie gestured emphatically for her to sit. This was no time for one of Gussie's long stories, but Annie sat down anyway.

"A lot of workers came up from the south to Morton River Valley for the brass factories which ran, I'm told, day and night. Some of the migrants brought the Ku Klux Klan along with them."

Annie dunked her tea bag, feeling antsy, and challenged Gussie. "To New England? No."

"Oh, but New England introduced that sort of thing to America. Remember the Salem witchcraft trials? Remember forced busing in Boston, Sacco and Vanzetti? New England is where *The Scarlet Letter* was set, Socrates. In the Valley there were the blacks and the Italian and Polish Catholics trying to learn English—and the Klan kept them all in their places."

"The good news is that you don't have a front yard to burn a cross on."

"You don't hear much about the Klan in Morton River these days," Gussie went on, ignoring her, "but that old suspicious anger is rooted deep. When Dusty and Elly, bless their souls, bought the diner, unemployment was almost as high as it is now. Word spread that prosperous gays from the city were taking over, even though Dusty's a native and put together a lot of helicopter parts before she could start her own business."

Annie listened with horror as Gussie described the harassment of employees and customers, gay and straight, the arson, the intimidating atmosphere.

"Why didn't anybody tell me this before I moved here? Morton River was supposed to be safer than the city."

Spooning her tea bag onto a flowered saucer, Gussie went on. "The rains came. The river rose. Dusty and Elly turned the diner into flood headquarters, gave away food to the sandbagging crews, helped the Red Cross—how could people hate them after that?"

Gussie blew on her hot tea, sipped. "But the economy's gotten worse again. The Valley never recovered from the closing of

Rafferty Brass. The houses being prettied up by yuppies who work in New Haven are pushing prices beyond what the locals can afford. That old Klan way of thinking is looking for an enemy to punish."

"And yours truly moved to town in the nick of time," Annie said. "Just what I always wanted, to take on the Klan."

Nodding, Gussie agreed. "The time is right—the *Valley Sentinel* is blowing our horn for us with headlines about gays in the army or adopting kids, scaring the squares half to death."

"Incredible. This woman who saw Lorelei kiss me, she's just defending her turf?"

Gussie set her cup hard against the saucer, her expression a mixture of amazement and anger. *"That's who she is!* Mrs. Norwood is the wife of that popular fundamentalist preacher. When I was stuck at the old people's home with my banged-up hip, Mrs. Norwood made the rounds doing bible readings. I practiced every rusty cuss word I know to get her to leave me alone. A royal pain in the derriere, though I know she was trying to do good."

"Worst case scenario," Annie said with disgust. She crumpled up a piece of junk mail and tossed it savagely toward the trash can where it bounced and fell into Toothpick's water dish. "I wasn't only in the wrong place at the wrong time, but I was there with the wrong person. Norwood must have a darling daughter on the other team."

"Her little darling. Mama keeps her hair long, femmes up the child's uniform—but that little tomboy has great promise— and I don't just mean in sports!"

"Serves them right."

"Have some more of this soda bread while it's still hot, Socrates. If I'm going to get my share, I'd better put my teeth in." She went toward the bathroom with a lively step.

Annie laid her head on her arms at the table. Toothpick pushed onto her lap. "You ready for this, tiger? Let's get 'em," she whispered to the little tabby.

When she'd visited her ex, Vicky, last fall, they'd driven from Eugene, where Vicky had her law practice, to the Oregon coast. They'd stayed for the gold and lavender October sunset—but not for the romance of it—they'd gracefully relinquished that part of their bond long ago.

The air had been damp and Indian-summer soft, smelling faintly but pleasantly of rotting sea vegetation. Pelicans had skimmed the waves, flanked by reeling gulls. She'd pulled the brim of her tweed cap tighter over her shaggy blonde hair and squinted at the glorious molten ball slowly immersing itself in the Pacific Ocean.

"I'd love to have you move here, Annie," said Vicky, stray silver obvious in the soft sweep of her short hair, sunglasses shading her eyes from the fiery sun that sat blinding and vaporous on the horizon. They were both past forty now, but Vicky had entered adulthood with more finality than Annie, who had flown out both to recover from her break up with Marie-Christine and to decide whether to leave New York.

Vicky went on, "You could stay with us until you got a job and a place. The way you attract women, you'd make the home you want within a year. The East Coast is in its death throes from crowds, dirt and pollution. It's making you so morose."

"Vicky," Annie had said, exasperated, "it suits me. I thrive on adrenaline highs. I'm not a laid back West Coast person."

Victoria Locke had lifted her sunglasses and Annie had searched those eyes, so troubled and fatigued-looking this year. But the law agreed with Vicky, gave her a framework for the world, a careful way of speaking that still seemed more about caring than caution.

Eugene had been tempting—until this year's visit. She'd argued, "These loony-tune right-wingers are trying to stuff you back in the closet. It doesn't much matter if you beat them at the polls; I don't think I could live in a place where the election signs and the newspaper headlines make it so clear how much I'm hated for wanting to puke at the thought of sex with men. I can see what a toll it's taken on you."

That night, in Vicky and Jade's guest room, she had wavered, hating as always to be parted from her best friend, but in the morning, as Vicky drove her to the airport through the darkness, she saw again that the lawns were a battleground of pro-and anti-gay signs. The heater had roared hot air, but Annie couldn't stop shivering. "Crap, Vicky, this is like seeing swastikas along the streets. It should be illegal." No, she'd decided. She'd take east coast boogeymen over this any day.

She lifted her head from her arms. Toothpick was nosing around the soda bread. She gave her a scrap. "I wonder," she asked the kitten, "if it would be better to live where you could name your enemies?"

Toothpick licked and nibbled through half the slice. Annie shredded her napkin and decided to move back to New York and be a cabbie again, go out to Vicky in Eugene, to some anonymous Midwestern city to start her own cab company, to the southwest where she would sell her little car and take the Amtrak anywhere it went. Was there a safe place for her on earth?

Satisfied, Toothpick circled on her lap and nested. Silently, Annie argued with Judy, then agreed with her decision to protect the Farm, then took her to court, then rescued Lorelei and Errol with her own agency, then begged for her job, or found a way to go back to school full time and decided that getting in trouble was a sign that she should move back to Chelsea and care for her ailing parents. She couldn't help but laugh at the thought that Chelsea, home sweet home to her parents' bitter marriage, might turn out to be safer than anyplace else.

Toothpick purred. Normally Annie would go upstairs and put on a jazz piano tape to soothe herself, but she wasn't up for diversion. Vicky had accused her of having turned into a sad sack.

"When," Vicky had asked, "was the last time you howled at the moon?"

"You remember that?" Annie had asked with delight.

"Could I forget? When we lived in our little toothpick house I'd watch you race over to the beach barefoot in all kinds of weather and streak along the sand baying your heart out into the night."

She was right, it had been a long time and it looked like it would be a long time again.

Gussie had wet down her cowlicks and come back patting them into place.

"Working with people at the Farm," she told Gussie with an incredulous smile, "forced me to be playful again, to laugh at how serious I'd gotten during that long struggle to keep Marie-Christine—to keep my head together in that wacked-out cabbie job."

The newspaper arrived with a thwack at the front door.

Annie brought it in and slouched over the want ads. "Hairstylist, Mold Maker, Motel Housekeeper. Maybe I could do that. No, it's in Upton. The commute would eat my wages. Nurse's aide, cafeteria help—even they want experience. I should advertise in the Work Wanted column—middle-aged dyke, recently canned for decent behavior, entire work history driving cabs—looking for meaningful job where she won't be a threat to heterosexuality."

"Nonsense," Gussie said, calmly buttering her soda bread. "Right after lunch I'll round up our troops. You've already told me you've got what it takes to slug this out. You're not going to be an ostrich like I was all my life."

She groaned. "Gus, I came here to turn down the volume. You don't know what a horror show this is."

Across the table, snowy eyebrows furrowed over round glasses, Gussie looked, not like a timid ostrich, but like some ancient owl. "Oh, yes I do."

CHAPTER 3

"I don't think this is such great idea, Gus," she protested as they pulled into a parking space near the diner.

"My timing may be off at that," Gussie said, heaving herself up out of the old Saab and into the first fat drops of rain. Within seconds, the sky that had glowed so brightly all day opened like an upended bucket.

Inside, they shook rain off themselves and dripped the length of the tile floor to the round table at the far end of the diner. "A-mazing! Look at all these people!" Annie said, stepping back. Gussie grabbed her arm.

America Velasquez, the high school teacher Maddy had tapped for advisor to a stillborn gay student group, called out with a wide lipsticked smile, "Maddy twisted her mom's arm to baby sit my Grandkid for me. Here I am!" America taught Spanish and, Maddy reported, made her lessons lively with Puerto Rican culture.

"You're fantastic," Annie said.

Gussie told her, "America's furious."

Whispering, Annie asked, "Did you tell these people that *I* wanted them here?"

"Why not, Socrates? You can't fight this alone."

"Watch me."

Elly, skinny Elly with her permed and tinted hair, her green eye shadow and decorated nails, her old friend Elly from the bar days, hugged Annie very hard. She was southern femme to her very soul, gracious and demonstrative, with a hard edge born of growing up in a world that labeled her white trash. "You poor honey-pie. Dusty's mad at me, but I made her promise to join us if the kitchen slows down. I skipped Verne's art class for the first time ever. I wouldn't miss this for the world."

"Just like old times, El, except Turkey's still in New York. It's you, Peg, and me against the world."

"And the world hasn't won yet! Come see my new drawing!" Elly demanded, preceding her to the wall behind the cash register. Annie smiled at the striking likeness to her earlier view of the diner roosting above the Morton River and the railroad tracks.

"I can't believe you were this talented all along and nobody ever knew it."

"It was my little dream, like yours, remember? You wanted to start a free cab company to help disabled people go places and to keep women off the streets after dark?"

"Then Peg and Turkey went to grad school and you moved out here with Dusty—and Rosemary, remember her and Claudia?"

"Whatever happened to that weird Rosemary?"

Annie had to laugh. She assumed a painfully erect posture, pulled her hair back from her face as tightly as she could and made a thin-lipped sour face. In Rosemary's clipped tones she said, "I've begun a wymmin's bank in Oakland. With my husband's backing. He's more of a feminist than Gloria, Betty and Andrea combined!"

"Just like her!" Elly cried in glee. "But poor Claudia."

"No, she's still thriving on that lesbian farm out in the Midwest. See, you're all doing something with your lives. It wasn't 'til I started the job at the Herb Farm that I felt like I was finally helping somebody."

Dusty emerged from the kitchen, just out of Elly's sight, as Elly asked in a manner both coquettish and pleading, "Will you come to our opening? Verne set up a show for all her students. You'll like Verne, she's—"

"A home wrecker," came Dusty's low commanding voice behind them. She pushed her white overseas-style cook's hat to the back of her head. Her short hair, grown over her brow and collar, was still a rich auburn though she must, Annie calculated, be in her early fifties.

"Oh, now Dusty. She's not wrecking any homes. You're just jealous—" Elly inserted her little finger under Dusty's collar, "because I'm not spending every livelong second here with you."

Dusty backed away from Elly's finger. "You used to want to be here with me," Dusty grumbled. "Now it's Verne this and Verne that."

Elly's blush went pinker against her wan face. She glanced at Annie from the corner of her eye and gave a nervous chirp of laughter. "Dusty, honey, us wives of workaholics can't just sit home and wait. And I can't work all the hours you do. I fall apart."

"The diner's falling apart. You've had an order up here for five minutes," Dusty barked, slapping the plate she'd been holding onto the counter. She marched back to the kitchen. Normally the most affable of women, she hadn't even greeted Annie.

"Giulia's covering for me," Elly said snippily to Dusty's back, but delivered the sandwich, then pulled Annie back to the group. "You will come?" she whispered.

"Sure, El," she replied quickly, further shaken by this discord in the institution that Elly and Dusty had become. She tipped her softball cap down over one eye and went into the old Bogie routine they used to do at the bar. "Hey, sweetheart, come over to my place if you want to talk sometime."

Elly tossed make-believe locks off her face. "Talk is cheap, stranger. Make me a better offer."

"That's more like it," she told Elly with a laugh.

Maddy arrived and gave her an affectionate bump with a hip. A high school senior now, Maddy had lived as a gay street kid in New York for some months before a network of dykes found her. Annie had given her a ride back to Morton River, then returned to the Valley to visit again and again.

As the group gathered, Annie felt overwhelmed. She escaped into a quick reminiscence of the day she first went to Dusty's Diner with Maddy.

A snowstorm had been raging, creating a white world that should have been all pristine stillness, but instead had been filled with the muffled scurrying of panicked people trying to get where they were going before they couldn't move at all. A train hooted, gliding into the Morton River Station on frosted tracks. A few minutes later a small mob of people in business clothing rushed the parking lot.

"This is way cool!" Maddy had exclaimed as she let go a well-packed snowball that thumped the shoulder of Annie's parka. They had run into each other near the diner.

"Cool? I've give you cool!" she'd replied, grabbing snow from a drift and packing it hurriedly. She'd hurled it at Maddy.

"No fair! You've been playing New York softball," Maddy accused.

"I'll teach you this spring!" She'd aimed a merciless volley at Maddy who toppled into a snow bank at the side of the road.

"You're in deep doo-doo now, dude!"

"I think you like the falling best of all," accused Annie, menacing her with another handful of the still-cascading snow. She leapt and washed Maddy's reddened heavy-browed face with it. Maddy was laughing too hard to do more than wave a feeble protesting hand.

"You win," Maddy panted.

She dropped the snow, pulled Maddy up and brushed her off. Before she'd even let her go Maddy was bending, like the kid she was, to scoop up more snow.

"Busted!" shouted Maddy.

"Uncle!" cried Annie, worn out.

"That's auntie to you!" jibed Maddy, but the last snowball came in an acquiescent, half-hearted toss. "Okay, I win. You buy the hot chocolate."

"I think I'd better, from the looks of you." She rubbed her burning hands in her wet gloves and threw an arm over Maddy's shoulders. "Your feet are going to freeze up and break off. Why don't you wear boots?"

"I have better things to spend my money on, paisan," Maddy replied, her voice still half-child's, her face incredibly young-looking.

"Like what?" she asked.

"Like saving for college."

Annie's cheeks burned from walking into the wind-whipped snow. "That's where I was headed at seventeen," she told Maddy.

"What happened?"

"I dropped out."

"Because?"

"If I wanted to be myself at work, I had to take what I could get. By the time I paid rent and my bar tab, there was no money for tuition."

Maddy had walked by her side, silent, intently listening.

Annie remembered digging a soft flannel scarf out of her jacket and wrapping it around her neck and jaw, but her breath had turned the melted snow to tiny ice pellets that chafed her lips. "Anyway, Mad, you can really go places," she predicted. "You don't have to drown yourself in liquor to feel good."

"But I'm a trouble-maker," Maddy had replied with no small degree of pride. She seated her baseball cap more firmly on her curls. "Ask anybody. Miss Valerie says I'm so disappointed that nobody's tried to tar and feather me I'll be disruptive 'til they do."

"Way to go, Mad."

"Dig it. Before I ran away, you know, when you met me, I was new to being gay and nervous about letting on to anyone. When I came back and refused to live in the closet I thought I'd get beat up once a week. So I came out at school and guess what happened?"

"What?"

"Nada. Zip. Hey, cool, a couple of the kids said. And girls? They're practically lining up to go out with me. I mean, this is red neck Morton River. What's the story? I checked it out with Paris. She said that people know me, they know I'm no threat. Maybe I want to be a threat."

The noise level of the diner brought Annie back from that snowy day. She looked at Maddy. Under the buzzing stark fluorescent lights of the diner the kid didn't look like much of a threat. Giulia, Maddy's sister, stood over Maddy a tray of dirty dishes threatening to topple. "You're supposed to be helping Mama tonight," the waitress said.

"I will, I will, ditz-brain," Maddy said.

She confided in Annie, "Living with hets is the pits. Especially when they're nothing but closet cases like my sister." She mimed sticking a finger down her throat.

"Then why did you come back from New York?" asked Annie.

"Think about it, paisan. With a crop of raving newcomers joining Act Up New York every week? I can see all the activists rushing to Morton River to defend your job. This is where I belong."

"You're something else, Maddy," Annie said, grabbing the kid in a butchy half-hug.

Jo Barker rushed up to them before Maddy could agree. Tallish, in her late thirties, her light-brown hair stylishly-shaped, Jo wore a navy business suit with shoulder pads and a cinched waist. She was delicately made up, fresh-looking and stuck out like an orchid in a field of weeds.

"I'm sorry about this," Annie whispered to Jo. "Exactly what you always wanted, a high visibility, unemployed sweetie."

Jo gave her a smile that looked like it was left over from her last loan turn-down. "Can we get started?" Jo asked with her take-charge air.

Annie felt too conspicuously queer in her jeans and rugby shirt to sit beside Jo. Always with Jo Annie felt awkward, frustrated and puzzled by Jo's old-fashioned cold feet when it came to sex. But she couldn't complain. She didn't feel altogether ready either.

Elly asked, "When are you going to let me come up and draw your new little pot belly pig, Jo? That's something Verne might want to paint."

Jo's delight showed as she answered, "Just let me know. Rexie'll want me to put on her ribbon."

Paris spoke as she and Peg squeezed behind Jo to reach chairs. "Sorry we're late. Peg had to find a substitute referee for the basketball game in Upton and I had to cover my English-as-a-second language night class."

Paris and Peg had only been together about two years, but they fit in a way that gave them an air of permanence. Paris was an active environmentalist, adept at obtaining permits and giving press conferences. She was also a femme from Texas, with a seductive air that explained much of her success in public relations.

Peg had about three inches on Annie, and held her spare body very erect. "It's been a long time since we tried to change the world together, Heaphy," said Peg. Always the most reserved of the old gang, Peg had become an adult of few words and many generous gestures. She stayed close to her wealthy family, but insisted on keeping her teaching job and was quietly active—and influential—in what passed for gay politics in Morton River Valley.

"Ready to rabble-rouse?" Elly teased.

"I retired from rabble-rousing years ago," Peg lied.

Gussie quieted everyone with a tap of her water glass. "I won't embarrass Socrates by claiming that I called on all of you to help only her. What happened today affects every gay person

32

in the Valley. I want you to hear it from the horse's mouth..."
Someone gave a neigh that brought friendly laughter. "...and
then I want to come up with a plan. I won't stand still for this
kind of treatment any more and I imagine none of you will
either." Gussie gestured to her. "Start talking, Mr. Ed."

But Annie couldn't. "Gus, it's like saying it makes it true.
You tell it. I mean, there's as much shame in the accusation as
there would be if I'd done something."

"Annie," America said, "it's better to spit it out than to swallow this poison."

Jo gave a quick encouraging smile.

"Okay," she said and went through it again, remembering
details she'd forgotten in the first hasty report to Gussie. When
she was done she could hear the group exhale almost in one
breath. She realized that her shame had transformed back into
anger. A napkin lay shredded before her.

At the end of the table a compact woman with a halo of
springy-looking dark hair and quick eyes said, "That is such
bullshit. I'm Cece Green—that's Cece like in cease and desist,"
compact, street-tough Cece told those who didn't know her.
Beside her was tall, ungainly, shy Hope Valerie, a route checker
for the bus company. Both were on the diner softball team. "We
were right next to you when it happened, Heaphy. You looked
more like Lorelei hit you upside the head with a bat than kissed
you. It wasn't your fault."

Annie shivered in her clothes, still damp from the downpour.

"Of course it wasn't," America agreed sharply. "It's an attack
on my kids when they harass you for being gay. And two of mine
are gay."

"Listen," Annie told them, "I didn't come to Morton River to
cause you trouble. This sucks, but maybe, before it goes any further, I just ought to go back to the city."

"No way," Maddy said, offering her hand for a high five.
"You're a Valley girl now."

They all thought that was hilarious. Willie Nelson began *All
the Girls I've Known* on the jukebox.

"As another Valley girl," Jake said, pulling at his blonde
beard, "I know these are the same inhumane jerks who won't
fund AIDS research. They can't see beyond their own issues."
Dusty and Elly's pharmacist friend, Jake was still weak from a

first bout with pneumocystis, but unwilling to relinquish his role as the resident one-liner.

Peg suggested, "Maybe you don't want to work for a place that depends on funding from homophobes."

Annie protested, "It was a great job, except for the money. Everyone really cared. I felt proud to be helping."

"But you can't just take that sort of treatment. Let's picket, let the world know they discriminate," said a college-age woman in a hugely oversized violet and yolk-yellow sweatshirt. "I'm Jennifer," she explained. "Peg's cousin." Annie had heard of this flashy college baby dyke. Peg bragged that Jennifer had been the only out high school cheerleader in the history of the universe.

"Picket?" exclaimed Cece. "I can't afford to be throwing away my job."

Venita Valerie slapped the table. She'd come out of retirement to teach math at the Adult Learning Center.

"I'll join your picket line," Venita vowed in her whispery voice. "I was the first black teacher here in the valley and believe me, I made the white folks nervous. The principal was threatened, a few parents switched their kids to parochial school, but I kept getting up in front of that classroom and I've taught almost every Valley native their arithmetic. They got used to me."

"This whole deal is dumb." Elly had covered her napkin with drawings of tiny cups and saucers. "Does anyone know a good lawyer?" she asked.

"I have one," said Jimmy Kinh, flashing a bright set of dentures too hardy-looking for his delicate face. Jimmy O' and Jimmy Kinh ran the after hours place. "But I think he works for aliens only."

Annie said, "I feel like an alien."

Jimmy Kinh went on. "Before I meet Jimmy O'—"

"Met," Paris corrected.

"English teacher!" Jimmy chided with a shy laugh. "I used to have trouble finding work. This valley is very afraid of people who are not like them."

"But picketing?" Peg said, palms up and outstretched. "I know I come from conservative stock, but I've paid my dues on picket lines and this doesn't seem like the time or place. One of our friends is an ACLU attorney in Upton," Peg offered. "I'll call her tonight."

Jennifer, eyes bright with devotion to her cousin Peg, said, "With us in the family, Peg, the Jacobs aren't conservative stock any more. At least let's go to the media. Annie needs her job back now, not after a courtroom battle."

Maddy jumped from her seat and cried, "If they don't run the story, then we picket!"

"Whoa," said Paris. "First things first. We go to Judy Wald and tell her we're going to *The Sentinel*. If that doesn't stir things up we get more rowdy."

The older people shushed her.

"I am so tired of fighting the whole damned world," Jake said. He looked close to tears. "We have to fight for our jobs, fight for our lives. Get *over* it, breeders. People like us are here to stay."

Paris took his hand. "I'm certainly used to doing battle with this town on environmental issues. If we want to go that route, I know my way around City Hall."

Annie scowled. "I don't want to draw the workers into this. Parading around out there with TV cameras on them would disrupt the whole Farm operation."

"So," plainspoken, crewcut Jimmy O' asked, "does this bitch who runs the Farm have a supervisor?"

"She's not a bitch, Jimmy." Dusty, who had finally left the kitchen, said with calm authority. "We've worked together on the Special Olympics for years. She knows which end is up with gay people."

Elly nodded in agreement. "She's a real nice woman. Maybe it's P.M.S."

"Oh, come off it, Elly," said Maddy. "Was the fire at the Iranian family's house set because the guy with a match had a headache?"

As if there to settle the issue once and for all, Jo Barker shook her head and pronounced, "There's something going on that we don't know about. Paris called when I was in the middle of ten things and I'm sorry, I didn't make the connection between this meeting and the Farm. I'm chair of the non-profits division for the United Way drive this year. Tonight's the big meeting with agency heads, including New Way."

Everyone at the table turned to look at Jo. In the rest of the diner, cups hit china saucers, spoons scraped soup bowls, a little kid slurped through his straw. Several booths down, Giulia called out an order. Annie had never noticed Jo's worry lines before, the shadows in her eyes. Would she lose her over this before they even got started?

"As a matter of fact," Jo added, glancing at a thin gold watch, "I should be on my way to the meeting this second." She looked at Annie. "Talk about a rock and a hard place—they're all town bigwigs I can't be out to and expect to keep my career. Except for Judy." Jo's frown got deeper. "She knows. We've been friends since grade school."

"Enjoying small town life, Annie?" asked Jake. "It took about a millisecond to get the word out that this fairy pharmacist down at Valley Drug might exhale the breath of death on some customer's laxative."

Jo nodded. "I don't know how to deal with this at all, Annie, but I'll bring it up to Judy after the meeting." She rose and pulled a trench coat on, smiling her irresistible smile. "I wish I could stay long enough to buy you a birthday drink."

"I'll deal with this, Jo. I don't like putting you on the spot."

"Gay people are always on the spot," Jo said quietly, casting a nervous look at the people in the booths. She left quickly.

Cece Green leaned toward Annie, her black jacket hanging open over a Tina Turner t-shirt. In her hoarse voice she said, "Listen, just in case your pretty lady can't fix it, I work over at Medipak. I happen to know one of the girls is leaving. She told the boss today. It's only picking and packing, you know, shampoos and band aids, like that, but the pay's okay and we have a good time. Why don't you come in with me in the morning and see if they'll put you on?"

"That's an offer I won't refuse!" Annie exclaimed. "Thanks."

Gussie cleared her throat. Her eyes looked tired. "But you love the Farm job."

Cece answered for her. "Not enough to mess with this town. Like Miss Valerie says, they're dangerous when they don't like you."

"You can call me Venita now, Cece. Third grade was a long time ago."

"But you were still the only black teacher in my school, Miss Valerie. And I worked twice as hard because it was you."

"You see!" Maddy cried. "That's why it's so important. What if there's a gay worker at the Farm and Annie's their only—"

"Keep it down, Mad," Dusty warned with her kind firm smile. "You're right, though. We stood up to them once and won."

Maddy lowered her voice. "Of course I'm right," she said. "If you back down now, it's like—"

"—Why should anyone else ever fight?" finished Jennifer, frowning at Annie.

Annie was sweating. "I'm not backing off. I need a job to fight this. Begging isn't exactly a position of strength."

"That's my paisan!" Maddy exclaimed. "This is why I came back home."

"The law is with you," Paris said. "You can't be dismissed or lose your home for being gay in this state. Period."

"But she hasn't fired me," Annie reminded them. "She left me hanging on this administrative leave."

America spat her words. "What a crock."

"That's down right sneaky," Gussie said. "The one time I was terminated for being gay, the owner of the business called me a lezzie pervert and a blight on mankind. I said, If you're a prime specimen of mankind, then a blight's just what the doctor ordered. I walked out. He'd just caught me with his tres gay daughter."

When the laughter subsided Jake brought them back to business. "I hate to tell you, honey, but I have a bad feeling about all this. We don't live in a vacuum. The military had hissy fits about Clinton trying to lift the ban and the fundies are bellowing "Onward Christian Soldiers." Queer controversies won't blow right over in this ill wind. You may get to be a living breathing lesbian martyr."

Wasn't anyone listening to her? "Come on, Jake. Joan of Arc I'm not."

Cece broke in with a smile, "If you're talking the saint part, babe, we know, we know."

Despite the humor behind them, Jake's words had rung all too true. Her stomach churned. "Crap!" Annie said, yanking off her cap and slamming a fist into it. "Why me? I've spent my whole life tiptoeing through het minefields without setting one off, and now I'm the gay lib poster girl. Dirty pool."

"You're not alone," Paris said quietly.

"Maybe today, maybe even a year from now, but what'll my job be worth if families pull workers out or the funding dries up? And even you guys have to draw the line somewhere."

"You'll have a place to live as long as I'm around," Gussie promised.

"And food to eat," Dusty added.

Annie set her hat on Gussie's head with affection. "Do you really think I could live like that? It's not the seventies anymore. I've got some yuppie blood in me and reliving the revolution could get old pretty fast."

Maddy leapt from her seat again and moved to Annie. "Don't be such a downer, Heaphy, you'll be okay. We'll disarm those het mines together. This may be the best thing that ever happened to queers in the Valley."

Annie said, "I don't want to be too ageist, but remember how crazed we were to change the world, Peg? Remember, Elly? That was a long walk down a dead end road."

"But don't you see? It's so cool," exclaimed Maddy. "You guys opened the road up."

Gussie laughed. "I've a feeling you're going to lead the way now, child."

Maddy grabbed Gussie's arm. "You know what I bet, Gramma Gus? I bet if we'd had a contingent from Morton River at the March on Washington and showed our faces at a press conference, people around here might think twice about pushing us around."

"Get real! We're talking about one job here, not taking on the world," objected Cece, glaring at Maddy with one eye while the other, which was always unmoored, seemed to survey the group. "These people don't like queers, never have and never will."

Maddy ignored her. Her cheeks were flushed and she raised her arms over her head in a gesture of victory. "We'll have a press conference to announce that we're fighting back!"

"Press conference?" Annie repeated. "I'll stand up for my job, but I'm not into seeing my face on TV with some guy in a rug calling me an accused molester."

America said, "You know what I'm going to do? I've been thinking about this a long time. I'm starting a chapter of PFLAG. *We'll* have the press conference."

"Sign me up!" Venita said, almost loudly.

Annie looked at them. "You're right. PFLAG could do this."

Maddy said, "Excellent, but I want in too."

"You want trouble—that's what you want," accused Cece, snapping her fingers and pointing at Maddy.

"Being dumped and not fighting is collaboration," argued Maddy.

"Hey, I came here to simplify my life," Annie complained with a sigh. "Not to start Valley Gay Pride."

"But you did, Heaphy," said Dusty. "You just started it."

CHAPTER 4

The next morning at six-fifty, Annie tucked her cap under her front seat, squared her shoulders and marched across the Medipak lot toward the measuring stares of Cece's coworkers.

Before the Farm, discrimination had been only a faint possibility in her life, now it felt inevitable.

The heavy night rains had cleansed Morton River. Each leaf on the nearby trees sparkled in the early sun. Annie saw Cece park her candy-apple red motorbike next to Annie's purple Saab. Cece had a barreling walk and rumbled past Annie, helmet under her arm, saying, "Come on. And remember, you used to date my cousin Tyrone in New York."

"Hey, hold on. Date?"

Cece wore a Nelson Mandela t-shirt today. She fixed one eye on Annie and relented, "All right. You worked with him."

A few of the smokers gave Annie encouraging smiles as she followed Cece up a steep staircase to a simply furnished, painstakingly neat office.

"Kurt!" Cece barked. Kurt was a slight white man of about thirty-five, with precisely parted early grey hair and a tie. He turned to them and shook Annie's hand, surprising her with an engaging smile. "Ever done this before?"

"No," she replied, her voice strong considering the night of worrying she'd put in. "If I can keep track of the streets and the traffic in the five boroughs of New York City, though, I don't expect any problems learning your products."

"No drug record?" he asked, scrutinizing her with blue eyes that held an unsettling mix of kindliness and doubt. "I'll know by the end of the week if you have one and you won't get paid if you lie."

"Not even a traffic ticket, Kurt."

"Good. I'd like to try you out. Cece, get your friend a jacket and let her follow you 'til break."

40

"Hey, that rates foreman pay."

Kurt gave Cece his stunning smile that belied a jocular threat. "If you're lucky it'll wipe out some of the stunts you've pulled and keep your job for you next time you're late." He turned back to Annie. "Fill out an application at the personnel office on your break. She'll set up a drug test for you. I hope you're not a clown like this one."

Cece laughed. "Count your blessings, Kurt. Everybody around here'd be curled up on the shelves sleeping if it weren't for me."

"You and that deafening bike of yours."

They went back downstairs, through the break room and into a room lined with shelves and lockers. A crescent-shaped industrial sink jutted from one wall, its communal spigots shiny.

"He's an okay dude," Cece told her, "for a part-time holy roller preacher."

"There's something creepy about him. He's like on automatic seduction mode. He gave me the charm, scoped me out, but he already knows he can't convert you."

"That's one place my black ass protects me. He's got to hire some of us, but he's not recruiting me to his church." From a metal shelf Cece pulled a back support and a jacket like Kurt's. "Happy birthday. The brace is required. After about a week they give you a name patch that sticks on here." She demonstrated by attaching a patch reading "Cecile" to the velcro on her own jacket.

"This isn't a jacket, it's a lifesaver, but this brace feels like the bullet proof vest I used to wear. And the building couldn't be more different from my grubby old cab company in New York. How long have you been here?"

"Me?" Cece squinted her good eye. "It'll be six years July. I remember because they were due to take my bike from me just when summer hit if I couldn't get some cash. Nobody messes with the Truth—Sojourner Truth—that's my bike. I was planning to take off for parts unknown with her. Medipak saved my life."

"Mine too, it looks like. Thanks, Cece."

"Hey. Family has to stick together."

She looked around. The workers were grabbing their blue jackets, slamming lockers, gulping coffee from thermoses and hurrying off.

"Listen," Cece said, "maybe a quarter of the kids here are gay or bi, but we don't talk about it because the rest are so straight they make rulers look crooked. Kurt only has a store-front church, but he likes to hire his people—and not all of them are very Christian if you know what I mean. So play it cool. Any questions?"

"Yeah. Where's the john? Quick."

She'd wanted some time alone in the bathroom, but Cece stood at the sinks filling her in on Medipak. Annie's insides felt like a coffee percolator. Nerves, Gussie had declared. It's just your nerves. All night she'd worried. Would she ever find a dream again if she took the Medipak job? If life was one big domino theory, what would fall next? If she did nothing, would nothing happen? Of course not. There was no such thing as doing nothing. She'd still have to choose not to act. Inaction had its own consequences.

She'd pulled her favorite old philosophy book off the shelf. Of all the thinkers she'd read, Bertrand Russell, kind of a pop lib-eral philosopher, was the one who'd stuck. Indecision, he'd writ-ten, is only due to conflict.

What conflict? She needed the income and, if the Farm took her back, there was nothing holding her at Medipak. Jo was the ticket. Judy would believe Jo.

She was light-headed as she followed Cece again, this time into the warehouse proper. Spring sunshine, not yet hot, but bright with the promise of good weather, streamed in through high windows over the eight-foot gun-metal grey shelving. The work was soothing. She was too busy to think about the Farm or her insides. It was also strangely gratifying to fill orders. She ran from one side of the big warehouse to the next, learned all the nooks and crannies, wrestled with the long-handled grab-bers, skirted near-collisions with the other workers and slid full bins onto rollers for shipment.

"Wouldn't it be more efficient to have each person fill from one section?"

"Not in the long run," Cece answered as she pointed to items for Annie to snatch. "See, this way you're responsible for your own bin. And there's too much down time the other way, waiting if the bin coming in doesn't need shampoo. See what I mean?

They keep you hopping and you get a quality control sheet at the end of the week telling you if your batting average is off. You'll get a lot of errors at first, but after maybe two weeks they drop right down."

Quickly, she learned to barrel down product-lined alleyways. The warehouse seemed to shrink as the morning wore on and she noted that she had been assigned, like most of the women, to HABA, health and beauty aids. The men worked with durable medical equipment—the urinals and wheelchairs and oxygen machines Medipak supplied to hospitals and rental outfits. Other men loaded and unloaded the trucks. Now and then the route men dashed in from their vans.

At lunch Cece led her outside where picnic benches lined the parking lot. The promising day had waned in the noon hour, as unstable-looking clouds drifted past the sun. Annie and Cece bought sandwiches from a truck.

"I feel worse than I did after the game," she groaned, easing herself down to a picnic bench at the side of the building. "I may be too stiff to work tomorrow."

"You won't want to cook supper tonight," said an extremely tall woman, a missing front tooth obvious through her warm smile. "Make him take you to McDonald's."

Cece looked a warning at Annie.

"Of course, even McDonald's gets expensive if you've got enough kids?" half-asked a short, gaunt woman. She and her companion sat at the next picnic table with three other women. "Want some cookies? My oldest baked them last night."

Annie took one with thanks.

"You're married?" probed the short woman.

She felt like she'd stepped into a time warp where matrimonial status was the most significant characteristic a woman could have.

"You've gotta be kiddin' me," she said, lapsing into cabbie banter. "When I can be free as a bird? Good cookie."

"You look familiar," the short woman announced. "Where have I seen you?"

She forced herself to swallow. "I must have a twin because I've heard that before," she parried. "I'm pretty new in town."

"Then come to church Sunday. We have potlucks and Bible classes," offered the tall one. Her smile was teasing now. "You

43

might meet someone."

She grinned back with gleeful wickedness. "Didn't you hear? All the good men are taken and the rest are g—"

Cece broke in saying, "Hey, birthday-girl, here comes the ice cream truck—my treat." She grabbed Annie's elbow to steer her away. "Don't be rocking the boat, babe, or we'll all go down."

"This closet stuff is going to get old real fast."

"It's that, Heaphy, or get poor real fast."

"Okay. Okay."

"Come on. I'll introduce you to some of our compadres."

Ice creams in hand, they avoided the picnic table and drifted to three women and a man leaning on a tiny electric-blue car. In the distance Route 83 wound through this newly industrialized zone. There was a sense of insulation out here, surrounded by trees, quiet clean businesses and suburban cul-de-sacs with well-mowed lawns far from the noisy railroad and the river. She could even hear robins, newly arrived, arguing over nesting locations and occasionally caroling out their joy.

"What's happening, Louie?" asked Cece of a tanned young man with a curly black forelock, tight black slacks and a chest-hugging knit shirt. "Not much," Louie replied.

"It's about time you introduced us to your new friend, Cece. I'm Chantal, after my French great-grandma, the only drop of non-Polish blood in my veins," said a spirited white woman who had short blonde swept-back hair, careful makeup and eyes the color of the sky on a hazy day.

"This is Annie Heaphy. Annie, meet Chantal Zak from the office. You be nice to her, she does payroll. And here's Nicole and Sheryl."

"You don't have to be nice to us, we're just packers," said Sheryl, dark-skinned, with close-cropped hair, plastic-framed glasses and a stand-offish air. "I saw you on the floor today."

Nicole, in dreadlocks, laughed, but had a compassionate look. "Almost creamed me once too!"

"Sorry," Annie said with a grimace of contrition. "I'm not used to it yet."

Nicole warned, "Maybe won't ever be. The pace just gets faster every day, I swear. Where do you live?"

"Rafferty Street," she answered.

"Mean little white neighborhood," Sheryl noted. "There's

44

some folks tucked away down there by the river I wouldn't want to be messing with."

"I've got bike buddies on Rafferty. They'll treat you right if you let them know you're Cece Green's friend. Meantime, this handsome honky dude is Louie. And this is his new sardine can."

"Nice little jalopy," Annie said. "What is it?"

Louie had an appealing kid-brother manner, and obviously, from his style, revered Elvis Presley's memory. "A Geo Storm. I work at a car lot in Upton nights and weekends and this one came in with very low miles."

"I'm trying to get him to take me for a ride," said Chantal in a throaty voice, moving her head so her dangling earrings flashed in the sunlight. Chantal Zak looked soft, her cheeks plump, her breasts ample, her hips generous. A comfortable sort of woman.

Cece whispered, "But he doesn't let fee-males in his car, do you, Lulu?"

"Female? What's that?" Louie asked, fluttering his lashes.

Cece lowered her voice. "You've met Louie's *friend*, Heaphy. John works nights at the diner? Hey, what's this about Dusty and Elly not hitting it off too good these days? My main woman, Hope, heard from her Aunt Venita that Elly's got a thing for that new art teacher, Verne something?"

"And Venita Valerie hears it from her best friend Gussie who gets it from yours truly," said Annie.

"Morton River's a small world," Chantal said.

Annie laughed, holding up her right hand. "That's all the dirt I have."

Cece crossed her fingers and with a solemn expression said, "They're in *my* prayers. They give the rest of us something to shoot for."

Then Cece pointed over her shoulder with her thumb and told the others, "Heaphy just got the third degree from Mutt and Jeff over there."

"Like they don't know just looking at you," said Chantal, her voice a purr pitched to Annie's ears.

Annie grinned and switched her hands from front pockets to back, rolling up and down on the balls of her feet. While Jo acted as if flirting was an intimate form of foreplay, Chantal was obviously a born flirt. "It was easier driving a cab. I gave the

45

Kamikaze Cabbie treatment to anyone who hassled me over being gay."

"Shhh!" said Nicole and Sheryl in unison.

"Crap!," Annie said, covering her mouth and stamping in a circle.

Sheryl explained, "Mrs. Kurt is here today. Everytime you turn around she's in your face with her church-lady smiles up front and her feet running back to Massa with tales."

Cece explained with her snap-and-point finger aimed at Annie's chest. "We call her Mrs. Kurt because she's like his shadow, but it's really Mrs. Norwood if you ever have to talk to her. She's pretty nice as long as you don't get her into a family values frenzy. Talk about a one-track mind."

"Mrs. Norwood? Not *Paula* Norwood," Annie asked, clutching Cece's shoulders. "Tell me it isn't so."

Cece asked, "Someone you know?"

"At the game? The complainer?"

"Uh-oh," Cece said. "You didn't mention her name last night. Sure, she's a Rockettes groupie. Her kid plays."

"I'm out of here. If that woman spots me—maybe that's where Mutt and Jeff saw me."

"Don't you dare leave!" Chantal protested, holding Annie by the belt. "I went to parochial school, but Mrs. Kurt is screwier than the nuns about religion."

"Paula Norwood is the reason I'm here." This time when she told the story of Lorelei's kiss, she let her anger out. "Damned ignorant hypocrites," she ended, stopping herself from kicking Louie's tire just in time.

"Man, oh man," said Sheryl.

"Don't be thinking about quitting though," Cece urged. "You need the bucks just like the rest of us working gals."

"Someday," Louie said with a big sigh, "my husband will be rich and I'll keep the sterling polished while I watch my soaps."

They laughed, but Annie complained, "This is starting to get to me. I feel like a criminal who doesn't deserve a job."

Cece snapped her fingers and asked, "How'd you like being told you're good for nothing but churning out little black welfare babies? Then getting your checks cut off because you think you're not good enough to get hired on a job so you don't try? Don't tell me about no self-esteem trouble."

Chantal's smile vanished. "I don't know who they think will take care of Lorelei and her kind if it isn't the poor people and us you-know-whats. We're the only ones who understand everybody's the same inside."

"You mean, we're the only ones who'll take shit wages," scoffed Sheryl.

"Should I stay away from you guys?" asked Annie.

"And deprive us of your company?" said Chantal, hands on hips. "If you stay away from us they'll know we're the rotten apples. Just act natural, be friendly with everybody." She smiled big. "Especially with me. You look like the sort of risk a single girl ought to take."

"You're one outrageous lady," she told Chantal. "And I like it."

Cece said, "Don't you worry about Mrs. Kurt. She mostly stays up by the offices, bugging the shit out of Chantal. You may not run into her for months and she'll forget by then."

"How do you stand working with bigots like them?"

Nicole answered, "Some of us are used to it."

Sheryl scoffed, "Like we can pass for white, right? Like Medipak is going to be writing in a domestic partner deal next week. Uh-huh."

"She's just trying to be a good parent," said Chantal. "I was there once. What did I know about homosexuals," she whispered, "that I didn't read about or see on TV."

"But I thought Connecticut was just a liberal New York suburb," she protested. "Like people here were already educated."

Chantal smiled again. "Where did you find this one, Cece? I didn't know—" she lowered her throaty voice and looked around—"butches could be so naive. Rush Limbaugh isn't going to broadcast why you're getting axed, but you have no way to check your bins, Sugar. If the error reports are coming down one after the other you have no proof that they're doctored. And you're only allowed three before they put you on probation."

"So has anyone actually been canned for being, you know, domestic partners?"

Chantal beamed and reached over to very gently straighten Annie's collar. "Isn't she adorable?" The touch gave Annie a chill of pleasure. Chantal folded heavy lids over her sleepy-looking eyes.

"Who knows why they can people? I can't swear I haven't made the mistakes they report," Louie said, with resignation in his tone.

Cece agreed. "I'd feel a whole lot better if we had someone on our side in Q.C."

"That's the plum job, Sugar. Kurt likes to give it to his flock."

The other workers started drifting toward the warehouse and Louie peeled himself from his car, combing his hair. "It's too beautiful to go inside."

"Car payments, Mr. Louie," Chantal teased, moving to walk with Annie. She had a swing to her hips like Elly's. Annie wondered what it would be like to fill her hands with those hips, then made herself look away.

"What's a girl to do?" Louie said and led them inside.

CHAPTER 5

"Celibacy," said Annie the next Friday evening, as she watched Gussie spoon chocolate sprinkles onto a mound of ice cream, "has never been part of my life plan."

Gussie licked her spoon and lifted an eyebrow. "It's pretty restful."

Despite a spring chill, Venita Valerie had brought them a quart of coffee ice cream from Dogwood Farms Dairy. Venita hadn't taken off her bright yellow cloche hat with its trailing tie. Hats, the wilder the better, were her passion. "Ice cream is a pretty good substitute," Venita commented.

"Celib-icy," said Gussie with a laugh. Her cowlicks were brushed down for Venita's visit and she wore a red-checked flannel shirt with her sweat pants. "Creamy, but no emotional entanglement."

"Gussie!" cried Annie as she loosened her belt. "This woman has a mouth on her," she told Venita.

"Isn't that the point?" Venita said, her embarrassed whispery words tripping over themselves, her eyes all slitted up in mirth.

"Venita!" cried Annie. "Gussie's a bad influence on you."

"I could have used her influence when I was younger."

"It's not too late to come out," Gussie said, her tone matter-of-fact.

"Tell my arthritis it wants to do bedroom gymnastics."

"Exercise is recommended," Gussie countered.

Annie pointed her spoon at Gussie. "I don't see you luring anyone into *your* bedroom for therapy."

"I've had enough," Gussie announced, pushing away her bowl.

Annie listened to a motorcycle's screeching brakes as it turned onto Rafferty Street and maneuvered the cobblestones. Would there be a time when she'd have had enough too? "I still can't imagine doing it with anyone but Marie-Christine," she confessed. "You get used to a woman. It's not like switching brands of shampoo. Or it shouldn't be."

"Are you saying you and Jo—," Gussie asked.

"Sometimes I wonder if I'm getting priggish in my middle years," Annie said, jumping up to distract Gussie. She did a quick disco dance shuffle to the big band playing "Chattanooga Choo-Choo" on the town's old-time radio station. "I think I was a seventies pebble swept up in the wave of sexual liberation. Without that I might have been as stodgy as my parents. About the only thing they ever agreed on was how unsafe the world was for a nice little girl like me. And they were right—about the unsafe part."

Gussie said, "And the nice part, maybe too nice. I'd be getting pretty frustrated if I were you."

"Nothing a cold shower can't fix," Annie lied.

Venita laughed. "There's no need for that! You're the most eligible bachelor in town."

Gussie took her bowl to the sink, poking Annie's arm on the way. "You should see the way the women cruise this one at the diner."

"She's blushing!" announced Venita.

Gussie laughed. "They like that too. Why don't you ever go out tom-catting?"

"You two are just plain lascivious."

"I've been called worse," Gussie bragged.

They played rummy until ten p.m. Annie offered to take Venita home. She u-turned in the middle of the street to avoid the gathering of cars, motorbikes and people with boom boxes crowding her usual turnaround at the end of Rafferty Street. But she could see them watch her, could feel their suspicious curiosity.

Too fitful to go home once Venita was safely in her lobby, Annie cruised silent, almost vacant Main Street. Morton River sometimes looked as if it hadn't left the 1940s—forget the fifties, sixties and beyond. Downtown was dark except for the Club Soda, a bar with an ancient neon sign. At the Mason's building around the corner men in suits and ties smoked cigarettes on the steps. The sounds of a band wafted up from the basement. She passed the silent grey stone railroad station and found herself sitting in the parking lot across from the Sweatshop, the Jimmys' after-hours gay oasis.

She closed her eyes, unable to deny her frustration another minute. She didn't want to rejoin the hunt, was disappointed in herself, but there it was; the blood through her body sang like the river at the end of the street.

Before Venita had arrived with the ice cream she'd called Jo—about seven times, hanging up on her answering machine every time. It was true, she and Jo hadn't gone further than heavy petting. Part of it was her own reluctance to get involved. The rest of it came, unexplained, from Jo.

She ground her starter, yanked the shift into neutral, then skittered out of the gravel parking lot, sliding around the corner onto Railroad Avenue without pausing at the stop sign. She rushed up into the hills above the Valley, feeling as crazed as a kid, on fire with restlessness, her thoughts splintered with distractions.

She hated this chronic love-sickness, this gnawing need for touch, for intimacy—for sexual release. Taking a break at work, falling asleep at night, she'd lose herself in labyrinthine fantasies of wrestling with faceless soft females. There were times when she felt like nothing more than a mindless embodiment of lust.

North of New Haven she found the cafe she'd heard about, amazed at how well she remembered the streets from her early cab driving days.

The DJ was playing some crazy punk music and the dance floor was packed. The heavy beat pounded through her, producing a jolt of lust. It was hot, the smoke was thick enough to sting her eyes, and she smelled rum through it, sweet, rich and astringent, as if someone had spilled a bottle of the stuff. She got a Coke, then found a space against the wall where she could watch, holding the cold glass first in one hand, then the other.

"Hey!" yelled a gritty voice at her side.

"Hi, Cece!" she shouted back. "Am I glad to see somebody I know!"

"Aren't these teeny-boppers a bitch?"

"Don't they card them?"

Cece looked at her with one eye. "Get real! They're old enough."

Annie tried to imagine herself out there dancing among the quick, supple kids with their lewd moves, their clown-colored stand-up hair like life in the 1990s was a constant shock, their layers of flannel, their baggy, many-pocketed pants or skimpy black leather skirts and flailing earrings. "Would we look like that if we were their age?"

"You better believe it," shouted Cece.

Beyond the dance floor two tables of jocky-looking women, a variety of ages, slopped beer in a cigarette haze, and laughed loudly enough to be heard over the crashing music. Jocks never changed.

The music stopped, the floor cleared. "They do jukebox breaks," Cece explained. "It's a great box. Come play a few."

She was surprised at the number of kids who returned to the floor for Martha and the Vandellas and the Temptations. Cece snapped her fingers.

Annie felt a gentle hand on her shoulder and turned. "Jo!" She felt like tossing her hat in the air and doing a little jig.

"In the flesh," said Jo, her lips going into their meltdown curve. In a loud whisper Jo said, "I saw your foot tapping. Will you dance with me?"

Formally re-introducing Jo to Cece, she said, "I'd have scoped out this place sooner if I'd known Jo hung out in sleazy gay dives."

Jo's gentle hand closed around hers like a fairy godmother's blessing and they moved to the dance floor. "Do you know Karen and Dawn? It's their eighth anniversary. Another couple and I took them to dinner up front in the restaurant."

"So that's where the old folks hang. I thought it was me and Cece lost in kindergarten land," Annie said.

"You can at least hear yourself think in the restaurant," Jo whispered, her breath cool on Annie's ear. "I came back here when I heard the old music."

They danced similarly, keeping the rhythm, but leaving the fancy moves to the kids. Annie thought about her yearnings tonight and wondered if she would've been better off with a stranger. At least the safe sex questions were out of the way with Jo, for all the good it did. They smiled and jounced around and watched the others until the slow old Rolling Stones song "Ruby Tuesday" came on.

This was the moment, she thought, an explosion of nerves and desire rising within her. Let the seduction begin. Jo must have sensed her mood. "Come to our table, Annie."

She was relieved and disappointed at the same time. She pushed through to where Cece was teaching some of the teeny-boppers to do the Bump and Grind and said goodbye.

"Fast worker," mouthed Cece.

She followed Jo to the relative silence of the front restaurant. Jo's friends were all dressed as carefully as Jo, in earrings, pretty pastel shells or tailored shirts that looked pricey. One, with a slight accent, was trying to teach the others Spanish, but they were all laughing too much to imitate her pronunciation. Annie, very conscious of the baggy chinos and unironed button-down under her black leather jacket, bought them a round of their fancy drinks.

"Did those two women who run the diner break up?" asked a woman with overpowering perfume.

Jo looked to Annie, eyes clouded.

"Not that I know of. Why?" Annie asked.

The woman nodded toward the tables behind Annie. She twisted to look over her shoulder. "Crap," she said. Elly and the art teacher were in a booth, Verne's hands embracing Elly's, eyes locked, whispering. She started to rise. Both of those traitors needed telling off. Jo darted a gentle hand to her arm. "This isn't the time, Annie."

"You're right." Annie sat down again.

"I hate to see something like that on our anniversary," said one of Jo's friends.

Annie turned away. "Twenty years. If Dusty and Elly can't make it, why bother?"

Jo's friends picked up their new drinks all at once. "I'm really sorry, Annie," Jo said softly.

There was a moment's silence from the back room and then the DJ kicked in a loud, thumping number. The two couples excused themselves to dance.

Annie growled, "I want to go over there and drag that amoral Lothario out by the collar."

"Oh?" breathed Jo, eyes on the illicit couple.

"But I'm a wimp," Annie confessed.

Silence stretched between them. Annie became aware of Jo's

hand on the table. Of the torrid beat to the back room music, like a not quite hidden agenda.

Jo asked, "What do you know about the immoral Lothario?"

"Verne?" Wasn't Jo feeling the heat of the evening? She told Jo all she'd learned.

"What an interesting woman."

Annie thought that was a strange reaction to the unflattering portrait she'd painted of Verne. They fell silent again, sipping their drinks.

"Jo—"

"Annie—"

They laughed. "Go ahead," Annie said.

"I wanted you to know that I'm still working on your situation with the Farm."

"What happened that night you went to their meeting?"

"Judy wasn't there. She was ill and I really need to talk to her first. Is your new job all right?"

"I kind of like it. There's a lot of us there. But something is missing."

"I guess the bobby pins aren't going to run up and kiss you."

"Or want to play softball." She hesitated to bare her soul, but Jo needed to understand what was at stake. "I can't get the Farm out from under my skin. I really liked working there. I never loved a job before."

"I envy you."

"I felt like I was into something important. A small part, but indispensable. Before, I've always felt like a misfit. Too smart to do drudge work, too gay to stay in school. So different from my family I thought Superman might be my brother, but so like my family I feel like a school dropout-street dyke around you. My parents own a house, but that was because of the G.I. Bill. I wasn't brought up to be a banker or even to go to college. I never saw any reason to invest time in getting ahead. Even if I did, I'd still just be a dyke cabbie with a degree."

"So the Farm wasn't just a job."

"Absolutely not. I might actually want to do MRDD work for the next thirty years. And not as a driver. I could go to school and get certified to teach, Jo. I could start up another Farm, some type of factory maybe. The Farm takes care of only a handful of people who could be out there working, feeling better about themselves. Feeling like I do because I'm finally part of something—like I did."

Jo's friends returned from dancing. Annie scraped her chair back, embarrassed about her disclosures. "I'd better go over to Puddle Street and see if Dusty's okay."

Jo rose too. "Are you huggable?" Jo whispered. Self-consciously chaste, she held Jo loosely, but Jo pressed her full body to Annie's for a moment, then a moment too long.

"Do you want to come along to Dusty's?" Annie asked.

Jo leaned back just far enough to look into Annie's eyes, then stepped away. "I admit I'm having a little trouble letting you go," she said with her dimpled smile, "but I don't know Dusty at all. If she's having a hard time it's not a good idea."

Annie realized that she still held Jo's hand. "I'd probably just make it worse, too."

"Then you'd consider one more dance?"

She could hear Gussie advise, Don't look a gift horse in the mouth.

"Here?" Annie asked.

"As opposed to?"

"Someplace more private?"

Jo gave a low, bubbly laugh and told her friends that Annie would give her a ride home. The Saab seemed to cut through the night like a Concorde on its way to Paris.

"Would you like a beer, some coffee?" Jo asked when they reached her condo. She turned on one small table lamp.

"Tea?" she said, just to break her own silence. With Jo out of the room, she sank onto the patterned couch and scanned the living room's country-style furniture and the large collection of pig portraits, pig toys, and pig carvings. As usual, there wasn't a lesbian title in the bookcase, or women's tape near the stereo—no sign that a dyke lived there at all. If Jo would just loosen up a little she'd be much easier to be with.

The first time she'd seen Jo, at a gathering Peg and Paris had held to introduce Annie to their friends, she'd been taken with Jo's contagious smile and big brown eyes. Peg, steepling her long slender fingers, had answered Annie's whispered question. "We went to high school together. Jo's branch manager for Valley Savings Bank. If you think these others are in the closet, Jo's in a fallout shelter." Peg had made see-no-evil, hear-no-evil, speak-no-evil gestures.

At her first visit to Jo's, Annie had been too nervous to think of witty seductive patter. She'd asked questions.

"So you bought this place yourself?"

"About eight years ago, when Marsha and I split. We'd been together since our junior year in college."

"So, uh, you made it quite a while."

"Long distance. Marsha works for an insurance company in Hartford. We'd planned a bonding ceremony." Jo lowered her eyes and shrugged slightly. "Then Marsha's other girlfriend heard about it."

"Yeah," Annie said. "Been there, done that, bought the t-shirt." She heard a scratching sound. "Your new friend, the pig?"

Jo beamed. "I'm crazy about her. Have you ever met a pot-bellied pig?"

"Different kind of wildlife in New York."

"Come." Jo took her hand and led her down some steps. Hugging the back door was a tall wooden enclosure strewn with straw. Rex had obviously been rooting in the dirt. About calf-high, black, with a short, wrinkled face, Rex greeted Jo with enthusiasm, then snuffled around Annie's sneakers.

"Is she full-grown?"

Annie kneeled to pat the bristly-coated pig. "Close. They usually go from seventy to one fifty pounds, but Rexie was the runt. Come, Rex!" Jo said and led the pig upstairs to a dog bed in the kitchen. Jo tapped the bottom of the bed. Rex stepped in and curled up.

Without the pig between them, the mood had shifted. They'd looked at each other. Annie had raised a very tentative hand to touch Jo's hair.

Tonight, when Jo returned with the tea she sat next to Annie on the couch, all brown hair, brown vest, long brown skirt, beseeching brown eyes.

"Tea's hot," Jo said, her eyes on Annie's lips.

"That's not all," she replied, tilting toward Jo. They moved together and kissed, then kissed again and again. "You're different tonight," she told Jo, who, ignoring the tea, had pulled her into a reclining position with unusual eagerness.

There was a commotion. Annie sat up, startled.

"Rexie's in the bathroom," Jo explained with a look of delight in her eyes. "She'll snort and blow bubbles and make all kinds of messes and racket in the toilet. What can I do? It's her new hobby."

They went to watch Rex blow bubbles in the bathroom, which was lovely. It was appointed with matching wooden soap dish, toothpick holder, toilet seat, and gold-colored scroll work faucets. The mirror was ringed by light bulbs, like a movie star's dressing room. The bathtub was oversized, half sunken and equipped with a Jacuzzi attachment.

Jo led her to the kitchen, heated more water and refilled the pig-pink mugs with curlicue handles. They sat on stools at a butcher block counter in the middle of the kitchen. Cast iron pots and pans hung from a ceiling rack. There was nothing early American about the stove top grille and double refrigerator with ice water, cubes and crushed ice dispensed from the door. Annie swung around, arms displaying the room. "Your place has always struck me like middle America."

"You know all of us gay yuppies have disposable income to squander."

What she read in Jo's eyes was, But money's not enough.

"At work," Jo explained, "I've pretty much hit that glass ceiling. Branch managers aren't much more than administrative secretaries."

"You do better than a cab driver."

"I'm not hurting, but not exactly on easy street. A big hunk of my salary goes to keep me in these togs—" Jo smoothed her long skirt over her knees—"so I can keep my job."

Very deliberately, Annie said, "They certainly become you."

The mood changed again. Rex was back in her bed. Jo looked as hungry as Annie felt. Annie touched Jo's no longer neat hair.

"Nice," Jo said as they kissed some more.

Annie felt deliriously light-headed. She'd follow these lips if they pulled her into Pastor Norwood's church. After a flutter of kisses, Jo came forward off her stool to press herself to Annie.

What a fine, fine feeling it was, woman to woman. Even behind clothing the charges of passion were alive.

They kissed until Annie pressed back against Jo. She felt the lines of pleasure that connected them rise up into her nipples, streak down through her thighs. She had a passing concern about Jo and closets and her job at the Farm, but she wasn't about to bring that up now.

"Here?" she asked, her voice not much more than a bark.

"Rex would think we were playing with her," Jo said as she paused between kisses.

Annie swung away and, hand at the small of Jo's back, propelled them to the couch. Jo lay down, arranging her skirt over her knees, the usual smile on her face. "Bankers need love too," she joked.

Annie knelt by Jo, hands poised. She blew the hair out of Jo's eyes.

"It's been a long time, Annie."

"It's okay."

"Years." Jo looked flustered.

"Why?"

"Why am I ashamed or why has it been years?"

"Yes," teased Annie, playing with Jo's skirt.

"There was only Marsha. It took a long time to even want anyone after I lost her. And then, well, it got scary."

She snuck a finger under the skirt. The scratchy feel of nylons turned her liquid. "All I can think of is getting to the top of your stockings."

"Pantyhose."

"Crap."

"Next time I'll wear a garter belt."

"Okay." She wasn't sure how to proceed in this start-stop seduction. "Okay," she repeated to buy time.

"Since we seem to be functional at the moment, would you like to adjourn to my bedroom?"

"Yeah. My knees are starting to hurt."

"Poor baby. Come up here off them." Jo kissed her chinos at the knees. Annie bent to kiss the back of Jo's neck, tracing a line across it with her tongue. Maybe, after all, Jo would be the one.

"Annie—" Jo warned, but Annie had found Jo's buttons and breasts and Jo had found her mouth. Their stiffness disappeared and by then the bedroom was too, too far.

She awoke jammed into the couch beside Jo, dog-breathed and sweating. Her sense of unease mushroomed with consciousness. When she heard the freight train whistle by she knew it was nearly two a.m. The sound made her long for her own bed even more. It was as if she were in her twenties again, rootless, desperate to flee from a one-night stand.

She extricated herself from Jo.

Jo stirred, opened her eyes, smiled wanly. "You okay?"

Crap. She'd never get away gracefully.

She answered by kissing Jo's hand.

"That was lovely," Jo said. "Want to come over and do it again some time?"

Didn't Jo want to hold her there for the rest of the night? "I think that could be arranged."

"Let me see you to the door."

"It's cool. I'll lock it behind me."

She raced into the fresh air, twirled her softball cap on her finger and skipped to the Saab. Jo let her go! What a woman! Smart, hot and—cling-free? She was too good to be true.

CHAPTER 6

She began to settle into this newest life, watching the Morton River swill by Rafferty Street each day, its spring currents mad for release. The May weather continued to alternate between near-torrential rain and days so clear and balmy she ached at the beauty of the world. From her bed at night she heard the trains run through the Valley, crying with mournful yet comforting regularity. In the warehouse, product streamed in, was shelved and unshelved and streamed out. She never saw Kurt, but he liked her work and kept her on. The gay packers warned Annie if Mrs. Kurt was nearby, sometimes forming a phalanx around Annie so she could scoot out of sight.

Jo hadn't been able to see Judy. Annie's messages to Judy went unreturned. If she'd learned anything from dabbling in those philosophy courses back in the city, it was that time resolves everything. On the other hand, time takes its time, and won't be rushed.

One afternoon when she arrived home from work, when the sky was threatening yet more rain, she parked her car and stepped out to find two white boys around seventeen in grunge clothing, strolling toward her from the vacant lot at the end of the street. One of them she'd seen on the porch across the street. The other was the noisy idiot with a trail bike who thought the cobblestones of Rafferty Street were an obstacle course laid down specifically for him.

She forced herself to move slowly, casually, and to meet their eyes.

The shorter of the two, with arrogant eyes and a shaved head, said to his friend, "Yo. Here's your new neighbor."

His burly companion, whose jeans hung lower than the band of his shorts, sniggered. "The dyke?" he jeered.

She stopped dead. "Is that a problem for you guys?"

They said nothing, but one brushed impudently against her

60

as he passed.

Her heart beat hard. Her breath came short. But she'd survived worse than these little shits. "I asked you a question."

The one with arrogant eyes turned to face her, but continued shambling backwards. "It's a problem, yeah," he answered.

"Why? I scare you?"

"Yeah, I'm, like, shaking in my boots."

"Then bug off about it. You do your thing, I'll do mine."

The boys walked off, sniggering.

In Gussie's alleyway she composed herself, dallying at the chorus line of tulips that Nan had planted alongside the house. Then a sound came from the street—the sickening impact of rock against metal. She sprinted back. No one was in sight, but when she checked her car the hood had been dented, the rock lying in the gutter.

She was clenching the rock in her fist as she went in the back door of the house. Gussie was red-faced again, eyes blazing like the headlight of a midnight locomotive. *"Look* at this!"

Annie reached for the *Valley Sentinel*, but wasn't ready for the banner headline: ABUSE CHARGED AT DISABLED FARM.

"Crap," said Annie, pressing the rock to the stabbing pain in her belly. Did those boys know it was her in the headlines? "This is what I get for not taking things into my own hands. Jo's too patient, too trusting."

"The paper," Gussie explained, "didn't use your name, but Lorelei's parents went to the paper because Judy hasn't officially discharged you yet."

"Oh, right. That's why I'm hanging out with hairpins and aspirin instead of my Farm folks. I'm going to the Farm to see Judy. I don't have to take this," she said, tossing the rock up and down, fumbling, dropping it on her toe. "Ow! If she fires me, so be it. The money's better at Medipak and there are fewer hassles. At least they're up front about hating gays. I know to leave my trust in the parking lot."

"Hold your horses. It's bigger than you are. This reporter looked into staffing at other places like the Herb Farm and says there is as much potential for abuse in those."

"Code for they hire queers too?"

"Not code at all. Next to last paragraph: The presence of

homosexuals on both staffs does not, according to management, increase likelihood of abuse. And then he quotes statistics about heterosexual men being the abusers over ninety-five percent of the time."

"So why carry on about this? I know, I know. It sells papers."

"I'm afraid that's not all." Gussie pointed to a headline on the other side of the front page: LEGISLATION URGED TO LIMIT GAY EMPLOYMENT.

"What the?" Annie asked, stomping from one end of the kitchen to the other as she read aloud. "'Representatives of several area churches are circulating a petition to urge the Board of Selectmen to draft legislation that would require employment screening on the grounds of sexual orientation in public and private agencies that provide services to minors or the disabled.' Isn't that illegal?"

"Illegal is just a sick bird," Gussie said, sounding disgusted. "Those ministers are rubbing their pious little hands, Annie. This will bring the wandering souls home. This will fill the coffers. The family that hates together enters the pearly gates together."

Annie noticed Toothpick rubbing against her. "What are you up to, you sweet little furball? You...," she said, picking her up and holding her high, "...you think dinner should be the minute I come home, even if my shift ends an hour earlier than it used to."

Gussie laughed. "She's still not much bigger around than a toothpick.

Annie bent to change the kitten's water. "I haven't been looking forward to calling Jo because—" She hated to admit it, even to Gussie. She'd spent one more evening with Jo, just talking, and since then Jo had been too busy to see her.

One Saturday noon she'd passed Jo outside her bank by the shopping center. She'd been about to call out when an old MG sports car drew up in front. Jo got in. The car had seemed familiar. Some imp in her made her trail the MG, but it took off up Route 83 so fast she knew she'd be flamingly conspicuous if she followed.

"Last time I called she was tired, the next time getting her friend. She hasn't returned my calls since. Is she afraid to tell me the bad news? Or is it just because I'm from the wrong side of the tracks?"

"There's only one way to find out, Socrates."

She tried to read Gussie's face, then paged through the phone book for banks and dialed. "Jo Barker, please." She tapped her fingers on the counter. "I wish she'd just tell me if she can't help."

Gussie fished through a tray on the table until her fingers found a pair of scissors. She clipped the piece from the paper. "If I were you I'd tell her off. But you won't. You'll be very polite and understanding, whatever she tells you. It's one of the reasons I like you so much."

"Don't be so sure." She turned to look out the front window. Those boys were gone. Two motorcycles jolted along the bumpy street. One rider waved to a long-haired man entering the house across the street.

A voice told her Jo was away from her desk. "Tell her—tell her Gussie Brennan called. And it's urgent," Annie said, supplying the number. "Is that all right, Gus? Maybe my name's not involved at all yet, but I don't want to blow the whistle on Jo."

"That's fine. There's no need to expose anyone." Gussie sorted a pile of papers on the table. "I hate to give you more good news, but you got a message from Peg's lawyer friend today."

Toothpick was making comforting crunchy noises at her bowl. "Go ahead, make my day."

"She can't do anything unless you're officially terminated."

"That settles it. I talk to Jo and if she draws a blank, then I pay a surprise visit to Judy."

Gussie said, "Listen to you, acting like the rock of Gibraltar."

"I wish I were a rock about now," she confessed. The man across the street came out onto his porch with a beer. He tilted back in a chair and seemed to settle into staring at Gussie's front windows. "Look at that subhuman specimen. Why do we even have to share the earth with cretins like him?"

"If you hate them your hatred will eat you up."

She was startled by Gussie's advice and told her about the encounter out front, showed her the rock. "Gus, you know what they're like."

"I haven't forgotten. But you can stand up to them without hating them, Socrates."

"I'm running on anger, Gus."

"Anger, hate—they're the flip side of fear."

"So I'm scared. Sue me."

Gussie joined her at the window. "Not a pretty picture, I agree."

Two other men lounged, smoking, on the steps.

Annie admitted, "I don't know that hate is the right word. I don't understand them at all. What do they get out of hassling gays?"

Instead of answering, Gussie said, "I wonder if your girlfriend's been keeping us away from the Farm to protect it?"

Annie didn't admit to having wondered the same thing.

Jo finally called back. "There's a New Way board meeting tonight, Annie. I thought you might have seen it in the paper. It's open to the public. I've been meaning to call you—but part of me wanted to protect you. It could get ugly."

"It *is* ugly, Jo."

Annie was fidgety with nervousness at dinner with Gussie. When the six-fifteen commuter train squealed into the station across the river she was out the door.

A drizzle had begun. She used it to scrub off the dirt in this first dent. The Saab had clearly been the car she had been looking for. It had been in a wreck, but Jimmy O., who spent his days doing what he called "gentrifying" battered cars, had bought it and rebuilt it, body and guts.

The first time she'd seen it—painted popsicle purple, she'd vowed to Jimmy, "She will be mine. Oh yes, she will be mine."

"No! A dyke *Wayne's World* freak?" he'd said with a groan.

She'd known she'd have to commit to years of payments, but she wasn't leaving without her Hot Rod Grape, Gussie's immediate nickname for it. She had to go on juggling mouthwash at Medipak if only to keep the Grape, although she was beginning to suspect that buying such a conspicuous car had not been the wisest of moves.

The meeting was at City Hall. She pulled behind Jo's Prelude with the PBPIG license plate. Something teased at the back of her mind—where else had she seen that old grey MG that had picked Jo up outside her bank? Then it came to her. Elly's art teacher had parked it across from the Sweatshop one night. Why would Verne have picked up Jo? Because she was from the right side of the tracks?

The room held a scattering of people. In the back row sat Hope Valerie, Venita Valerie, Maddy Scala, Dusty Reilly, Louie's boyfriend Jon and the pharmacist—what was his name?–Jake. America Rodriguez rushed in behind her with five non-gays, all of whom greeted Venita with hugs.

"What are you all doing here?" Annie whispered.

Maddy leaned forward. "I spotted this in the paper and I thought fuck this shit. They don't get the last word, right?"

America said, "Even on short notice we have, what—seven PFlaggers here."

Hope quietly applauded.

"That's my baby," said a balding black man, loving eyes on Hope. "They mess with us because we're black, they mess with us cause we're poor, now they messing with us cause my child has a girlfriend. What do they think, God only gives love to some in-crowd?"

Judy Wald was at the front table, with an array of white men in suits and ties. She looked wraith-like, pale and skeletal.

"I'm Jack Plant," said a robust man in his sixties. "Judy's not feeling too well tonight, so I'm going to wield the gavel for her and try to fill her more than competent shoes."

The usual droning reports, budget discussion and announcements seemed to go on so long that Annie wondered if Jack Plant was trying to outlast the back rows. Finally, he asked for old business and a gravel-voiced short guy with a grey crew cut and military bearing stood.

"I move that we open the meeting here to the public."

"Can we do that Judy?" asked Plant.

Judy shook her head. "Public comment is welcome after the Board completes its business."

The retired soldier grumbled his objection, but raised his hands toward the front rows in a gesture of helplessness when Plant asked him to be seated.

Annie just wanted to get this over with before someone from Medipak showed up. Down the row Jake's foot was jiggling at about 80 m.p.h. and Venita resettled her red felt hat for the dozenth time.

Plant had barely opened the meeting to the public when a heavily perfumed woman with a matronly figure stood.

"I want to know what you people are doing about improving

your hiring practices."

"The staff out at the Farm is doing a bang-up job." He displayed a sheet of paper. "Worker productivity is at an all-time high and contributing one third to the Farm's budget. My understanding is that this is a phenomenal achievement."

"All right!" Annie whispered.

A red-faced man with the beefy build of an ex-football player who'd let himself go, rose next. "Is that all you care about? Number crunching? I'm Leon Simski. You've got a bad situation down at the Farm. So bad I may pull my kid out. And you know why. I want to see some action taken to get the wrong element out of there."

Annie was at the edge of her seat. She'd stripped off her jacket partly because she was sweating so hard, partly in an effort to look more respectable to Jo, though Jo hadn't looked at her since Annie had first entered the room. Now she wanted to respond to Simski's unspecified accusations, but no words came to her except a shouted "NO!"

Everyone in the room turned toward her. She was half standing, half-sitting, poised to tell her side of the story.

Behind her, a chair scraped. Hope Valerie, unfailingly silent in a group, said clearly, in a shaking voice, "You don't know what you're talking about, Mister. I was there. I saw what happened at the ballfield and you have it all wrong." Briefly, plainly, with a shaky voice, she gave the Board the truth, unflinching, though every eye in the front row seemed to be scrutinizing her with disdain. Hope sat abruptly. There was silence in the room. Annie, still on the edge of her seat, knew that if Hope had found the guts to stick up for her, it was time to end her own silence, but again, just as she began to rise, someone else spoke.

"Are you going to take *her* word against that of my minister's wife?" asked the outraged matron.

Annie felt two hands on her shoulders, pressing her back into her seat. "Don't be a jerk," Dusty whispered. "We're here to do the talking." Aloud, Dusty introduced herself and asked, "Is there some reason we should believe Paula Norwood over Hope Valerie? The Valeries have been in this Valley for generations. They've been ministers and bankers and teachers. Hope holds a responsible position with the transit company and volunteers her time to help the whole community." She paused. "I know you're not referring to her race."

"No!" sputtered the woman. "Of course not!"

"If I may have the floor just a moment longer. I can confirm what Hope said. Nothing happened at the ball game that could harm anyone. As team manager, I may have used poor judgement in allowing an excitable, troubled young woman to have the bat girl position, but I honestly thought it would help her adjust to some difficult changes in her life—and she was so proud."

A male board member said, "That's very moving, but I think we've gone beyond one incident here. I emphatically agree, Ms. Reilly, that you displayed misguided pity rather than sensible judgement in your decision. Surely you knew the environment into which you were placing this young woman."

Annie jumped up then. "Yes, sir. Sunshine, competitiveness, fun, physical exercise, teamwork and a sense of accomplishment. If that's suspect, then I think the city ought to take these Norman Rockwell posters off the walls." There were two of them, one actually depicting a sandlot baseball game with smiling players and a fluttering American flag.

"Those," said Leon Simski, "are normal people. My kid could play with those clean-cut fellas any time and I'd be rooting in the stands."

"Like," cried America Rodriguez, "the clean-cut suburban jokers who got caught having sex with a developmentally disabled girl looking for love and acceptance?"

That story had been in the papers for weeks.

"What's the difference?" a board member asked.

The back row burst out. "Oh come on!"

"What's your problem?"

"I don't believe this."

Annie noticed that Judy looked uncomfortable. What was wrong with her? Why didn't she stop this?

"I move," said the soldier, "that the board review personnel policies and add specific criteria to guard against this happening again."

The front row applauded. Annie felt sick.

Plant said, "That's a big undertaking. We'd have to get some legal help to understand employment discrimination laws. They've added that sexual orientation clause, you know."

"Damn government," said a lean man in a fatigue jacket. "Nosing in where they don't belong. Just fire the son-of-a-b and get this over with."

Finally, Judy spoke. Her voice was strong, but speech seemed to be an effort. "I'm not ready to fire anyone, Mr. Knight. We've heard contradictory stories. I've interviewed both the staff member and the worker. I can see no wrongdoing on the part of either. The worker has a history of these attachments as well as a pattern of inappropriate though harmless behaviors."

"Harmless!?"

"No harm was done here except a good employee is on administrative leave for the six weeks we agreed on to investigate the incident, which unfortunately falls at a difficult time for me and consequently had to be extended. You will have to come up with some more compelling justification for termination or I fully intend to reinstate the employee."

"We'll justify it all right," the matron said with a self-righteous bitterness. "The United Way and your other benefactors will be hearing from a lot of concerned citizens. And if they won't listen, the Board of Selectmen knows who keeps them in office. They'll rewrite the licensing codes to require screening for sexual preference in day care centers, schools, camps and disability facilities—or hear from the voters."

Jake had managed to be quiet all this time, but now he rose, as thin and pale as Judy, and let them have it. "Excuse *me*," he said. "This is all very civil, but there are so many innuendos floating around I'm beginning to think I'm at a seance. I want to say a few words aloud. Brace yourselves. Gay. Reactionary. Justice. Prejudice, discrimination and bigotry. Hysteria. Manipulation. Compassion. Truth. Political agendas. And *that's* the worst one, because I think all of you up front and some of you on the board are trying to use this incident to manipulate the voters and the funding sources. You throw your puritanical tantrums and get your way or else you punish the Farm and you punish our city government. This is not the American way, folks. And you're not getting away with it. And thank you, Ms. Wald, for standing up to these storm troopers!"

The back rows whistled, stomped and cheered Jake, who sat daintily back down with a stern proud gaze fastened on the front row.

"ENOUGH!" shouted Plant, banging the gavel.

Judy stood again. "That was very articulate, sir, and I appreciate all of your comments. I think we have to guard against name calling and escalation. Let's remember it's the workers at the Farm who've brought us all together, and it's a workable solution for them that we're seeking."

The meeting ended with the board agreeing to review the personnel policies. Judy would keep a temporary worker in Annie's job, but would reinstate Annie unless she was thoroughly convinced that there had been willful misconduct.

No deadline was set, but by the time Annie reached the front of the meeting room to ask when she could expect to hear, Judy had vanished.

CHAPTER 7

The little pig was in its enclosure out back. Jo called down that the door was unlocked.

A vanilla-scented candle burned, as usual, on the highly polished coffee table. The precisely placed floor lamps cast a homey light. On the wall was a new piece of art, a cloyingly adorable watercolor of Rex. Ah-ha, she reassured herself, that's the connection with Verne.

"Can I get you a cup of tea? I just put the water on," Jo said with her meltaway smile, cutting short their hug.

Jo had stopped her outside City Hall and invited her over. Annie had been hoping to process the meeting at the diner with her supporters, but Jo was insistent.

Now Annie surprised herself. "No. No tea and sympathy. I want to know when I get to stop being afraid a mob will come for me."

Jo didn't hesitate. She patted a space beside her on the couch. "This must feel like it's taking forever, Annie, or like I'm not trying, but it's really complex. You saw tonight that I can't just walk up to board members to demand anything." She moved closer and reached for Annie's hands. "I called after we talked this afternoon. Judy's been really sick. You got lost in the shuffle."

"Then I guess I'll just have to go down there and help her find me—and the law that protects my job."

Jo sighed as if Annie were a sulky and frustrating child. "She knows the law, Annie. She agrees with the law. Try to understand the position she's in."

"I know, I know, Lorelei and Errol and the rest need protection. They do. I'm not arguing with that. But if I didn't know it before, I do now—I need protection too."

Jo withdrew her hands. "Please try to be fair. That's not as obvious to straight people."

"I lose my job and you want me to be fair. Who's side are you

70

on, Jo?"

"Come in the kitchen. I can't take that kettle whistling any longer."

Annie became aware of its insistent screech. Jo, complaining about the Boards' capitulation to the front row, poured water into a creamy pink tea pot with a foreshortened spout and a curlicue handle.

"A piggy-pot?" She had to laugh.

Jo joined in. "Poor Annie. How are you doing with all this? I'd be absolutely terrified my name would be released to the whole world."

"It's like I told you the other night. It's been a long time since I had a dream. I thought I could get a degree, teach Special Ed. There's got to be more to life than earning enough money to have a place to sleep so I can earn enough money to have a place to sleep—you know?"

Jo smiled. "You're a sixties kid, still hanging on to your ideals. Dreaming over there on your cobblestoned street."

"Bingo. I want my life to matter! Maybe my real job isn't to make a difference to the workers at the Farm or to teach. Maybe I'm supposed to make a difference for gay people."

"I'm not willing to dip you in chocolate and throw you to the radical right. They're the enemy—not Judy. You know that, don't you?"

"Who fired me?"

"Annie, this is definitely confidential information, okay?"

"Sure."

"The Norwoods' church is small, but it's part of the biggest denomination in town."

"Point being?"

"The church has a lot of money. When the Farm had a balloon payment on its mortgage a few years ago—"

"Oh, shit."

"I'm afraid so."

"They own the Farm."

"No, but they do hold part of the mortgage."

"Aren't there public funds involved? What about separation of church and state?"

"You'd have to ask the attorneys."

"Oh, man. Now what?"

"I know what I'd do."

"I know what you'd do too," Annie scoffed. "The closet's a temptation, but I'd suffocate."

"No. I'd go back to New York. What better solution than hiding out with eight million people."

"Hey! We could get an apartment together!" The look on Jo's face told her that wasn't in her plans. "Not a good idea," she said, backing off. "Besides, cabbies have the highest death rate of any occupation. At least dodging Mrs. Kurt isn't likely to be fatal."

"I didn't realize driving was so dangerous. Of course you have to stay here," Jo said, looking concerned. "I'd never thought of that."

She wondered just how much thought Jo had given to the possibility that Annie might flee the Valley.

As if to distract Annie from her suspicions, Jo smoothed her skirt over her legs and asked, "Is Lorelei Simski still bat girl for the diner team?"

"Are you kidding? Lorelei sneaks over to Dusty and Elly's place late at night. She's guilt-ridden about not being there for the team. Her mom drives her to and from the Farm and keeps her practically imprisoned the rest of the time. What is wrong with those people? I enjoyed Lorelei, but does her family really think we recruit kids or the mentally retarded?"

Jo poured more tea from the pig pot into Annie's mug. Annie stared at it.

"The Simskis sincerely think they're doing what's best for Lorelei, Annie. They think being gay is as bad as a cancer diagnosis and that they have to protect her from people like you."

Her anger, as if waiting for a spark, flared again. She rudely pushed the tea cup away. "Like me? You mean like us, don't you?"

Jo hesitated. "Of course. It's just... Mrs. Norwood took Lorelei's parents down to look at the diner team and, well, everyone looks so *masculine* on the softball field."

"Right. Like femme-of-the-century Paris Collins?"

"No, but Mr. Simski has a little backhoe company and Paris is a known environmentalist—"

"So the only one who looks like their take on a woman is a subversive." As she spoke, she tried to convince herself that Jo was on her side.

Jo sounded annoyed. "Talking to the Simskis is like talking to something more solid than a brick wall, Annie. They were just so freaked to have had a disabled kid in the first place, then to learn their adopted kid is a lesbian who obviously gave it to their daughter..." She smiled weakly. "It's probably shaken their pro-life faith."

"The crosses they must bear," Annie said. The last of her tea tasted bitter.

"I'd miss you, Annie, but I certainly wouldn't blame you for leaving a town filled with Simskis."

She forced her question past a dry lump in her throat, trying to ignore Jo's body, her own desire. "Is that what you want, Jo, for me and my problem and my factory job to disappear? Would that be better for you?"

"Of course not," Jo said hastily as she dropped their tea bags into the trash.

The telephone rang. Jo looked at it, seemed to hesitate, then answered.

"*Hello*," said Jo, her tone so intimate Annie went to the living room window and looked across at the reservoir to give her privacy. Under the illumination of a street lamp a Mallard waddled onto a narrow strip of bank and disappeared under some bushes. The drizzle was like a fine fog. Annie fingered her hat, trying not to hear Jo's low words, but she knew that flirtatious tone. She'd tell Annie if she were seeing someone else, wouldn't she? The old MG. Tell me it's not Verne, she thought. She couldn't take any more humiliation.

Rex pawed insistently at the downstairs back door. At a particularly loud snort Jo cut off her conversation.

"Sorry," Jo called to Annie as she hung up the phone. "It's getting late. Would you like something to eat?"

"No, go ahead, I barged in on you."

"I'm feeling good about working this out, Annie. I still think you're wise to..." She was obviously choosing her words carefully. "...keep a low profile. This isn't a good place, or time, to make waves."

Angry again, she declared, "One more week, Jo, and if Judy hasn't talked to one of us, I'm going to track her down. She can fire me or put me back to work, but I want to stop this now. For my sake, but also before she gives the right wingers a taste for power—the power to win elections by stirring up homophobia— like their cohorts out in Oregon and Colorado have. It wouldn't take much to repeal everything you've gained here."

Jo bit her bottom lip. A piece of Annie wanted to stop her from hurting it. "I don't know, Annie. You'd be taking on the whole Valley."

"Then I'll take on the whole fucking Valley. Meanwhile, I'm history. Thanks for playing mediator. I really hope it works."

She pulled her team cap on and paused at the door. Should she at least kiss Jo's cheek? Acknowledge their intimacy at all? She found that she didn't want to. The flaring anger had replaced desire. When she looked at Jo's smile, no one was home but the bank manager. She tipped her hat.

The gesture felt like a reminder of all they hadn't promised each other.

CHAPTER 8

The next night, while the *Sentinel's* letters-to-the editors raged about gays ruining the moral fiber of America, Annie had to get out of the house.

The Sweatshop was supposed to be an after hours club, but when the diner was mobbed, or the gay crowd wanted to dance or play pool without drinking, everyone drifted early the few blocks down toward the river to another cobblestoned street, where the trolley once took dreamers to the old promenade along Morton River. She imagined girls with white parasols batting their eyelashes at—did butches wear striped blazers and straw boaters back then? All carefully averting their eyes from the factories where they forged brass all week, faces to the river where friends waved from rented rowboats.

She was at the jukebox when she heard, "Sugar!"

"Chantal Zak!" she said, adding, to her own surprise, "It's really great to see you!" The payroll clerk from Medipak, with her swept-back frosted hair and constant smile, reached with a delicate hand to guide her to the empty chair beside her, then introduced her to two friends.

"Come sit up close. I never get to feast my eyes on you enough out at Club Med. I'm going to start messing up your paychecks so you'll come visit me."

"Thanks, but no thanks. I'm trying to avoid the boss' wife, remember?"

She'd forgotten the sultriness of Chantal's voice and noted her over-sized deep gold sweater, black slacks and the splash of black scarf knotted at her throat. "You look really nice," she said, feeling something like a drumming begin deep in her gut. She confessed, "I seem to have a thing for French women."

"Just a quarter French. The rest of me is Polish as the pope."

Chantal's friends got up to dance.

"Don't they look good together?" asked Chantal. "I just intro-

75

duced them."

The two dancers took a minute to find their rhythm.

"Yeah," she agreed, not bothering to hide the pining from her tone.

They both watched the women. "It'd be a great coup if it worked for them, wouldn't it?" Chantal mused.

"For any of us," Annie said, turning to study her.

Chantal's smile had gone a little sad. Her chin rested on a dimpled hand. The dreamy light blue eyes, when they turned to Annie, belonged to another lonely person looking for the same thing Annie wanted. Companionship, maybe love down the line. Not quite as far down the line as Jo seemed to be headed. Annie didn't want to be pushy about it, but Jo seemed about as interested in her last night as Mrs. Kurt. It looked as if Jo didn't want to share her closet any more. Not with Annie Heaphy.

Chantal interrupted her gloom. "So what brings you to the Sweatshop tonight, Sugar?"

"I usually hang out at the diner, but when there's all this tension between Elly and Dusty the service gets crummy and the customers are crabby. Not to mention the staff. I wouldn't have thought Maddy's sister Giulia could get any snippier. I don't need the extra stress."

"You're meeting someone here?"

"Only you, unless you're booked."

"Oh, I have so many beaus, you know, but I pencil my dates in. Consider them erased," Chantal announced with a dismissive flick of her hand.

"You're a joy to run into, Chantal." She relaxed in her chair and looked around.

The Sweatshop was an enormous space, converted from a factory. Jimmy O' and Jimmy Kinh had purchased it with the idea of refurbishing cars full-time, but first they'd given Jimmy O's other dream, a gay club, a chance. Weeknights like this a lot of straights came in and weekends they got gays from Upton and New Haven, more than enough customers to keep the place going.

She told Chantal, "It's nights like these when a gay watering hole is a lifesaver. I need to be with my people. I never felt like a skulking pervert before."

"Sugar! You're the most worthwhile thing to hit this town in about five years." Chantal straightened the table where her two friends had been sitting. She mopped up a minor puddle with a napkin.

"Right," she scoffed. "Is that when you moved here, five years ago?" she asked. The table of straights next to them was noisy. The men dressed like Rafferty Street's vacant lot crowd. Annie turned her chair away.

"Not me," Chantal answered. "I was born and raised and condemned to stay in this old ghost of a town."

"I thought things were picking up."

"You mean industry? If I'm employed they must be. I'm talking about high society in Morton River. The same old faces year in and year out. It gets dreary, dearie."

"What ties you here?"

"My kids, for one."

"Kids? You?" Chantal wore just enough eye makeup to draw attention to the extraordinarily light blue of her eyes. Her cheeks were pink without makeup and made her look like a kid herself.

"Wait, I want to enjoy this. I have a twenty-year old and a twenty-two year old."

"You don't look old enough—" Annie said, starting to laugh.

"I love it! I love to hear this part! Keep going!"

"—to have kids in their twenties."

"I made my mistakes young. It takes time to be perfect."

"Seriously."

"Seriously. And they're the loves of my life. Ralph is the oldest. I think he's going to decide to go gay too. And Merry, my daughter, has a pretty nice husband. She started as early as me, but she was smart enough to stop after my granddaughter Merrilyn was born until they have some money set by. If you think it's hard for whites to get work in this town, you ought to talk to my son-in-law. He might tell you a thing or two about being hated for loving."

"I'll bet."

"And I peeked at your personnel file—not that there's much in it—but I learned that I did all that in two years less than it took you to do whatever you've done."

"Are you really forty?" Chantal's face looked completely unlined. Maybe she was good at makeup. "It's hard enough to accept that I'm forty-two, but to hear that women my age can be grandmothers? Grandmothers are supposed to look like Gramma Gus."

"Doesn't it get to you to see the kids graduating from high school? They look like they might be thirteen, tops." Chantal leaned to her, smiling eyes probing. "So fill me in on what you've done with your life. And don't leave out the sexy parts."

Annie exaggerated a sigh. "I can't wait to be an old-timer in Morton River. Do you know how often I've told my story since I moved here?"

"Then leave out everything but the sexy parts."

"Come on, Chantal, I hardly know you."

"All the more reason. No, really, I'm just kidding, Sugar." She slipped the napkin out from under her glass, carefully smoothed and replaced it. "Am I coming on too strong? It's just that when you came in you looked like someone burnt your supper and then told you your dog was terminal."

This sigh was real. Thinking of Jo was too sad. "I visited Jo, the New Way board member."

"I remember. The one who's getting your job back. I hate her. Why don't you stay at Club Med, Sugar? Don't go where you're not wanted."

"We're not *wanted* anywhere, Chantal." She shared the gist of her exchange with Jo and pulled out the clipping.

Jimmy Kinh was serving the raucous table. One of the straight men flirted with Jimmy while the others laughed.

"You know, my Mom's a good Polish Catholic," Chantal said. "She's as conservative as those right wingers even though they hate Catholics almost as much as queers. She doesn't know about me, but this makes me want to tell her she's got a rooster in her own hen house. They all want to put sex in a big old box and leave it there. What they don't want to face is we're talking jack-in-the-box. Pop! goes the weasel."

"That's what I want to tell them, damn it, and everybody keeps trying to shut me up."

"They wouldn't hear you, Sugar. God told them they have to save us if they have to kill us to do it. We can protest 'til we're blue in the face, but they only listen to God."

Annie shook her head. "You know, as much as I'd like to protect Lorelei and Errol," she bit her lip to keep from getting teary-eyed, "if I don't stand up for myself, what kind of teacher could I be?"

Chantal nodded. "I kid around a lot, Annie, but whether you go back to the Farm or not, I really think something good can come of all this. The Valley's big enough for all of us. Maybe you're here to teach us that lesson."

"Why me?" she groaned. "Don't answer that. I always said I wanted to do something good in this world. Maddy's right. There's a surplus of do-gooders in the city."

"When I read that you'd last worked in New York City, I knew what was exciting about you besides your irresistible shaggy butch femininity. Don't tell me, you left because of some dopey dame who didn't know how good she had it."

Annie let out a loud laugh. "Bingo! Sometimes I just want to run back to her on any terms. It's been months and I'm still so goddamn mad at her for being who she is, for not being able to dig in her heels and stay put." Then she grinned. "I don't think I ever heard anyone call Marie-Christine a dopey dame before."

"If she's what drove you to Morton River, I love the dopey dame. You don't have to answer this—was she cheating on you?"

She almost gagged on a swallow of Coke, "Not *exactly*."

"What a jerk."

"It was more complicated than that."

"Isn't it always? Isn't the bottom line that she wasn't capable of appreciating you?"

"That's a little hard to accept, but I guess I need to hear I was right to tell Marie-Christine that I wanted a marriage, and damn it, some commitment, especially with AIDS raging. We're all grown women, after all, more than old enough to know our minds, aren't we?"

Chantal looked skyward. "You'd think so, by now," she said.

"Well, I stuck my neck out and said that I not only wanted to, but would work at staying together through thick and thin for the rest of my life."

"Good for you, Sugar."

"Marie-Christine took months to decide she wasn't willing to do the same." She shook her head and crumpled a napkin. "I don't want to, but I miss that wacky, enchanting, incurably selfish woman like crazy. I just couldn't take her waffling. I felt like I deserved more than she was willing to give. I'm not cut out to live forever on crumbs from a lover. She just wasn't the settling-down type."

"And you are?"

"Absolutely."

Chantal arched one pale eyebrow. "Never even a little fling when your heart isn't looking?"

"Yes, well," she answered evasively into her Coke, her heart skipping with a charge of lust.

"With this woman who's supposed to be going to bat for you at the Farm?"

She was surprised when the charge drained. "You mean Jo?"

"Oh, I hear it in your voice. You'd never give her this much slack if your soft spot for her wasn't bigger than your soft spot for yourself."

"I—" It was true, she realized with a shock. Her voice came out as a squeak. She cleared it. "I wouldn't?"

"This is your reputation on the line here, your future in the Valley that Jo Barker's been holding in her white-gloved little hands. If it was me on that board I'd be raising hell, demanding your job and a public apology." Chantal studied her nail polish. "Of course, that's why nobody'd ever ask me to be on their board."

Even talking about the Farm, Chantal made her laugh. "You can be on my board any day! Meantime, Jo's gotten my job back. It's just a matter of when."

"She'd better be quick. I don't like Miz Hotshot's idea of soft pedaling you to the old boys' network. If you wait too long on something like this, word gets out and you're the one who's up the creek without a paddle."

"But *is* my reputation more important than letting the Farm get on with its business? Besides, Lorelei was coming on to me in her own way. Sometimes I wonder if I had the responsibility to hear the alarm bells long before I did."

"Annie, I've known retarded kids," Chantal said with a sudden passion, "watched a couple of them grow up. They like sex as much as the rest of us. They feel attractions just like we do. How about Lorelei? How about a lesbian softball team being the only one that'll make room for her because we're special people too? Give up your own rights if you want, but don't speak for her."

Annie just stared at Chantal, "Crap, what a dummy. I never

thought of it that way."

"What if Lorelei is a dyke? Shouldn't she be able to love? There's so much going on here it's way out of your hands now, Annie."

"I have a sinking feeling you're trying to tell me I don't get to just walk away from the whole thing."

"Maybe I'm not one to talk, as closeted as I've been at work, but I like to think if Kurt did fire me, I'd shout it from the hillside—for all of us."

"So while I'm trying to figure out what to do, you think I'm betraying every queer in the galaxy."

Chantal just smiled.

"Maddy's the activist, not me, Chantal," Annie pleaded. "What am I supposed to do, run for mayor?"

"I don't think so, Sugar. Just don't run." Chantal studied her face and nodded. "No, I don't think you will."

Annie drained her Coke, put down the glass, checked out the loud straights from the corner of her eye. They made her nervous.

"Do you see me running? I love the Valley," she told Chantal. "It's full of crazy old houses and miles of old brick factories. It's got a soul of its own. All those years in New York I thought being anonymous and uncommitted was so tough and cool, when really I had a mega-hole to fill. That's not something you can ask one person to do, Marie-Christine or anyone else. Here, I started to fill the hole. Then I'm laid off and, boom, there's the hole again."

"So it's the end of the world? Haven't you always bounced back from this kind of thing in the past?"

Annie flung her arms high. "I've never been forty-two before. The crazy right wing never felt like a threat before. I never felt this middle-class, middle America craving for settling down before. And I never had work that made me feel anything but drained at the end of a shift."

Chantal said nothing, just held Annie's eyes, like she was watching her thrash it all out inside.

"Want to dance?" Annie asked, not waiting for an answer, but recklessly swinging Chantal into a fast number. She laughed as Chantal shimmied, then led her into the old bump, each of them careening off the other like wildly swinging metronomes. When the music stopped they fell into their seats laughing.

"You're right," Annie admitted, "I'm not going anyplace. I've waited long enough for my life to start. Those crazies are not going to get in my way."

"That's the best news I've heard since Merry had a girl," Chantal announced, fanning herself with a napkin. They were both pretty sweaty. "This friend of yours may be a pretty lady, but she doesn't sound like she has any more idea of your worth than the one you had in New York. But then, I'll bet you always chase pretty ladies that give you a hell of a time. Being comfortable is what girlfriends should be about." Chantal paused for a moment, then asked, "Want to come over to my place and get comfortable?"

She felt her face blaze red. Wasn't comfortable just the word she'd pinned on Chantal? "I'd—"

"Scared the socks off you, didn't I?"

"Yeah," admitted Annie, pulling the brim of her softball cap over her eyes. Was the game really over with Jo? Was she ready to step up to the plate again so soon?

Chantal reached to flip Annie's hat up, adjusting the brim exactly in the middle of her forehead. "No hiding. Come on, no strings attached. We'll have fun. Unless you want to go to your place."

"Not 'til you've met Gussie. And she's gone to bed by now."

Chantal extended a finger and gently tapped Annie on the tip of the nose. "Is that anything like taking me to meet the family?"

"Oops, caught me," she answered with a laugh. "How about a lift home instead?"

They both looked toward the dance floor. Chantal's friends still danced.

"That's so inspiring. I don't want to disturb them," Chantal said. "I'd love a ride."

CHAPTER 9

Chantal wanted to stop at the diner to pick up a Boston cream pie she'd promised her mother. Maddy rushed at Annie and grabbed her coat as they stepped inside.

"Annie! You've got to help! Dusty's gone to kill Verne!"

"Hush!" Elly said, joining them, steering the group into the kitchen, away from the haunted face of Maddy's sister Giulia, who watched them with frank alarm.

"What's going on?" Annie asked against the clatter of pots being cleaned.

Maddy looked to Elly in panic. Elly's hair was disheveled. She held her pink and white baseball-style jacket together with her hands, the zipper torn loose. Her eyes were frantic, but she took a moment to speak, as if by choosing the right words she could hold her life together too.

"Annie, thank goodness you're here. I've been trying to think who to call. I stopped by on my way home from class to see how things were going. Dusty was still here, mad as a hoppy toad in a drought."

"There was no chilling her out," Maddy said, voice filled with amazement, still wild-eyed. "I never heard Dusty yell before."

"This was how she acted when she drank. She hasn't had a drink in, God, years!"

"She wasn't drinking," Maddy objected quickly, darting a hand to Annie's sleeve. "I would have seen her, or smelled it. I'm filling in for the dishwasher tonight."

"She said I smelled like Verne's cologne. I was in Verne's class all night—art teachers have to get cozy to check your work—why wouldn't I?"

"Maybe tonight, Elly," challenged Annie, "but everybody knows something's going on. Dusty isn't totally paranoid."

"If you don't mind my two cents' worth," Chantal said, "even I've heard about you and the art teacher."

"This is Chantal Zak. Chantal—Elly, Maddy."

Elly frowned at Chantal and seemed to notice for the first time Chantal's hand on Annie's arm. Annie hadn't been aware of the firm grip before either.

"Look what happened when I tried to keep Dusty here!" Elly pleaded, displaying the tear in her jacket as if it could explain everything.

"Where is she now?" asked Annie.

"I'm sure she's home."

Maddy's voice was pleading too. "She sounded dead serious about hurting Verne. We have to do *something!*"

Elly shook her head. "I know my Dusty better than that. And I can't leave Giulia alone here crabbing at all the customers."

The anger Annie had swallowed hours before now burst out. "I love you, El, but you've driven Dusty nuts with your flitting around. If she's not drunk on liquor, she's drunk on rage and misery. You can't keep acting like you have and expect her not to explode. Where does Verne live?"

"No!" Elly said, covering her face with her hands. "Verne and I haven't done anything, I swear it! I got so lonely these last few years, I had to have something. Just because I can't spend every living hour here, Dusty thinks I'm wasting time and money, but I've never loved anything as much as drawing—except Dusty. And Verne, well, she's more than a teacher to me, but only because she *talks* to me, about art and artists and the places she's been." There was a glitter in Elly's eyes that Annie hadn't seen since they'd bar-hopped together in their early twenties.

"Where—does—Verne—live?" Annie asked.

Elly's eyes swung from Annie to Chantal and back. She looked cornered.

Maddy, punching the crown of her Mets cap in and out with nervous hands, spoke up. "Verne has this cool loft in the old Cooper Rivets building. She converted it, like in Soho. Nobody else would live in that old firetrap except an artist."

"You don't think she'd really—" Elly asked. She shook her head as if seeing a vision too horrible to face. "No. Dusty can't get up there without a key anyway."

"You've just told us what Dusty's acting like," Annie said. "If I were you I wouldn't put anything past her."

"She's not drunk," insisted Maddy with simple faith. "Dusty

told me she'd never do that again."

"I think you're right, Mad," said Annie, half out the door, "but she shouldn't be alone now." She turned to Chantal. "Shall I run you back to your car?"

Chantal, one hip thrust forward, looking taller than usual, finished retying the black chiffon scarf around her neck. "I hate to sound like we're in a movie, but, Annie, I'm comin' with you."

They were nearly silent as she maneuvered the Grape under the highway and over railroad crossings, rushing between ghosts of factories set along trolley tracks so ancient the narrow cobblestone streets had swallowed them almost entirely.

Chantal interrupted the silence once as Annie braked for a stop light, then rolled through the red. "I'm glad to see you have gumption when it comes to other people's battles, anyway."

Annie scowled, then sputtered, "I *know* what to do here, Chantal. It's a little harder to mount a defense against mass hatred."

Cooper Rivets was next to the river. The bottom floor was a custom lamp factory on one side and outlet shop on the other. There was a light on in the second floor windows, but the street was otherwise dark and deserted except for Verne's old MG.

She killed the Saab's engine and took off her glasses.

"You *look* like a philosopher in those," Chantal whispered, tapping an edge of the frames.

Annie whispered back, "I hope that's a compliment." She got out, warily, listening.

"Anything?" asked Chantal, halfway out of the car.

"Music. Sounds like Verne's playing opera loud enough to serenade the river ducks."

"Would Dusty park out of sight so she could—"

"Never. With Dusty, if she's mad enough to fight she's going to barge in and do it. She's no sneak." They watched Verne's windows. "Geez, I hate this. Why can't we just grow up? The grass is never greener on the other side. It's all got weeds."

"Maybe she's come and gone already."

They walked toward the next corner. Annie chortled. "To tell you the truth, I can't picture anything better than good old street-fightin' Dusty scaring the butch-gel out of Verne's hair."

"Sugar!"

"It's true. I know she's no saint, devoting all her energy to the business. Elly's just as much to blame, fawning on Verne. But Verne is the worm in the apple, the snake in the grass, the dirty dog—"

"The slime bucket!"

"The beetle-headed, flap-eared knave! Shakespeare said that."

"The two-timing double-dealing sidewinder! I always wanted to call someone that."

"The wolf in sheep's clothing!"

"Good one, Sugar! Lecher! Swine!"

Annie paused at the corner and looked up and down the street. "Still no old Dodge Swinger."

"Know anyone who drives a Prelude?" Chantal asked.

They walked closer. She squinted. "Speaking of swine. PBPIG," she read.

"PBPIG? Does that mean anything to you?"

"Pot-bellied pig. Jo Barker's car." Annie felt stunned. "What would Jo be doing with Verne?"

Chantal gave her a disgusted look.

"Oh," said Annie. "But Verne's too out for Jo."

"From what I hear, that art teacher is so outrageous she crosses into a safe zone."

"That would explain a lot. And you know what?" She told Chantal about Verne meeting Jo outside the bank. "It's so obvious. Jo's got a line on a lot of funding sources in this valley. This Verne would naturally cultivate a woman like that. And would be willing to keep a low profile—for profit."

Chantal took her arm. "I'm sorry, Annie."

"Actually, it's good news," she said, ignoring the wail of disappointment inside. "Elly really wasn't with Verne tonight."

Chantal looked at her and asked, "You think the three of them are up there?"

Annie shrugged. "I guess I better go up just to be sure Dusty's not. But it feels even more awkward now."

"There's no one else Jo could be visiting?"

"You heard Maddy. Verne converted this for herself."

"The neighborhood is creepy."

"You're welcome to lock yourself in the car."

Chantal looked up and down the street, laughed nervously, then stood tall again, those light blue eyes darker with worry.

"Cece would call you my lily white knight. I feel safer with you."

She checked Chantal's shadowed face. The woman was absolutely sincere. "No one ever said that to me before. I like it." She took Chantal's small hand and they marched to the double door together. Annie pulled at it. "Locked."

"Just like Elly said it would be," Chantal whispered. "Dusty could have come and given up."

"Could have."

Chantal looked upward. "What's Verne like?"

She almost laughed aloud at the wave of anger that rushed over her. "Pretty obnoxious. The Goddess' gift to women. A beetle-headed, flap-eared knave."

"All too common in these parts," Chantal commented. "What does Elly see in her?"

"Elly has real talent. Verne's given her all sorts of strokes for her drawing. Plus Verne's from out of town, sort of glamorous, and I'd say she's stirred up Elly's yen for excitement after years of slaving away at the diner and being settled down. Voilà, you have an affair—or a flirtation—waiting to happen."

"And Verne?"

"Doesn't look to me like the type to turn down any reasonable offer."

"Too bad I didn't meet Verne first," teased Chantal, batting her eyelashes. Annie dropped Chantal's hand and cocked an eyebrow at her. "Because I'm so gorgeous—and single, and available—and single," explained Chantal, grabbing Annie's hand again.

"You're too smart for someone like that weasel. Elly's just in a place where she's susceptible."

"Are you this understanding about your own lovers' roving eyes?"

They'd been standing in the open, Annie half-listening for the sound of a car approaching. It started to drizzle. She pulled Chantal under the lamp shop's awning. The window was lit by a lamp with a red and yellow Tiffany-style shade that lent a living-room coziness to the dank night. "Do you have a personal stake in my answer?" she teased, not taking her hand away, wondering if she was playing with the right woman this time.

Chantal stepped closer. "I might."

Their faces were close enough for a kiss, but Annie froze.

"Chantal," she said.

"Ooh, you never said my name like that before."

Annie pitched her voice lower. Her heart was doing that wonderful pounding thing it did when she was really into someone. "Chantal." Their eyes kissed, but Annie pulled back. She heard an unmuffled car revving nearby. "This isn't safe."

Chantal stepped back too. She bit her lower lip, eyes still fastened on Annie's. The cloak of seduction that had surrounded them dissipated. "Damn," said Chantal. "I really found a good woman this time, didn't I? I had every intention of being the responsible one if this ever happened to me again, and then—I forgot. Isn't that ridiculous? I tell Ralph not to be irresponsible, but do I stay cool in the heat of the moment? Hell, no."

Annie was confused."Oh," she said, "you mean AIDS."

"Isn't that—"

"I hadn't even got that far yet." Noticing the embarrassment on Chantal's face, she added, "but I was headed in that direction. I was thinking more about social risks than health risks."

"Oh, those little things."

"You want to go talk in the car? Hang around in case Dusty shows up?"

Chantal looked thoughtful. "Have you considered calling Dusty at home to see if she's there?"

Annie shoved her hands in her pockets and looked to the sky with exasperation. "Crap! Why didn't I think of that? Better still, let's run over there." She took Chantal's arm. "We'll come back if she's not home, okay?"

"Sugar, I can't imagine a better way to spend the first evening with my white knight than rescuing a dyke in distress. Can you?"

They laughed as they hurried through the drizzle to the car. Annie opened the door for Chantal, then looked up at the loft and listened. "I still hear the opera," she reported before she raced around the car. "And that was definitely Verne's punk-haired silhouette crossing the window just now."

"At least she's alive," Chantal said, raising an index finger. "One crisis down."

"And I need something to help me face the next one." Annie got the heater and an old Marian McPartland piano tape going, leaned across the stick shift and pulled Chantal to her. "I think hugging is considered safe on every level." She slipped her arms around Chantal's shoulders, aware of a breadth of softness under the gold sweater. It was a shock to feel the difference from the slenderness of Marie-Christine and Jo. A pleasant shock, like settling into bed after a hard day's work. They touched cheeks and she smelled Chantal's natural scent, something faintly peanut-buttery. "I like it that you don't drench yourself in perfume. The stuff makes me sneeze."

"My last girlfriend wore Brut by the quart. It cured me forever."

Annie shifted to ease a cramp in her thigh. "I'm getting too old for awkward positions," she said, "but I'd do it all night if I weren't so worried about Dusty."

"Giddy up then."

"Yes, ma'am." She was disgusted with herself. Here she was, drummed out of a job, the woman she'd been dating possibly stolen away by a creep, ready for the whole town to tar and feather her, and she was cozying up to the first nice woman to come along. She tried to feel miserable, but she loved retracing her cobbled way through the dark, nearly-empty, rain-polished streets, heart racing to the romance of "You and the Night and the Music." She loved speeding off on a new adventure, though she'd rather Dusty's heart wasn't at stake.

Chantal's quiet voice sounded studiously casual. "So, have you been tested?"

"Yes, I was fine. That was one reason we split, Marie-Christine and me. I wanted to keep it that way. And," she said, uncertain of the proper etiquette, "the woman I've been seeing?"

"Yes?" responded Chantal with a hint of mockery.

"There's nothing to worry about there."

"I see. I was afraid to get it done in Morton River. Getting tested is proof of guilt around here. So I went to the Upton health department."

"Morton River isn't exactly dyke paradise, is it?"

"You expected that?"

"No. But everybody seemed so happy here."

"Compared to what?" asked Chantal. "Connecticut is pretty liberal, but these crazies that want to change the laws, the newspapers say they're cropping up everywhere."

"That's what my ex said about Oregon. When I visited a few

months ago she begged me to bring the message back that it can happen here. And she was right."

"Another ex?"

"Vicky. I guess you'd call her my great love. But, you know how it is, our paths diverged."

"You have been around the block, haven't you, Sugar?"

Annie, giving her a sly grin, revved the Grape and sped completely around a block.

"You're a trip, Annie Heaphy!" Chantal said, holding onto the roof strap as they careened onto Main Street. "Don't worry," Chantal assured her. "I've got settings other than full speed ahead, but it's hard—I've never had more energy. The kids are gone and there's no man to make demands on me. Coming out's been like a tonic, though I've been without so long maybe I'm not susceptible anymore," Chantal teased, running a finger along Annie's arm.

Annie got goose bumps and stalled the car at a traffic light. "You are one helluva sexy lady, lady."

"It's all stored up for somebody like you, Sugar. I don't mind waiting." Chantal squeezed Annie's thigh, high up. "And by the way, I'm negative."

CHAPTER 10

The Saab splashed onto Puddle Street. Dusty's was the only light still burning in this old residential section just the other side of town. She turned off the car and sought Chantal's startling eyes. They seemed to glow in the dark, right along with her mischievous little smile.

"So do I get that kiss?" Chantal asked.

Annie was all shaky inside, but managed to run a finger slowly along Chantal's jaw. "I thought you liked anticipation."

"Maybe I like a little anticipation."

"Can't you handle it?"

"Sugar," said Chantal, massaging Annie's upper arms with deliberate slowness, "I'm just beginning to get ideas of how waiting could turn out to be fun."

Annie smiled, but she felt abysmally sad. "I just don't know what I want, Chantal. I haven't even been able to digest, you know, Jo and the swine—no disrespect to Jo's pet pig."

The drizzle had become a fine warm rain. Annie pulled a plastic poncho from her trunk and they held it over their heads as they hurried up the flagstone path. One of Dusty's ducks quacked back at the little pond. Music Annie couldn't quite place pounded inside this house too, and Annie's shaky feeling was no longer excitement, but apprehension.

Dusty opened the door. "Heaphy? What are you doing here?"

At the sight of her friend, Annie realized she'd been holding her breath. "Are you all right, Dusty?"

"Don't tell me the scene at the diner's all over town already."

"No, we stopped there, then went to Verne's to make sure you didn't do anything foolish. This is Chantal."

"Glad to meet you, Dusty."

Her tone gruff, Dusty commented, "It's a funny time to be saying that, Chantal."

"It's true anyway. I've always admired you from afar."

"Not much to admire these days."

"You're hanging in there."

"I don't know how much longer. You two want to come in out of the rain?"

"Do you want company?" asked Annie.

"Hell, yes. I'm about to go insane. Did you see her?"

"Elly?"

"No, Lily Tomlin."

"She was pretty scared that you might have been drinking."

"Was she now. You'd think after all these years she'd know she can trust me, even if I can't trust her."

"Maddy stuck up for you like a kid for her mom."

"She's a good kid and a damned hard worker. We keep her weird sister on mostly to make sure the family has that income."

The main room was beamed and spacious. It would have been barn-like in the flickering light from the TV except for Dusty's paperbacks in homemade bookcases and Elly's matted but unframed drawings clustered on every available patch of wall. Two bulky white and black cats slept soundly at either end of the couch, one on its back, legs in the air, the other slopping over the sides of a small pillow. They snored and wheezed.

"I've been watching M.A.S.H. reruns and playing some of my old albums that she hates to listen to."

Annie and Elly had once had a friendly little one night stand before Dusty appeared on the scene. Though over twenty years had passed, the memory of that quick intimacy always made Annie feel squirrely around Dusty.

Dusty broke the silence. "By the way, I haven't been drinking."

"Annie stuck up for you too," Chantal said.

"Thanks. It gets kind of lonesome."

"I know," Annie said. "I'm sorry I haven't been in touch more. It's this darned am-I-fired-or-not business."

Dusty peered at her and replaced her glasses. A car approached the house. Dusty stood stock still, hope so palpable it filled the air like a fog. The car's sound gradually died and left an audible stillness. In the basement the furnace kicked on and Dusty jumped. That seemed to return her to them.

"You have news about your job?"

"Dream on. No, it's the memories. I'll be grabbing a bubble pack of eyeglass repair kits at work and remember Kim. She was blinded and brain damaged in a car accident. I remember the feel of her hand clinging to mine and how hard she cried when a whole patch of wintergreen she'd babied was trampled by mistake." No one said a thing. She looked at Chantal. "But I enjoy the new job."

"Right, Heaphy, and I'd rather manage a McDonald's."

As far as she could tell, Dusty really hadn't been drinking, but in the dim blue light of the TV her short hair was uncombed, her stained white work clothes smelled sweaty and her face was old with grief. The gruff, jovial manner she usually presented to the world was only gruffness tonight.

"You really stirred up a hornets' nest, Heaphy. I thought we were over and done with that gay-bashing stuff. Now all of a sudden, between the military and the politics out west and the Norwoods' outrage, gays are in the papers every night. I'm seeing queer-hating graffiti around town and some of my customers, well, they look at me like a germ under a microscope."

"What can I say, Reilly?"

"I know it's not your fault. It just puts me on edge, feeling like we're all going into battle when we don't want to and don't know much about fighting. Elly and me may have our problems, but I was at least keeping it together at work before I got turned into a dangerous dyke overnight. Now—well, there's always more breakups when life gets harder."

"With any luck," said Chantal, "we'll hear some wedding bells too." Dusty looked from Chantal to Annie.

Annie opened her mouth to protest, but nothing came out except a spurt of nervous laughter. She cleared her throat.

They went into the dim kitchen, a neglected-looking room that smelled of cat food and obviously was used less for cooking than as a repository for gardening tools, how-to books, rain gear and junk mail. The room, with one of the ceiling bulbs burned out, had an out of control feeling, like Dusty's clothes and manner. The cats meandered after Dusty.

"Let me make you some coffee. Usually El—" Dusty's voice went thin as she stumbled over her words "—does those little things." Dusty trod around the kitchen trailing her sneaker laces, pulling mugs from the drain board. "I know we've got instant here someplace."

Annie wanted to cry for her. She blurted, "Dusty, you don't

have to be a woman of iron tonight. I know what it feels like to have your lover want to be with someone besides you."

Dusty leaned forward over the sink, back to them, and covered her face with those battered, big-knuckled hands. Her shoulders heaved once like hurricane waves. One cat leapt onto the counter and stared at her. The other flopped over on her feet. This shouldn't happen after a dyke passes fifty, thought Annie. Voice muffled, one hand stroking the counter cat, Dusty said, "I don't fucking cry, Heaphy. It takes the end of the world to make me cry." She straightened, blew her nose into a paper towel and exhaled noisily.

"This type of thing fucking feels like the end of the world, Reilly," said Annie, her voice breaking.

"Chantal," Dusty said, pulling a chair out from the kitchen table, "Why don't you have a seat?"

Chantal bobbed her head in a way that made Annie think of a curtsy. "Thank you. It's been a hard night."

"I'm sorry if my little upset made it harder."

"Even if it did, it was worth it," Chantal replied. Despite the circumstances, the woman obviously couldn't stop smiling at the two butches. Chantal told Dusty, "The best way to get to know someone is to live through a crisis with her."

"I guess I'm having one of those all right. Damn it, sit down, Heaphy. You look like you're standing on hot coals." Annie obediently sat. Dusty rubbed the fist of one hand against the palm of the other with a dry-sounding, anguished motion. There were innumerable small burn marks on her forearms and hands from cooking at the grill. Her eyes darted toward the front door. "What was I looking for out here?"

"Coffee?" suggested Chantal.

Into the silence that accompanied Dusty's preparations Annie nervously chattered, "Tonight's been intense. I'd say Chantal and I have crammed about two years of getting to know each other into these few hours. Plus I spent the early part of the evening with Jo."

"Nice woman," Dusty commented absently, spooning coffee into mugs, "but isn't she a little on the snooty side?"

"Not that I've noticed," Annie lied, annoyed with herself for doing so, annoyed with Dusty for bringing it up.

"That's right, you and your ivy league women."

"What's this?" asked Chantal, her tone playfully taunting, her eyes mischievous. She straightened a stack of napkins in their holder.

"She just means Vicky, the woman I told you about in Oregon. She went to Yale. Vicky and I were getting together about the time Dusty and Elly met. We all hung out at the same bar. I guess I have a slight history of getting in over my head. I would've liked to have finished college back in Boston, but, you know, it was the drop-out era and I got tired of being a starving student with a dyke agenda. No education, just educated girls."

"Like the last one," Dusty said, sliding steaming mugs onto the table. "I always felt like us Morton River types were like quaint villagers to her."

"Marie-Christine was from France, Reilly." Her loyalty to the woman might no longer be reasonable, but she'd loved her hard and long. "For her, Morton River was like walking into American history—the old factories, the mill houses."

"She was nice enough about it, but you couldn't talk to her. She was so artsy-fartsy," concluded Dusty, setting one foot on a chair, leaning on her knee with both hands and giving Chantal a conspiratorial look. She turned to Annie. "Remember when you brought her over here, Heaphy, and she got a gander at my bookshelves? Who's the reader? she asks, like she's surprised we know how to read."

Annie had been embarrassed by that, even though she knew it hadn't been what Marie-Christine meant. "You're exaggerating," she objected. "I remember her trying to talk books with you. She was just looking for what you had in common. And you said, I don't talk about 'em, I just read 'em. Marie-Christine thought you were the original Butch National Monument. And you are, Dusty."

"Yeah, the original asshole. Or I wouldn't be putting up with this shit from Elly like you did with ol' M-C."

Chantal asked, "What happened?"

Dusty hugged a cat to her chest. "The beginning was no big deal. El went to this art class."

Dusty set the cat down and walked from window to chair, back and forth. "She stopped telling me the truth. She had to stay late at school. She had to make a call to somebody in class and whisper on the phone like a teenager with secrets from her mother. Like I was the enemy! I told her to have her friends over, but no, she *needed* something separate from me. True, but I know enough about lying to recognize it."

There was a sudden sharp tapping on the back door. "Oh, nuts. Lorelei climbed out her window again." She went to unlock the door.

"Annie!" cried Lorelei. "I saw a purple car!"

She found herself with her arms full of a crying, smiling Lorelei in flowered pink flannel pajamas. "It's great to see you, Lor!" Then, as if Lorelei were a great electrical bolt, she dropped her arms. "Okay, let's back up here. This is what got us in trouble in the first place." She took a few steps away from Lorelei. Although she still hadn't a clue how to act with her, she figured that she'd better learn. "Sit down here, and I'll sit across the table here."

"You're mad at me," Lorelei said, eyes downcast.

"No way," Annie said, struggling for a way to explain. "I'm glad to see you. It's just that people like your parents get upset when you hug me."

"Why? Are they afraid you'll die too?"

Annie looked toward Dusty for help, but it was Chantal who leaned over and took Lorelei's hand. "Lor, I'm Chantal. I'm a friend of Annie's too."

"You have a pretty name. Chantal."

"Thank you. So do you." Lorelei smiled. "You know how softball has rules?"

"Yes! Balls and strikes and outs. Dusty taught me." Her head fell again and she mumbled, "When I used to go."

"Lor, life has rules too. They don't always make sense."

"I break the hugging rule a lot."

"It's a hard one. Knowing when to and when not to and how hard and how many hugs you can give someone. Even whether someone would be sad that you didn't hug her."

"I like to hug everybody."

"You know what might help you to keep from breaking the rules?"

"I don't know if I can remember any more rules."

"How about asking?"

"Asking?" Lorelei watched Chantal's face. "You mean, ask can I hug you?"

"Uh-huh."

Lorelei looked at Annie and at Dusty then back at Chantal. "Can I hug you?"

"I'd love a hug, Lorelei."

Annie thought she'd fall in love with Chantal that second.

"Nice and soft," Chantal coached. "It scares people when you slam into them and hang on tight."

"Can I hug Dusty?"

"Ask her, Lorelei."

Lorelei couldn't meet Dusty's eyes, but mumbled, "Can I?"

"Not tonight, Lorelei. I feel sad. I'll probably be in a hugging mood next time I see you."

"Can I hug you, Annie?"

"How about a little one, just for practice." They embraced briefly. Annie touched nothing but Lorelei's shoulders, but she gave them a firm squeeze. "Good hug, Lor. That was just my style."

"Thanks," Lorelei said.

"I really miss you guys, you know," she told Lorelei.

Someone pressed the door buzzer and didn't stop.

Dusty looked at her watch. "What is this, Grand Central Station?"

Lorelei whispered, "It might be my Pop. I better go."

As Lorelei slipped out the back door, Dusty went to the front. Annie, ready to lambaste Leon Simski, followed.

"Mr. Simski!" said Dusty.

"Have you seen my daughter?" he demanded. Tall, beefy, eyes hard, he looked from Dusty to Annie, studying each face as if to memorize it. Chantal came to stand by Annie. "Bad enough you have your friends trooping up and down the street at all hours. Don't think I don't know who you are," he said, looking at Annie.

"Who am I? Jack the Ripper? Son of Sam? The Hillside Strangler? Look at me, Mr. Simski. I'm just a woman, not a monster."

But he wouldn't look at her again. "Where's Lorelei?"

Chantal was right. He couldn't hear her.

Dusty said, "Don't be coming to my house and making trouble, Mr. Simski. I don't keep tabs on your daughter."

He turned and stomped into the yard shouting over his shoulder, "That better be the truth. If I ever find her over here," he muttered something unintelligible as he disappeared.

Dusty closed the door. "How do I tell Lorelei she can't come here?" She looked at Chantal.

"If something doesn't get resolved in that household soon," said Chantal, shaking her head, "you may need legal protection, Dusty."

"You were so good on hugging," said Dusty. "That'll really help."

Annie pulled Chantal close and squeezed tight. "This one's a great hugger!"

Dusty worried aloud. "It would ruin me to fight some stupid lawsuit. Simski could accuse me of anything." Dusty sat heavily in her chair. "You know, guys, sometimes life feels like one kick in the pants after another." She looked at her watch again. "Where the hell is that woman? The diner's closed. When I got here I turned up the music so I wouldn't be listening for a car in the driveway. I had the TV on to force myself to look at it and not at Puddle Street." She raised her face to the ceiling and cried, "Puddle Street! Everything I love hurts now. Will she ever come home?"

"Dusty," Annie blurted, "I can't swear to it, but I don't want you going through so much pain for no reason. Elly probably wasn't with Verne tonight."

"She tell you that, Heaphy?"

"Yes, but I also know it's true." She swallowed her feeling of humiliation. "Jo is with Verne."

"Your Jo?"

Chantal chimed the words, "Jo-Barker-the-banker-with-the-pot-belly-pig."

"I don't know whether I want to read her the riot act for fucking you over or thank her for saving my marriage."

"I ought to thank you for showing me the light, if that's what's going on. Her car was near Verne's place. We didn't go up."

"Hell, nobody but that puffed up peacock would live around there. What else was she doing, checking out the twerp's etchings? Shit, Heaphy, I'm sorry. Is there a good woman left in this world?"

Both Dusty and Annie's eyes drifted over to Chantal.

Chantal fluttered her eyelashes. "I love listening to you two butches dish your femmes."

Dusty sat heavily at the table. "Dish nothing, these are the facts of life as we know them. It's a bitch living with a woman and it's a bitch doing without, right Heaphy?"

Annie grinned. "In a nutshell."

"I sit here racking my brain: is she bored, did I do something to turn her off, was she really no good all along and should I cut my losses? I know she says I work too much, but that's what small business is like. I thought we would work too much together."

"If you think you've put up with a lot, you ought to have lived in my shoes a while."

As if to demonstrate Chantal slipped her shoes off under the table. A toe crept up under Annie's chinos. Annie had to stifle a grin of pleasure.

Chantal went on. "I had one woman live with me who made my mouth water every time she came in the room, but she was hell on wheels when it came to pulling her weight. I might as well have called her your royal highness. Like I should be glad she'd chosen me to sponge off of. Proof, Annie, that I know first-hand how dumb love can make people. I'll take a roving eye over a faithful couch potato any day." She looked at the kitchen clock and laid a hand on Annie's, toying with her fingers. "We've got to be up in a few hours, Sugar."

"You going to be okay, Reilly?"

"As okay as I can be until she gets that fancy-pants from the city out of her system. Not to put what you're going through with Jo down, but this isn't any two-months' worth of fooling around."

Annie interjected, "She claims she and Verne haven't done anything, Dusty."

"Does that matter, the way they flaunt themselves all over town? I feel about two inches tall. El's paying court to that worthless dauber just like she's the royal highness on your couch, Chantal."

"Is there anything we can do?" Chantal asked. Annie could hear her asking the same question, the same way, of her children—what were their names? Crap, she couldn't remember.

"No. Pretty soon she'll come dragging her ass in here all sweetness and light and talk me into some sleep. Tomorrow night it'll be the same unless the little turd is seeing your woman. Er," she corrected herself, eyeing Chantal, "your friend. I tell you, it feels so good to have her home where I can see her, I just about roll over and do tricks when she's around."

"No wonder she's not mending her ways then," Chantal counseled.

"What do I do? I don't want to keep losing it like I did earlier tonight. What would bring you home for good?"

Chantal shook her head, her sprayed hair never losing its shape. "I'm not the one to ask, Dusty. I can't imagine leaving a good woman like you for a minute. What have you tried?"

"Tried? I don't have any miracles up my sleeve. I just keep the business going and try to keep the house up since she lost interest in it." Dusty bent to pick up one of her cats from a pile of newspapers on the table. "I never even got around to taking the Sunday paper out this week." She reached for it.

"Wait," Chantal said. "May I see that travel section?"

"This? Bermuda? Ireland—wouldn't I like to take off and see Ireland tomorrow. Maybe absence would make a certain heart grow fonder."

"Go," Chantal said quietly.

"Sure, just like that. And leave El here with Rembrandt, Jr."

"You butches can be as obtuse as men sometimes," said Chantal, lining up some pencils and pens she'd found on the table, from large to small, then pointing at one after the other as she spoke. "Take her with you. She's looking for excitement—take her on a trip. Ireland, Bermuda—it doesn't matter where. *You* give her excitement, Dusty. You take her romantic places. Verne's charms will fade the minute you put the tickets in Elly's hand."

"Genius!" Annie cried, dancing Chantal around in a little circle. "You're a living genius. That's one of the things I hate about being single. No femme to just turn things around and make them work like *that*." She snapped her fingers.

"It's the view from the bottom, girls," Chantal said.

Even Dusty cracked a smile at that one. "Yeah, right," she said in a skeptical tone.

Annie squeezed Chantal's hand. "It's hard to be morose around you, woman." She felt a flash of jealousy. Chantal and Dusty would be a natural match. "Dusty, I think you ought to take Chantal's advice. I'll bet Elly hates herself for how she's acting, but it's the only way she's ever known how to play."

Dusty scratched her neck, her lips pursed, eyes scanning the article on Ireland. She flipped the paper open. "Look at these ads for tours to Ireland. Bargain rates. I suppose people are afraid of the troubles, but, you know, Elly's as Irish as I am. That wouldn't stop her if she wanted to go." She tore an ad off the page. "On the other hand, I'd hate to be all the way over in Ireland and get a call that the Queen of Hearts had been torched."

Chantal rearranged the milk carton and sugar bowl. "What about making it an art trip? She could take her pencils with her."

"Maybe," said Dusty slowly, "that would convince her that I respect her talent. It's just this damned Verne that gets in the way so it looks like I don't want El to draw. But I do. She's never had a passionate interest before, like reading is for me." She fell silent as a car pulled into the driveway. "El's home."

At the door Chantal said, "I'll be glad to help out at the diner after work if you need me while you're in Ireland."

"Me too," Annie volunteered without hesitation.

"You've got me packed and on my way already, you two," Dusty complained with a small smile.

"Hey," Annie said, flicking her cap at Dusty with affection. "What the heck are friends for?"

On the front walk they met Elly, wan-looking under her umbrella. She seemed to drag herself past the wet, bright azalea bushes. "What's going on? Did you bring the ferocious bulldagger home?

"Didn't need to," Annie said, her annoyance with Elly gone at the sight of her drooping spirit. "Take it from me, sweetheart," she said in her Bogart voice, "lover girl was here the whole time." She lifted her cap and said seriously. "And, El, I told Dusty that you weren't with Verne tonight."

"You didn't have to take me on faith, Annie."

She smiled. "I wasn't being a great hero, El. We went over to Verne's. Jo Barker's car was outside."

Elly's eyes got wide. "Oh," she said. "Does Jo like art?"

Damp, chilled through, disillusioned and tired, she was damned if she'd cushion this blow for Elly. Tugging Chantal's hand to follow, she told Elly over her shoulder, "I never got a chance to ask."

CHAPTER 11

"It's rough coming back to Family Valuesville," Maddy complained. "How about finding something on the radio? I could use a Violent Femmes tune about now. They kick."

"A what?" exclaimed Gussie.

They had been to Maddy's Gay Alliance meeting at Yale. The ride home under the just dark May sky was a straight shot on Route 83. The quarter moon was still faint. Gussie and Chantal were tired and needed the heater on, but Maddy had enough energy for all of them.

Annie laughed and tooted her horn. Maddy Scala always lifted her spirits, even when she pushed beyond where Annie wanted to go.

In the spring night, as the four of them drove back into the dark Valley, Annie wondered aloud, "Maybe this right wing hullabaloo is the last rallying cry of a losing culture. I can't picture their kids carrying on like this."

Maddy agreed. "I wish the straight adults in this town were half as bright as their rugrats. It'd be nice to live somewhere people don't write ugly things about queers in the letters to the editors. This place is getting surreal."

Chantal asked, "Did you see that disgusting letter last night?"

"Didn't people learn anything from World War II?" asked Gussie. "It should be illegal to talk about exterminating anyone."

Maddy answered with a cynical snigger, "They learned that genocide's easy. Anybody want some excellent gum?"

"Grape?" asked Chantal, as she took a piece. "I was out of my mind when I read that letter. I tore the paper into a million pieces. When Merry came over with the baby, she said the writer was not a well man and I should ignore him."

The car began to smell like spilled grape juice.

"*Easy* for a straight to say," Maddy burst out.

"That's what I told her. If they can get away with threatening to kill us in the paper, what can we expect next?"

"Laws against us," Maddy told them. She'd talked at Yale about the upcoming meeting of the Board of Selectmen. The right wing petitioners planned to fill the chambers with people who supported what the New Haven paper had dubbed gay screening. Maddy's group was discussing arriving en masse and giving them some competition.

"I was afraid all these years of marching in the streets for gay liberation would come to no good," Gussie said.

Maddy, with manic youth, declared, "Hey, Gramma Gus, it's not over 'til it's over." She popped a large lavender bubble.

Only once had Annie seen Maddy discouraged. Annie remembered looking out the kitchen window at a late winter rain, her arms plunged to the elbows in sudsy dishwater, when Maddy had appeared outside Gussie's house, hurling down her old lavender cruiser.

Maddy had flung herself into the kitchen. "I'm tired of being shot down!" she'd cried. She wore her usual ripped and faded jeans and a rugby shirt frayed at the collar. "I mean, it's not like I'm asking for the solar system on a platter." She tore off her soaked jean jacket and flung it on the back of a chair. "Oh, mama!"

"Want to dry your buttons?" Annie had asked, offering a dish towel, amazed as always at the variety of slogans festooned on Maddy's jacket. "They might rust."

"Get a life!" squealed Maddy just before she burst into tears. "Shit. I didn't want to do this. I've been down at the river for two fuckin' hours trying not to act like a baby about it."

Gussie picked up her teacup, lips drawn into a long narrow line.

"I know, I know," Maddy said. "You don't like my language. I'm sorry."

"If crying makes you a baby, then I should be in diapers." Gussie said.

"You don't have to tough it out, Mad," Annie added. "What happened?'

"He shot me down. The principal won't let me start a gay youth group."

"Crap." Maybe nothing had changed since she'd first come

out. "One more reason to launch an attack."

"We need a gay youth group big time!" Maddy said through her tears, pacing now.

Gussie shook her head. "I should have known better than to have high expectations. It seemed like the world might be ready."

Maddy blew her nose into a lavender bandanna. "It is ready, it's just in denial."

"And after all the hoops they put you through."

"It's the pits. I finally got an advisor last week."

"I'll bet you dollars to doughnuts it wasn't a gay one," Gussie said.

"No, America Velasquez."

"Your principal said he'd approve if you came up with a willing soul. What excuse did he give this time?"

Maddy's voice went nasal and mocking. "First he said, it's just me and it's silly to have a group and an advisor for one little ol' student. I told him the rest were in hiding, waiting for their chance. Second, he says it'll look like he's promoting homosexuality and he reminded me how important family fucking values are to the Valley. Shit." She winced and looked up under her eyebrows at Gussie. "Sorry."

Annie went to her and kneaded her shoulders. Maddy honked into her bandanna again and said in a voice still squeaky with tears, "Do you think if there were five of us, twenty-five, a thousand, he'd care? He probably wishes we'd all get AIDS. What's the big deal about starting with me? We need a place to find each other. I think I'll go home and cry into my Janis Joplin tapes for a while."

Gussie suggested, "Can't you have your group outside of school? You could use the kitchen here. What do I have to lose?"

Maddy stood abruptly and threw her arms around Gussie. Annie grabbed Maddy's chair to stop it from clattering to the floor.

"Thanks, Gramma. You're a good buddy. We talked about meeting somewhere else, but then we lose the school's protection. At least in a school no gang of skinheads is going to come beat up on us. Outside, we'd be a direct target. And I wouldn't put you in danger for anything."

"So you need more kids."

"Up front. It's like, I know this dude Esteban who's gay. He said he'd join if I started it. And Trang, that outrageous girl in black boots and short skirts I was seeing."

"For two weeks," Annie reminded her.

Maddy scowled and plunked her baseball cap on the table. "Chill, paisan. She's a babe."

"Maddy!" chorused Gussie and Annie.

"It's just an expression," Maddy said with a whine. "Anyway, Trang doesn't know what she is, but she'd come to our meetings just to dare the school to tell her what she can't be. And there are others. Maybe the girl who turned red when she saw my 'How Dare You Assume I'm Heterosexual' button. There's that football player John saw cruising. If only they'd all come out."

"If only," echoed Annie.

Toothpick chose that moment to join them. Maddy lifted her high in the air. "How's my main feline?" she asked. Toothpick got her paws in Maddy's dark curls and started chewing.

"So what do I do now? Come on, we have to come up with something—the conservatives are coming."

Gussie rubbed her chin. "I wonder if your Yale meeting would be a safe place to get together."

"I can't get to New Haven. The last bus leaves to come back out here way too early. Plus, I want to make my stand here."

Gussie nodded in her judicious way. "And even God didn't create the world in a day. Just let the other kids know you'll be there. When you have three, or ten, go back to your principal en masse."

Maddy pouted, Toothpick still kneading her head.

"It could work, Mad," Annie said. "It's taken a year to get turned down. What's another month or two if you pull it off?"

"I'll be graduating in another month or two."

"Don't you need to plan your graduation action?"

Maddy snickered.

"If you get enough kids to do one good action this year," Annie said, "and teach the juniors what you know about organizing, the next class could carry the torch."

Maddy's eyes had grown crafty. "Speaking of the next generation," she said, "you wouldn't be willing to give me a ride to the meeting at Yale to plot my great revenge conspiracy, would you?" Maddy had asked.

"In The Trojan Grape?"

Annie snapped back to the present, to driving what had indeed become the Trojan Grape, when Maddy shouted, "I'm jazzed, gang." The kid bounced on the back seat of the Saab as if to demonstrate the resilience Annie envied.

"I can't wait for graduation day."

"You'd better," Annie advised. She yawned, always bored at this long dark stretch of 83, and gave the Grape more gas. "If you get kicked out of school now, dingbat, you won't be able to zap them."

"I'll wait, don't worry. This is too good a chance to blow. Besides, I'll need the rest of the term to write my speech."

"I can't get over how you sat on this for so long, mum as a clam," said Gussie, her voice thin.

"I was figuring the angles," Maddy admitted. "I want to get the most I can out of it politically."

"How do you get to be salutatorian anyway?" asked Chantal. "I was thankful my kids didn't try dropping out of second grade once the thrill was gone."

Annie felt Chantal play with the hairs on the back of her neck. She felt herself respond even as knew she should pull away. Was she going to use Chantal, just for comfort, until the real thing came along again? Was there any such animal as the real thing? Surely this plump grandma wouldn't turn out to be—

"They give salutatorian to the student with the second highest rank," explained Maddy. "You know, the meat and potatoes of school—dumb grades. That's why I worked so hard, so they couldn't ignore the numbers and shine the queer on. They've got to give me my turn at the microphone. And am I going to let them have it! I'll guilt trip them into letting the gay kids meet next year."

"Say, Annie," Gussie said, reaching over to slap her knee, "let's throw a graduation party at Rafferty Street and invite everybody—the Yale group, Maddy's mom. What do you think, Maddy?"

"Way to go, Gramma Gus! Thanks! I can't believe how much more fun it is to live out than in the closet. Look at all the goodies I'm getting for being little old pervert me." She pulled the bill of her Mets cap down further on her neck. Her springy curls made it hard to keep in place. "I wonder if the gay Yalies really can get me a late acceptance and a full scholarship. I never even thought of applying there. Maddy Scala at Yale. Can you picture it?"

"There's no doubt you got your Gramma's brains," teased Gussie. "But would you last? Can you stop being an agitator for four years?"

"Nope. Fuck 'em if they can't take a joke. Sorry. I was planning to go to the community college anyway so it's no big deal if that's where I end up," said Chantal.

"But how wonderful if you could get a Yale education free. It was never in my mom's Green Stamp catalogue."

"It may not be so free, Chantal." Annie rubbed against Chantal's fingers instead of discouraging her. "I remember how rough it was on Vicky. The price may not be in money."

"That was twenty years ago, dude. They try to change me and I'm out of there," Maddy promised. In the rear view mirror Annie saw Maddy cross her arms. "You know, I have to hand it to you older dykes. If you hadn't started marching there'd be no student groups and without the groups we wouldn't be helping each other now."

"It's getting to be a regular old gays network out there," Gussie joked.

Maddy and Chantal sang a giggling improvised duet of "When the Gays Come Marchin' In."

Annie basked in this one-big-happy-family feeling. By the time the flashing lights caught her eye it was too late to slow down. She eased her softball cap from her head—no use antagonizing the state trooper.

She slumped in her seat while he checked to make sure she wasn't a mass murderer. "This is humiliating," she groused.

Chantal said, "A purple Saab does sort of catch the eye."

"He's taking a long time," Maddy said with an ominous tone.

"They're probably sending him Annie's life history."

Annie groaned. "Don't even think it. There's probably some form of tag placed on the records of troublemakers. Am I considered a troublemaker?" She lowered her voice. "Watch out for the bulldyke in the purple imported job."

"Why not be truly paranoid," Maddy teased. "They've been told to harass you 'til you resign from the Farm…, 'til they can arrest you for something and then, WHAM, the old what-is-it-a-boy-or-a-girl routine?"

"I can see it all now," Annie predicted. "At their mercy in jail—you know it wouldn't be good for my health. Am I nuts to stay in the Valley, where too many minds are stuck back in the 1950s?"

Citation in her glove box, driving slowly toward the valley, she half-listened to Gussie entertain them with a tale about her one brush with the highway patrol, out in Kansas.

"I'll bet it wasn't so funny then," Annie sulkily accused.

Gussie taunted her. "We'll laugh about this night one of these days, Socrates."

Maddy lived way up on the hillside. Annie dropped her off first, then swooped down to Rafferty Street. She watched until Gussie locked herself in the house and waved from the front window that all was well. A clump of cars was gathered at the end of the street and kids, wine and beer bottles in evidence, were gathered around the cars.

"What address is that?" one yelled.

"Sixty-nine!" shouted the group.

Annie revved her engine. "Damn them." She screeched into a u-turn and, ticket or no, sped out Railroad Avenue to the parking area by the dam.

For a while Annie and Chantal were silent as they watched the water fall all over itself in its eagerness to reach the river below the dam. The moon was bright now and hung above them, a lover's lantern. Annie cracked her window and a damp mossy fertile smell stole in, strangely sensual.

She'd come to enjoy talking with Chantal. They spoke the same language was the way she'd explained it to Gussie, patting the area of her heart to demonstrate which language.

"Originally," she confessed to Chantal, "I invited Jo to come tonight but, true to form, Jo was busy. She's been busy every time I've called since the night the Prelude was outside Verne's. I know I should just give up on the woman. What'll it take—a wedding announcement?"

"Could be," Chantal said.

Annie looked at her, touched her hand. "Ah, Chantal. I shouldn't be thinking out loud. It's not that I wanted her to come more than you. I just can't believe I blew it again so I keep trying to prove I didn't. Two in a row. First Marie-Christine, then

Jo. Am I losing my touch or what?"

"Maybe," suggested Chantal, looking at the dam, not at Annie, "age forty-two is about time to start looking before you leap, time to let your head—and more of your heart, less of those hormones—have a say."

"But," Annie complained miserably, "the thought of Jo jumping into bed with Verne when I was practically a saint not to push her makes me even more hesitant about starting anything with—someone else. There's got to be something wrong with me."

Chantal took her hand and used one finger to trace lines she surely couldn't see in Annie's palm. Annie felt that old melting feeling that traveled to her wrist, her forearm, her shoulder. She went as weak as the falling water, plummeting into she had no idea what. Chantal might be just what she needed, though not exactly what she wanted, especially the package deal that came with two kids and a grandchild. Then there was that hint of nervous neatness, the way Chantal squared every object on a table. She'd just centered the little mirror Annie had clipped behind the passenger visor in the Saab—could she stand that all the time?

"I haven't made out here since high school. Would you believe in an 1958 Edsel?" said Chantal, with her husky laugh.

Annie closed her hand around Chantal's and pulled her closer. "Gosh, I like you," she whispered.

Chantal looked up at her in the shadowed light of a distant street lamp. Annie had never had a lover shorter than herself. It made her feel magnificently butch. They rubbed noses, their lips like magnets about to draw together, just inside the safety zone. A millimeter closer and they'd pull together. Hard.

Chantal lowered her head as Annie touched her light hair with her lips. "I think you're pretty nice too," Chantal said against her shoulder. "And your friends. Except for you-know-who-with-the-weird-pet."

"Aren't they something else? Except for you-know-who-with-the-weird-pet. Who do you hang out with when you're not seducing the new girl in town?"

Chantal sat up. "Seducing—*moi*?"

"Seducing, *tu*," Annie answered with a smile, though inside she was torn. How could she even think of getting involved with someone in Morton River Valley when the Valley seemed intent on evicting her?

"I'm not sure I like that."

"I do."

"Then I guess it's okay."

"It'd better be."

Chantal took both Annie's hands and nibbled on the finger-tips one by one, planting lingering soft kisses on the palms. Annie squirmed, felt her underwear grow uncomfortably damp.

"To tell you the truth, I don't have many friends," Chantal confessed. "Maybe there's something wrong with me. That meeting tonight at Yale? I've never seen so many gay people together before, even at the Sweatshop. I've been pretty much a one-on-one queer."

"That's the whole point, isn't it, one-on-one?" Annie slipped fingers under Chantal's sleeves to touch bare skin. Chantal shivered visibly. "It takes attacks to bring us out of the woodwork. You've never gone to a gay pride march?"

"Only in my heart when I see them on TV. I spend my time working and keeping up my house and yard, visiting with Mom and my kids. I'm a devoted catalogue reader. It's how I satisfy my shopping addiction—I make out extravagant orders and throw them away. The best part is adding up all the money I save. There's my oldest and best friend Lynn. She's married, a hairdresser. She likes to bellyache to me about her hubby and her job and she listens to me complain about my non-existent love life." She looked up under her eyelashes at Annie. "That takes about all my time."

Annie had butterflies about the straight friend as well as the kids. How she longed for the taste of Marie-Christine's lipstick on her lips, a crowded piano bar where she could, for a cover charge, rent a table for the night and feel at home. Did she have it in her to start all over, so differently, including putting up a fight for her job? Was Chantal's pull strong enough to energize her when all these other forces seemed to be tearing her apart?

"Is there room for me?" Annie asked, her voice embarrassingly small.

Even over the leaping river she could hear a train come into town. Chantal's voice sounded small too as she looked toward the falling water. "Well, I suppose if I didn't have to spend time complaining about my love life I could fit you in somewhere. For a while, anyway, 'til you went back to your exciting ivy league women."

"Why would I go back?"

"Be realistic, Annie." Chantal ticked off points by poking a finger at Annie's knee. "I'm just a divorced gal in a dumpy little factory town. I'm fat and forty and I'll retire as a payroll clerk for some dinky operation like Club Med. I don't expect romance. I never expected a good-looking, smart woman like you to look at me twice. There'll be another Jo in your life, guaranteed. I'll enjoy you while I can and then we'll both go on." She turned to Annie and traced her lips with an index finger. "As a matter of fact, I'll be satisfied getting you into bed."

"That's all you want?"

"No, but I don't think it's wise to be too optimistic."

"Geez. I always want this to be It, Chantal. All or nothing. Sophisticated women have their good points, but it never works out for me. I'm just a common, garden-variety dyke."

"So maybe we could be It. I don't know. I've learned not to count my chickens 'til the Kentucky Fried scouts leave town."

"I guess I get married in my head every time I kiss a woman."

"You haven't kissed me yet."

"Not because I don't want to. Just because of where it would lead." She slammed the heels of her hands against the steering wheel. "You're right. I want, for once, to look before I leap."

"When's your birthday?"

"April 30."

"Taurus. It figures. Hold me again, Sugar. It's getting chilly."

Annie leaned over the shift and wrapped her arms tightly around Chantal. "Wouldn't it be nice if—"

"We got trapped together on a desert island in the tropics?" Chantal suggested.

"Well, yes, but—"

"I won the lottery and could invite you to visit me in my New York penthouse or my beach house in Provincetown?" Chantal nuzzled Annie's neck with a cold nose. "You always smell so clean."

"That too, but—"

"We were the kind of people who didn't worry about tomorrow and we could you-know-what each other silly?"

"That's more what I had in mind," admitted Annie.

Chantal grinned. "That's the good thing about you Taurus women. You get what you want or die trying."

Annie pulled away. The moon had drifted just out of sight. She opened her window wide, stuck her head out and howled at the dam.

"All right!" cried Chantal. "Do you know how many times I've wanted to do that?" She howled too as Annie rolled up the window.

"I'd settle for a howling partner in my life about now," Annie admitted. "Oh, crap, no!" She slammed her cap onto the seat.

"What?" asked Chantal, whipping her head around to look out the back window.

"Another damn cop. This isn't my night."

Chantal moved to the far side of her seat. "He probably thinks we're a couple of kids."

"Yes, but what if my speeding ticket is already on their computer? Or the dispatcher remembers my name. And who's to say he doesn't already know who I am?" Though she didn't want to be right, it did feel like they might be hounding her.

But when the city policeman reached the Grape he peered inside and asked, "You ladies need any assistance?"

"No," Annie said, trying to sound on top of things. "We're just talking."

Chantal laughed, and used her flirty voice. "It's so hard to get any privacy at home for, you know, girl talk."

The officer, no rookie, cocked a finger at Chantal and grinned. Annie could see that Chantal had piqued his interest. "Then I'll leave you to it, little lady. Just keep your doors locked. We get some rough customers out on the streets this late at night."

"I'm sure you do," Chantal said, leaning across Annie, one hand, out of sight of the cop, behind Annie, under her shirt.

"You're awful!" Annie said, laughing as she rolled up the window. "He didn't even ask for I.D."

"I lived with a lunk like that for a long time, Sugar. That's all you have to do to keep them in line."

Chantal hadn't removed her hand and was delicately kneading the small of Annie's back.

"I think I'd better get you back to your car, Chantal, before he has any second thoughts about us."

"I'm sure you're right," Chantal said with a sigh, getting out of the way of the gear shift. "This isn't the time or place, and we deserve a better start than this, don't you agree?"

Annie just smiled and pulled her cap back on.

CHAPTER 12

That Sunday afternoon Annie scooted the Saab into the last parking space behind Rafferty Center where the art exhibit was being held. A mass of grey clouds had been haunting the day. She didn't notice Peg and Paris until they'd come up beside her.

"Penny for your thoughts," said Paris.

Annie jumped. "Hi. I was thinking."

Peg laughed, settling three fingers in her vest pocket. "I thought you gave that up."

"Philosophy? Like you gave up three-piece suits," teased Annie.

"Philosophy," Paris teased, "is only institutionalized worrying."

"Disciplined worrying—it trains the mind," Annie defended herself. "Look at you two. If you aren't a dyke fashion statement."

Paris glanced lovingly at Peg. Peg examined Annie.

"Hey," Annie said. "This happens to be my best blue button-down and these are my newest chinos."

Paris laughed. "A tweed jacket and elbow patches and Turkey could get you a job teaching philosophy in New York."

"My ultimate dream," she jabbed.

Once, when Annie and Paris had been waxing nostalgic about the unsettled nature of their otherwise very different younger years, Paris had explained why she had finally put down roots in Morton River Valley. "Missing that freedom is not quite the same as wanting it. And the periods of wanting it are getting briefer." Her words had encouraged Annie to move in with Gussie.

Above them the sun peered through clouds as if mulling over a grand entrance.

"What's all this?" Paris asked.

Several people with signs circled in front of the steps, looking angry in dark suits or pastel dresses.

"The Rush Limbaugh Fan Club," Peg grumbled.

Annie pulled her cap over her eyes, but she'd seen a sign that depicted a circle and slash around the word pornography. Others read, Save Our Children and Out of the Army/Out of the Schools. She felt cold with fury.

"They've gotten wind of Elly's lesbian drawings," Peg explained, stopping to watch.

Paris added, "They pulled Verne Prinz out of the junior high. The parents objected when she showed some sixteenth century nudes."

"Is there a back way in?" Annie asked, talking to the sidewalk.

"Why?" asked Peg. "They're just a bunch of no-brain reactionaries."

"I don't want to run into anybody from Medipak," she muttered.

"Whoa," said Paris. "Once burned, twice shy?"

Peg said, "As long as we're doing clichés, lightning never strikes twice."

"Better safe than sorry," countered Annie.

"Come on, then," Paris said. "I can get us in the back way, though I hate for them to run us off like this."

Annie balked. "You're right. I shouldn't give in to them. That's just what they want, isn't it?"

"Art becomes pornography if we let them call it that," Peg agreed. "Let's go." She dashed through the picketers, head down.

"Hey, you!" called a man's voice.

Annie made the mistake of looking up. Lorelei's father had hailed her.

"Where's your friends?" he hissed. Then he turned to the person behind him and said loudly. "All the sickos will show up for this, wait and see."

She stopped to shut him up, but froze with a groan. Behind Mr. Simski was Mrs. Kurt. The woman, plump with bouncy blonde curls and little makeup, squinted suspiciously at her. Annie looked around for Kurt, but evidently she was to be spared that confrontation.

"I wanted to speak with you when my daughter wasn't around," said Mrs. Kurt, in a voice carefully not hostile. She still only knew Annie by sight from the ballparks.

Annie stepped boldly up to the woman. "Listen, it wasn't what it seemed at the game that day. I was as surprised as you."

Mrs. Norwood's face registered genuine shock. "Surprised? Surprised? Don't try to blame that poor innocent."

Annie's face felt hot and red. As soon as she said it she knew she'd gone too far. "I suppose you think lesbians are so irresistible your kid's going to throw herself at one of us too?"

"I don't want you speaking of my daughter. She's been raised to resist the temptations of Satan."

"What're you calling me, you hateful, narrow-minded bigot?"

"Evil! I'm calling you evil! You and the pornographers in there!"

Peg put a restraining hand on her arm. "Let's go inside."

"Are you another one?" accused Paula Norwood, her almost cherubic face transformed by some combination of terror and aversion. "Are you?" she screamed after them. "Corrupters! Filth!"

Propelled forward by Peg and Paris, Annie called back, "Bless you too. Thanks for your Christian charity and goodwill!"

"Heaphy!" admonished Peg.

But Annie stopped. The cherub had returned. "You're right. God hates the sin, but loves the sinner. You're welcome at our church. Come and be saved for Christ!"

She felt the mesmerizing conviction of the woman, a ray of a kind of heartless purity like a tractor beam trying to pull her aboard a phantom rescue vessel. Chantal was right. She could explain to Mrs. Kurt until doomsday and never even be heard, much less understood. And vice versa, she chided herself.

"Crap!" she said once inside the entryway.

"You're really letting this get to you, aren't you, Annie?" asked Paris.

Annie pulled away. "Didn't you hear her?"

"She can't do anything to you, Heaphy."

"She already has, Peg." Her two friends had almost matching concerned expressions. "Listen, I'm not the crazy one. I need to protect myself."

Venita Valerie came through the door. "Aren't they horrible?"

"Scared Heaphy here half to death."

116

Venita looked sympathetic. "They're harmless, Annie. Just a lot of noise."

"What can I say to make you guys understand where I'm coming from? I'm not scared of those wackos, I'm scared of their crazy power, of living with no cushion between me and the unemployment line. You try it and then see if they feel so harmless."

She noticed the shock on Venita's face. "Venita, I'm sorry. I shouldn't have said that, but women who grow up in Chelsea, Massachusetts don't very often lead gay pride marches and if they do it's when we're too young to know what's at stake."

"There were stands I should have taken, I suppose," Venita said in her quiet way, "but for me, being the best teacher I could be was going to change the minds of more white people than any march. I never had to choose between my job and my race. I think I understand, though. You're walking a tightrope and if you fall there's no net for you like there would be for Peg, or for a retired person like me."

Annie nodded. "I'm sorry. I'm getting confused about who my friends are. My job now is to be even more careful Mrs. Kurt doesn't see me at work. And to stop putting off confronting Judy."

A small black man in a suit, tie and green, red and black crocheted cap joined them. "What are you doing, Paris, importing troops? This one," he said, looking Annie up and down, "must be a hit with the moral majority outside."

Paris introduced Thor Valerie, Venita's nephew and director of V.O.W., Valley Opportunity Watch, the town's community action program. Where Venita was soft-spoken and self-effacing, Thor was a fast-talking, assertive, gifted spokesman for the poor. He and Paris were soon deep in grant talk.

The building itself was a work of art: French doors, mahogany wainscoting, decorative tiling around the fireplace and stained glass windows. A lemony furniture polish smell was strong. About two dozen people wandered through the main room, looking at artwork, sipping wine and nibbling hors d'oeuvres as they talked. Annie stood for a while watching, trying to regain her calm.

"You came," Elly said, her voice breathy and low. In her patterned dress and high heels, she appeared to have shed yet more pounds. She was almost frail-looking except for the same old stubbornly forward-set jaw and jauntily up tilted nose. "I was afraid no one I knew would be here for the biggest night of my life. I feel like the parachute jumper who just passed by the edge of the earth."

Elly took Annie's arm, her hands bony icicles, and led the three of them to the hearth. "This is Verne Prinz, my instructor." Annie noticed an incredible level of excitement in Elly's eyes.

Verne did not offer to shake hands. "I've been hearing a lot about you," Annie said, studying the woman who leaned, no, lolled against the mantlepiece, the picture of sang-froid. Her eyes were a striking grey and her hair, short on top, had been dramatically thinned and left long down her back. She smelled of red wine gone sour.

Verne said, "Not from my Southern belle, surely."

Elly laughed softly, eyes downcast, eyelids lavender-hued. Her fingers, nails under a glitter polish, fly tapped a small beaded purse as if echoing a heart beat out of control.

"Where's Dusty?" asked Paris.

Elly rolled her eyes. "Working," Elly answered. "I'll bet that woman came out with one hand stirring a pot of stew and the other..." She stopped, and clapped a hand daintily over her mouth. "I do run off at the mouth when I get nervous, don't I?"

Annie scowled at Verne. No one said anything, but even Annie's obvious hostility could not suppress Elly's excitement. "Did you know," Elly asked in a proud tone, "that Verne studied at the Art Institute of Chicago? And she lived in a loft in SoHo!"

Annie asked Verne, "Did you get lost?"

Elly laughed, casting a tender glance at Verne. "She makes her living doing residencies in places like this."

Peg moved smoothly between Verne and Elly. "Show us your work, El."

"I'm so nervous. I can't." Downcast eyes, tap-the-purse. It was as if Elly's outgoing soul, the heart of the Queen of Hearts, had been consumed. No wonder Dusty was worried.

Peg led them to the nearest wall where they studied a strikingly realistic self-portrait of an old man, then several messy abstracts. They moved on to an arrangement of photographs of the Valley and its people.

Paris commented in a low voice, "Verne serves a purpose,

though. She brings some semblance of culture to backwaters."

"And polishes gems like Elly," Peg added.

Elly's drawings were on the next wall.

"She's so good," Paris said.

"I can't get over it," said Annie, opening her arms wide to indicate Elly's work. "All this talent just waiting for the light of day."

The Valley scenes—factories, river, railroad—had the look of finely detailed etchings. The controversial drawings were softer, both of the same couple. In one the two women kissed, pressed tight together. In the other, they walked along a road holding hands, a suggestion of arms swinging between them, a dark dog bounding behind, leafed trees meeting above.

"But at what price?" asked Peg. Annie followed Peg's eyes. Verne was accepting wine from Elly as if used to being served. In the doorway, Dusty, in grey slacks and white shirt, stood watching with narrowed eyes. As Elly poured, Dusty clenched her fists.

"I'm not standing here doing nothing," Annie declared and crossed to Dusty.

"Did you ask her?" Annie led Dusty toward Paris and Peg.

"Ask who what?"

"About Ireland," Annie said, able to answer her own question by the stubborn look on Dusty's face.

"I think maybe I'd better find someone else to ask, the way things are going."

"No, Dusty—"

"Heaphy, this has been coming for a long time. She's been restless. I should have done something right off, but I didn't figure it out for a while, and then I suppose I hid out at the diner rather than own up to the problem. Now, I don't know if I care enough myself."

Annie felt as if someone close had just died. While Paris hugged Dusty hello, Annie tried to shake off her sadness. Dusty must be doing enough grieving for all of them.

"So, are we talking great artist here or what?" Dusty asked in a raspy voice, peering at Elly's drawings. She cleared her throat. "Hey, that's our place," she declared a little too loudly and added, as if to distract everyone, "We've had two Canadian geese on the pond this week. They're so big it's getting crowded.

I'm afraid they're planning to settle down and raise a family."

"Dusty!"

Elly came across the room to her lover with a half-skipping step, her color even higher. "Do you like them?" she asked.

"They're as good as the last time you showed them to me," Dusty answered, but she straightened her collar with nervous fingers.

"You really think so?"

"I tell you all the time."

"You did at first." She turned to the group with a smile, but she was tapping her purse. "Now she doles out praise like it's bad for me."

"Your drawings," Annie noted, "are full of light."

"Everything is full of light," Elly said in a passionate drawl. "I just never knew it 'til Verne said it out loud in our first class."

Dusty grimaced.

"I know you don't like me talking about her, Dusty, but it's true."

There was a silence. Annie remembered Dusty in her thirties, stewed to the gills, a big, rugged charmer playing a penny-whistle at the open back door of the bar on a hot summer's night. Two or three femmes would drift away from the jukebox and listen, dreamy smiles on their faces, passing cars stirring hot breezes. Now Dusty was more solid, not an aggressive entrepreneur, but the sort of unflagging small businessperson who embodies the American dream. Elly was her stanchion. Annie watched them for a sign of hope.

The Director of the Learning Center, a balding man with a quick high-pitched voice, had just begun his speech when Paula Norwood cried, "That's not art, it's pornography!" The Director stepped back, clasping the portable microphone to his chest.

Jo's panicked eyes caught Annie's.

Mr. Simski and a man in a white shirt and tie flanked Mrs. Norwood and some other women. One man yelled, "Take them down!"

All over the room people looked at one another. "What jerks," said Dusty. Annie was shaking. She felt helpless.

"Take them down or we will!" Everyone in the room seemed to be in shock. Dusty watched the protesters and Elly intently. When no one moved, the man advanced on Elly's drawings, but

Elly, in her heels, ran at the wall.

"Oh no you don't!" she cried.

"Are you going to let her get in your way, Jerod?" challenged one of the women, approaching. She reached past Elly, but Elly knocked her arm back.

Dusty seemed to teeter, as if hesitant to stay or to go. Then, she strode across the room and stood with Elly. "Why don't you folks just calm down," she said, her gruff voice soothing.

Annie had never admired Dusty more and strode to stand beside her. Venita followed, along with most of the rest of the gathering.

What about Verne, why wasn't she defending her show, her artist? She spotted her leaning against a window, a smirk on her face. Jo stood beside Verne, gazing at the artist. There it was, the wedding announcement for which Annie had been waiting. Jo and Verne together in that fitted stance only lovers achieve. Damn it! What about *me,* she wanted to shout. She'd smash Verne's face in. Yeah, like she'd stand up to the picketers. Annie'd out her to the school board. Sure, like she'd really do that to another gay person. She'd make her life so miserable Verne would have to leave town. Good plan, Heaphy, like that would win Jo's flitty little heart?

Annie returned to the scene before her. Two little armies lined up to defend and attack a piece of art, and here she was wanting to attack Verne. Priorities, Heaphy, she told herself.

Thor Valerie took the microphone from the Center Director. His voice leapt across the room, startling the line of Elly's defenders as much as the line of attackers. He boosted the Rafferty Center's cultural program and praised the artists and the multi-culturalism of the show. Meanwhile, Peg and a bearded black man, who Paris whispered was a history teacher, talked the troublesome group to the hall.

Elly was staring at Dusty with the look of a woman rescued by a prince on a white horse. Dusty, once the troublemakers had left the room, motioned for her to pay attention to the judges on their inspection. Elly tapped her purse at a furious pace as she hung onto Dusty and stole glances at Verne. The judges went to the offending drawings and placed a first on the hand-holding piece.

Elly looked pale as a smattering of applause grew to a strong ovation. Dusty hugged her and let her go.

CHAPTER 13

Thursday evening Annie and Gussie were digging into their meatloaf and lima beans when the phone rang.

"Good timing," she muttered, reluctantly getting up to answer.

It was Jo.

"No," Annie said. "I'm not into coming over, but you're welcome to come over to Rafferty Street."

"Funny," she told Gussie after she'd hung up, "how spending time with Chantal helps me know what I'm willing to put up with."

She had honorably driven Chantal back to her car the night they'd sat at the dam. For the next few nights, while she battled back and forth with herself about whether her Herb Farm dilemma made her crazy or saner than everyone else, she'd indulged in comfortable Chantal fantasies.

"Jo can just bring her banker's butt across the tracks if she wants to talk." She'd told Gussie about the way things looked between Jo and Verne at the art opening. "I have a few things to say to her, too," Annie grumbled.

"Are you sure you've lost Jo?" asked Gussie. "You don't want to alienate her if there's still a chance."

"I don't even care."

"If that's true, don't waste your energy fighting for her then. Or being angry. Be glad you found out now."

"I suppose," Annie replied. "But without Jo's connection to the Farm, I'm up the creek without a canoe, much less a paddle." She speared a bean and studied it, exhausted with frustration. "I've been up to the Farm twice. I left three phone messages for Judy, but she's still on sick leave. It's a little hard to press my case when nobody's home."

The day was muggy. Gussie had all the windows open. Annie saw Jo step out of her car with her alluring smile, her crisp navy slacks and a soft-looking yellow v-neck sweater. Neighbors across the street stared openly. Then some mutt gave a wolf whistle.

"Hey, baby," called another, "come over to my house!"

Jo didn't know to come through the alleyway. Annie, enraged and embarrassed, rushed to the front door to let her in, but not fast enough to avoid the last hurled comment.

"What do you want with dykes when you could have me?"

"Get lost!" Annie shouted ineffectually into the night.

Gussie was pulling down the shades. "Annie! Don't let them know they get your goat!"

"I know, I know." A can hit the front steps and rattled onto the sidewalk.

Gussie peered past a shade. "There's just three young thugs, pulling up clumps of grass and heaving them over here. Laughing." Gussie raised her voice, "There's no call for behavior like that!"

Annie could see the men mime terror. "Three? Look at the backups on their porch, laughing their butts off."

She noticed that Jo stood well back from the window. "This is bad, Annie."

"Yahoos always love an excuse to bait gays. The politicians and the Norwoods are inadvertently encouraging them. I'm sorry I asked you over. This never happened to a guest before."

"I'm afraid this isn't a social call. I'm here as an emissary for Judy. She goes in for surgery in the morning and wanted this cleared up just in case something unforeseen happens."

"Surgery?" asked Annie.

"Gall bladder. At least we hope that's all it is. Here's your formal offer of employment, Annie, complete with apology. She'll stand by you if you decide you want to be a part of the Farm's work."

Annie skimmed the papers and didn't try to hide her sarcasm. "She's sorry for the miscommunication. So that's what it was! Well tell her I'm so very grateful for the explanation."

"She called it that so none of the details—about your life—or her panic—have to go on paper."

"And they need to know my decision, like, yesterday?"

"The guy filling in for you needs to look for other work if you're coming back."

"I appreciate that Judy figured out right from wrong, but I may want to stay where it feels safe. Safer, anyway."

"But your career. Special Ed."

Annie passed the papers to Gussie. "I don't want my emotions to get in the way," she explained. "How does that look to you."

Gussie commented, "This doesn't undo the harm already done. Or end what the whole mess started. After tonight's paper I don't blame Annie for being cautious."

"Thanks for not ruining dinner with whatever it is," said Annie, taking the newspaper. "'FAMILY SUES HERB FARM FOR FAILURE TO PROTECT DAUGHTER,' she read aloud. "Why do I feel like I've been bopped in the head? Like I can't win for losing. Maybe I have my job back, but isn't it my fault the Farm's being hassled?"

"Sit down." Gussie ordered. "You look like you havebeen bopped in the head."

"Why? Because my ears are ringing? Because I'm sweating like a pig? Because my mouth tastes like the inside of a garbage can? Sitting won't help. Grinding clumps of dirt into those clowns' faces might. Rushing their porch with the Grape at top speed might. Blowing up Medipak might. But my legs are shaking too much."

"Gussie's right," Jo said, her face very pale.

Annie sank into a chair. "Judy's still willing to take me back, knowing what's going on in Morton River?"

Jo's tone was solemn. "She convinced the New Way Board to reject running and hiding. This was coming whatever they decided. Your incident was the tip of the iceberg, Annie. I see papers from all over the country at the bank. Momentum's been building for years against the legislation gains we've made—and fear of AIDS."

Annie was as glum. "I still can't believe this." She counted on her fingers. "First, nothing happened. Second, the thing they think happened was after working hours and off Farm property. Third, I was so careful not to do anything that would hurt the Farm, like sue for my job back, and I'm the bad guy? Do you guys mind if I whine a little? This isn't fair!"

"I feel so helpless," Jo admitted. "What good is getting your job back? That was only the beginning. If I'd been able to resolve this faster. If—"

Gussie wrestled a cowlick down. "You did what you could, Jo. What you young people call homophobia has a life of its own."

Annie said, "I feel like running back to New York as fast as I can go." She lifted the cat to her shoulder. "What do you think, Toothpick? Want to go home?"

Gussie was picking up crumbs and setting them on a plate one by one, saying nothing.

Annie looked at Jo. Jo looked from her to Gussie and back. Annie found herself reassuring Gussie as she had Chantal. "Aw, Gus, I'm not going anywhere. They hate us in New York, too. They just can't be bothered showing it on a daily basis. Besides, this *is* Toothpick Cat's home now."

Gussie looked up. "I'd be fine," she said.

Jo advised, "This whole situation has gotten out of hand. Don't do anything drastic. It'll just give energy to the bigots."

Annie took her softball cap from the back of her chair and spun it on a finger. "I keep trying to ignore it. I guess now that we know what's what we'll get the gang together again and see. You want in?"

Jo bit her bottom lip. "Yes. No. Maybe," she said with a small laugh. "That is, I want to, but I'm not sure it's wise."

"It won't make much difference now that they've seen you here," Gussie cautioned. "Hold your head up and walk right past them."

"You're more paranoid than I am!" Jo said with a laugh.

"I've had more practice," Gussie joked. "And lived through more difficult times."

"I'm not sure of that at all," Annie objected from inside her deepening cloud of gloom.

"Don't I get credit for the two world wars? The war to end all wars?"

"Did it?" asked Annie. Silence threatened. "Jo," Annie said with some apprehension, "would you like to come upstairs to see the palace suite?"

The sky was just beginning to darken. The voices were loud on the porch across the street.

"Maybe waiting for dark is a good idea," said Jo.

She led Jo slowly up the stairs, leaning heavily on the rail, as if she were dragging the carcasses of her old loves along.

Vicky had told her last fall that she was becoming a sad sack.

"I just know who you were, Annie, when we were together," Vicky had said gently as they'd walked the beach. "A cuddler, a teddy bear, a day-in, day-out kind of woman who wears well and gives more and more over time. Even with your boundless enthusiasm, your excitement had to do with us, or with you. You didn't need much outside. I never had to worry whether you'd come home at night, whether you'd go off with another woman."

To herself Annie thought, like I was banking on you getting over your love affair with the West Coast. In her fourth year with Vicky, just before Vicky's last year at Yale Law School, they'd driven out to visit their friend Rosemary Harris in San Francisco. Rosemary had left Yale with an M.B.A. and taken a job in banking.

Vicky had fallen for the glow of the West Coast light, the softer air, the slower pace of life. The next year she'd passed the Oregon bar and accepted a job with a hippy-dippy law firm of boys in Eugene who wanted a female presence. It still rankled that Vicky chose to leave her, but Annie hadn't been willing to move west.

They'd dubbed themselves bi-coastal lovers and spent vacations together for another ten years, until Vicky and Jade Winter had their ceremony of commitment. Jade was one of those typical west-coasters-with-a-lesbian-name at whom Vicky would once have scoffed. A little scornful, a little amused, Annie and Marie-Christine had flown out for the occasion. It had been easier to finally let go of Vicky because Marie-Christine had been so large in Annie's life.

Now not only were Vicky and Marie-Christine gone, but as she stood back to let Jo precede her into the room and saw the blankness in Jo's eyes, she knew that within the hour Jo would be gone too.

"I've only had one other guest up here," apologized Annie. "I don't keep it ship-shape. And it kind of collects heat during the day. Have a seat." She offered the old green nubby easy chair to Jo. She'd bragged to Chantal about the good deal she'd gotten on it at a tag sale, but now it just looked shabby.

"So this is the famous Toothpick Cat." Jo said, bending to lift the kitten into her arms.

"Haven't you met her before?"

"She's never shown her face when I've been around."

"Toothpick!" Annie cried. The kitten had launched itself from Jo's arms onto the bed where it sat licking its fur back into order. "I'm sorry. She's always friendly."

Jo was smoothing her sweater. The heat didn't seem to affect her. "No harm done."

"No. She pulled your sweater."

"It's okay. I'll work it back in."

"I'm really sorry."

A promising little breeze blew through the window, stirring the curtain just enough to catch Toothpick's eyes. In a flash she attacked one panel and hung on it, claws caught, until Annie disentangled her.

Jo looked around. "How wonderful! You can see the diner from your window."

"When Nan was still alive, she and Gussie were the ones to spot the arsonists who tried to burn it down."

"I remember. Some boys who didn't like gays. It got so bad I almost moved up to Hartford to live with Marsha, but then the flood came and everybody loved Dusty and Elly for practically saving the town. We need another flood!" Jo said with a laugh. "Or maybe I just need to relocate someplace where I don't feel so exposed."

"It's funny," Annie said. "I was telling Venita that most of the women around here who have professional jobs or a pension, who have some type of security, that they're the ones who aren't worried, who can afford to take the risks. But maybe I'm wrong."

"Maybe you think my job comes with more security than it does. When I lost my parents, they left just enough insurance for me to finish college. The only close relative I have is Uncle Claude and he's done well, but he has five kids of his own. The banking industry is so conservative I couldn't have made a worse choice, except maybe teaching."

They fell silent. Annie imagined that Jo was watching the sky grow more and more dark so she could make her escape.

Jo broke the silence. "This is a nice room."

"There isn't really a common space where we can talk in private."

"Annie, stop apologizing. I'm the one who has some apologizing to do." Jo balanced on the edge of the easy chair while Annie sat next to Toothpick on the bed. "I thought I could accomplish the impossible—save your job and keep Mrs. Norwood and her friends from swarming all over us," Jo said, twisting her gold watch back and forth on her wrist.

"Right. Now blame yourself because Mrs. Kurt's crowd is starting a chapter of the Traditional Family Values Coalition. After all the stories I've heard about the Klan around here I was surprised that Morton River didn't already have a chapter."

"The worst of it is that some United Way people are talking about pulling support from the Farm. They want agencies that receive funding to write veiled anti-gay policies into their hiring procedures in case the Selectmen won't pass a city-wide ordinance."

"All because Judy unfired me?"

"It's the timing. You gave them an issue. This is where the radicals have chosen to take their stand. Every step you, Maddy, Paris or lawyers take to resist their stand, escalates the conflict and exposes the Farm more. If you're working there it could get even worse, for you as well as the Farm."

Annie felt so discouraged she might as well be wearing cement shoes on quicksand. She couldn't help being defensive. "I didn't get myself laid off on purpose, Jo. I have to fight this to feel okay about myself, never mind plan for a career. This whole deal has circled around on me and I find a tiny part of my mind agreeing with Mrs. Kurt—Paula Norwood."

"Don't be ridiculous!"

"I wasn't recruiting Lorelei, but I was a magnet. If I hadn't been gay maybe she wouldn't have felt that way about me. So I get to thinking that the queer inside is to blame. With that kind of thinking, next thing you know I'll be writing my senator to oppose lifting the military ban, right? Silence doesn't buy safety—or sanity."

Jo's pert haircut was a bit shorter than usual, Annie noticed, though just long enough to escape any hint of dykeliness. Geez, she ought to introduce Jo to Giulia. What a great closeted couple they'd have made if Giulia hadn't gone off and married that nice old man. Did Jo practice that deeply apologetic look in her eyes to use at work?

"I tried, Annie. I threatened to quit United Way if they dared influence any members to discriminate. That held them at bay for a while. I even considered coming out to stop them. It's gotten your job back, but who does that help?" Jo looked so distressed that Annie's annoyance dissipated. "What do I do, Annie? I want to fight this and I'm terrified right down to my toes."

Annie moved to hold Jo, to smooth her brow, but words were all she dared. "You know what made Bertrand Russell tick?"

"What?" asked Jo.

"He said it was a longing for love, the search for knowledge, and unbearable pity for mankind that were his governing passions."

"Yes," said Jo with a sad-eyed nod. "We are pitiful, aren't we, with our big dramas and our heartrendingly simple needs. It's not as if I couldn't get another job somewhere."

Annie drew back. "It never occurred to me that I could keep my job and you could lose yours." She went to the window, her hands jammed into her pockets so hard she felt her chinos tug on her hips. The breeze had not kept its promise and the near dark was, if anything, more oppressive than the day had been. "This hatefulness is everywhere. Germans killing refugees. Bosnia's ethnic cleansing. Apartheid. Isn't preaching fear of a group of people how it starts?"

"And we're in a little microcosm here. My uncle warned me when I came back to Morton River. He said that a good business person always saves her first dollar and her first words. I've got the dollar, and there are a lot of first words I've had to swallow to pass."

Annie smiled out the window. Rafferty Street looked very peaceful from here, where there were only Nan's flowers and the Santiagos' neat cottage next door.

Annie turned. "In other words, don't come out for yourself or anyone else, no matter how much you want to? Don't stand up for what's right because if they don't hurt you they'll hurt the ones you love?"

Jo looked up. "I want to shout it in their faces, Annie. But I know that some people can't listen to reason when they're dealing with homosexuality. Coming out to them won't change their minds about gay people; it would only change their minds about me."

As much as Annie didn't want to believe it, her own choice

was swiftly becoming one of limiting the damage.

Jo reached a tentative hand to Toothpick, who watched her every move. Toothpick stood, stretched mightily and ambled to the other end of the bed. "I really have been considering moving," said Jo.

"I thought the Valley was home."

"It was always a choice between Morton River and New York. Now I'm wondering about other cities. Chicago?" Her face was pained.

Annie couldn't help but wonder, if they were together, would she move to Chicago with Jo?

"Verne Prinz is from Chicago," Jo said in a small voice. "Her family has holdings in one of the big Midwestern banks."

Annie lay an arm across her stomach, trying not to bend from the sudden cramping. "And she's going to get you a job?"

"She'd introduce me around. Morton River has gotten too small for her too since your incident stirred up the rednecks."

Annie stared out the window, stifling a sarcastic remark about it all being worth it to run that creep out of town. "Jo, have you been staying away because you're afraid to be seen with me, or because you're seeing Verne?"

Jo was behind her, but Annie could hear her catch her breath. "You're a wonderful woman, Annie. You deserve a partner as courageous and colorful as yourself."

She turned and caught the look of relief on Jo's face. "But that partner isn't you."

Jo didn't look away. "I think you're right, Annie. I like you so much. You pried me from my rut and I'll always be grateful to you for that. This is a corny thing to ask, but I'd hate to lose you as a friend."

"You mean like go-to-the-movies and long-walks-in-the-park friends? Or do you mean see-ya-around-friends?"

"Don't be that way, Annie," Jo replied, looking away. "Some kind of friends. We can see what develops."

"Thanks for letting me know."

The silence in the room went unbroken for an intolerably long moment.

"I guess it would be better if I left now. I'll call you," Jo said. She hesitated, looking at Annie, seemed about to say more, then was gone.

Annie checked her heart for breakage, but found only a trace of disappointment. What a cold fish Jo had turned out to be. Jo'd done her best, that was clear. She'd stuck her neck out, but scared herself right out of Annie's arms.

Annie lay down next to Toothpick. The cat purred. "It's a good thing it's Chantal you like," she said, burying her face in fur.

CHAPTER 14

There was no remedy for pain better than the thump of ball against bat and the cheers of softball fans. As Annie and Cece Green warmed up, late May game smells were on every breeze—mowed fields, coconut-scented sun screen, an anticipation of hot dogs and popcorn. It was one of those promising days when summer became more than a memory. Annie settled the lavender-brimmed team hat, its crown white and pin striped, squarely on her head.

Peg limped onto the slightly soggy field to gather them all together just as Maddy came careening up on her lavender bike. Maddy leapt off, slid her glove from the handlebar, let the bike fall by the makeshift dugout, and jogged over to the team. "First base-*wo*man reporting for duty, cap'n!" In her team t-shirt she looked like the least political lesbian on earth.

Annie and Cece tossed a ball back and forth. Hope Valerie did leg stretching exercises as Peg, who had taken over when Dusty decided not to coach this year, gave a pep talk. It was the first season for Paris. New to softball, she'd quit the team twice in tears of frustration but was back again, sporting an Amazon rain forest t-shirt. Annie missed Lorelei's sweaty excited face.

"We can beat these Rockettes, team!" said Peg with her professional optimism. The diner team had won just the one game all season. "You don't want a bunch of straight girls pushing you around."

"If it'd only stop raining so we could have a dry field to play on," complained Paris, scraping mud off her sweat pants.

"This gay-bashing shit's got us all down, Peg," Hope mumbled.

"Why?" asked the great unruffled Peg, zipping her immaculate lavender windbreaker. Even on the ballfield the crease in Peg's slacks wouldn't relax. "Straights are just saying aloud what most of them have always felt. Nothing's really changed

132

except both sides are talking. Too bad it's not to each other."

"They ought to mind their own shit," Cece complained, wiping sweat from her face. "I can't sleep nights, worrying what they'll pull next. I tell you, if one of them messes with me, I'm pleading justifiable homicide."

Everyone, not just Annie, was jazzed about the post-game strategy meeting scheduled at Rafferty Street. She wondered if Jo would come after their last visit.

"Check it out," Cece told her. "That's Kurt's kid."

Annie laughed aloud. "If that gum-chewing, glove-smacking teenager in a bulldyke crouch doesn't grow up queer, it'll be a major feat of mind-control. Is she really a Norwood?"

"Ruth Norwood. Her pals call her Babe."

"Babe. A good old dyke name. Too bad she's too butch for you, Maddy. You'd bring her out in a Morton River minute."

"I know her from school. She's got this deal with her parents: they let her play ball, she goes to church. But Mom has to escort her to every game."

Cece slapped a knee and laughed. "Look at Mrs. Kurt over there, fussing with Babe's ponytail so no one thinks she's walking around with short hair. Oh, Mama's gonna save her from the lezzies, yes she is, Lawd Almighty!"

Chantal was on the grass with her daughter and granddaughter. Her daughter Merry was a soft-looking bashful young woman whose life was focused on her baby. Her relationship with Annie consisted of shy smiles.

Except for some crude anti-lesbian comments from teenaged boys, the first innings were routine. Mrs. Kurt hovered over her sulky teenager like the diner team would swallow the kid whole. To Annie's relief, Kurt himself wasn't around. Probably home writing this week's anti-gay sermon. Small town life, she marveled, was full of strange bedfellows, yet Mrs. Kurt *still* hadn't figured out that Annie worked at Medipak. Annie had tried to reach Judy to find out when to give notice at Medipak, but, she was still out sick.

In the sixth inning a Rockette made a hit to the second baseman. Babe, on first, bolted toward second. Annie ran for all she was worth. The second baseman tossed the ball to her. Annie leapt to tag Babe, then gave a whoop of elation. Chantal went crazy cheering. Annie grinned over at her, proud.

If there had been some dykes around that hadn't known about the possibility of her and Chantal, they knew now. But, hell, who needed Jo Barker's closet with Chantal wearing her heart on her sleeve? It gave Annie a rich, warm feeling, like a taste of butterscotch pudding before it cooled.

"She was safe!" she heard from the batter's mound. It was the Rockettes's coach, his face in the umpire's, disputing Annie's out. The ump was agreeing. Peg stepped in to protest. Annie looked back to where she'd made the tag.

"No way!" she shouted at them.

The hitter glared at Annie from her coach's side. Annie glowered back, heart pumping rage.

Babe sprang at Annie. "Cheat!"

"Hey!" Annie said when the kid gave her a two-handed push that almost knocked her off her feet. "What'd I do?"

"Messed up, that's what."

She hated this. Anger made her cry. It took all her will to choke out some too-civil words. "Uh-uh. Sorry, you're mistaken."

"You think you're good enough to get me out? You're so over the hill you probably can't see a base." The kid pushed her with one arm.

The umpire finally stepped between them.

Still swallowing tears Annie yelled over the ump's shoulder, "What's with you? This is a game. G-a-m-e. Comprendez? Take it easy."

"Leave my daughter alone!" screeched Mrs. Kurt, coming at them full speed.

Oh no, thought Annie. Instant replay. She was beyond crying. "Excuse me? Babe here starts pushing on me and I should leave her alone? I don't think so."

"Her name's Ruth. And you stay away from her."

She knew she should back down, walk away, toss the hot potato back in the woman's lap before she got burnt, but she lost it. Her ears rang, her eyes seemed to cloud over. Her knees shook and she wanted nothing less than to have a bat in her hands.

"Fuck off, bitch. I was minding my own business when your little darling came at me. Maybe if you didn't keep her on a leash she wouldn't froth at the mouth."

"How dare you! Ruth, go to your bench."

The umpire was trying to get a word in, but Mrs. Norwood

kept moving in front of him.

"No!" said Babe, "This is between me and her. I hate these sneaky queers."

"Ah, Babe," Annie pleaded. "Don't you see why you're so mad? Look in a mirror."

"Ruth! Do as I say!"

Babe slouched back to the bench, and the umpire, Peg and the Rockettes' coach reached Annie before Mrs. Kurt could start in.

The umpire told Annie, "Sorry, I should have called her safe. The sun was in my eyes."

She was stunned. "Peg! Say something! My best play since coming to the Valley shot to hell?"

"Ump's call, Heaphy. I don't agree, but he's not backing down."

"Crap." She threw her glove to the ground. "I don't get it. I put my all into my work, into the game, and what happens?"

The umpire said, "I may throw the both of you out for fighting."

Annie couldn't stop. "That was a wrong call, buddy. Why're you letting these people tell you your job? Are they queer-baiting us, Peg? And what about the Babe over there? I have a little complaint. Like about her coming up to me and shoving me around."

"Coach?" asked the umpire.

"That true?" the coach called to the bench.

Babe spit out her gum like a wad of chewing tobacco. "What of it?"

"It's true," the Rockettes's coach admitted.

"She's grounded for the rest of the game then," the umpire ruled. "She was safe, but she's on the bench. Okay?"

Peg agreed. "Let's play ball, Heaphy. Keep up the good work."

Annie retreated to her position shaking. For all her questions it was clear what was happening, all too clear. Babe Norwood was a baby dyke in torment, scared of what she felt inside, but more afraid of hellfire, damnation and her parents. By pushing Annie, she'd been pushing away the queer inside.

The next batter walked and then Cece, who'd had a screaming match with three Rockettes during the conflict, missed a ground ball. It was all downhill from there. When the game was over, the score was 4 to 3 for the Rockettes. That rotten call had made all the difference, both to the score and morale of the diner team.

Dusty ambled over from the stands. "That was a great catch, Heaphy. Peg, you're doing a fine job with these gals. You'll have the team in such great shape we'll waltz into the championships next year. We'll take our revenge fair and square."

"With you at the helm," Peg said, laying a hand on Dusty's shoulder.

"Maybe," said Dusty, "just maybe."

Annie looked more closely at Dusty. The woman was almost smiling. "Okay, Reilly," she said, steering her away from the others. "What's going on? Did you run the art teacher out on a rail?"

"Heaphy, I don't know what's happening, but life's gotten a little easier."

"That's a switch. Every other queer in town has the heebie-jeebies."

"To tell you the truth, I think these hard times are helping."

"I'm glad it's doing somebody some good."

"No, really. It's taken my mind off Elly. I think it's shaking her up a little bit too." Dusty's smile seeped out even more. Annie felt the great damp patches on her t-shirt. She felt her anger draining. It really was only a game. "Come on, Reilly, tell me the rest."

"I can't explain it. That night at her art show—when those protesters came in I was going to let her stew in her own juices. Let that poor excuse for an artist get her out of that mess. But something snapped. Elly's my—my whatever, just like I'm hers, complete with art and overwork and temporary insanity. Not," Dusty added, a stern look in her eye, "that I condone her shenanigans."

"Has anything changed?"

"Apparently, along with all the time her highness Verne the Great is spending with your old pal Jo, she's talking about breaking her contract and high-tailing it to a more civilized place. She can't hack life shoulder to shoulder with the bad guys, Heaphy. This doesn't exactly impress El. I mean, the cur's not gone yet, but a woman can dream, can't she?"

"Hey, Verne out of town could create more complications than someone you can keep your eye on. Especially, Jo or not, if she's managed to pack Elly's heart in her soft-sided suitcase."

But Dusty's confidence was back. "Okay, I know. It wouldn't really solve anything. But between that and Ireland—I haven't dared broach a trip yet—what if she says no? But I'm doing my research and when the moment's right I'll pop the question."

Chantal had joined them. "I'm jealous. You wouldn't have to wait for the right moment to ask me."

"Me neither," agreed Dusty with a chuckle. "Those names that always sounded like poetry to me—Dublin, Limerick, Tipperary—I want to rent a car and see them all."

The spring twilight lingered. At the bleachers crows cawed over spilled potato chips. Dusty's news had buoyed Annie.

Mario Genero, Maddy's sixtyish brother-in-law-to-be, helped Giulia into a car as spotlessly white as his shoes. Annie had the urge to ask Mario to hang out until they were safely in their cars. She'd noticed, these days, that the players seemed reluctant to leave the field until their opponents had packed up and gone. Then, in a subdued knot, they'd hasten to their vehicles.

Tonight was different. Before she'd finished making plans with Chantal the whole team was headed for the street and their cars, as if, despite their worries, they felt more powerful because the meeting lay ahead. Not her. She wished they could play another game, then another. She wished life were one unending spring softball game.

With a mixture of admiration and exasperation she watched Babe Norwood swagger next to her mother. The Babe had an athlete's thick thighs and muscled calves. She dwarfed her mother not so much in height as in brawn. That was going to be one powerful woman, whichever way she landed.

"I'll run Merry and the baby home, then come over," Chantal decided.

"Fuckers!" came a cry from the street side of the field. "Honky fuckers!"

Annie and Chantal ran toward Cece's voice at the same moment. Cece was pounding on the ruined seat of her bike.

"You're dead meat!" Cece shouted into the street, "You think I won't kill you pale-ass breeders?"

Annie swallowed bile. "Cece—" she said, laying a hand on her arm. "I can't believe we didn't hear anything."

Someone had battered the bike into junk. There were dents

on every possible surface. Gasoline dripped out of a puncture in the tank. The tires and seat were slashed, mirrors smashed and dangling.

"Oh, Truth, oh, my Sojourner," Cece moaned, arms outstretched as if to fold the broken thing to her. "My bike, my bike, my bike."

"Poor Cece." When Annie looked closer she saw that someone had scratched a word into the glossy red paint—lezzie. She slung an arm over Cece's shoulder while Cece cried. There was an aching sorrow in her chest where anger had earlier raged. "We'll show them, Cece." Her eyes swept the street for vandals. "They're not getting away with any of it. I promise."

Later, the crowd overflowed from Gussie's kitchen into the back hall, the bedroom, doorway and part way up the stairs. The original ragtag group was swelled by some Morton River liberals, the whole softball team, the Club Med gays, PFLAG and the anti-poverty group. With fists clenched, Annie told them about Cece's bike.

There was a loud silence before Dusty burst out, "And that's not all! My cop regulars are avoiding the diner like the plague! One of my firemen stopped by to tell me the Department bought them a microwave—just this firehouse. There goes a big chunk of our take-out business."

Gussie, dressed for the occasion in a black turtleneck sweater with a tiny rainbow pin that Maddy had given her, broke in. "This morning someone chalked insults on our front sidewalk!"

Annie looked at Gussie with alarm.

"Sunday someone paints fags outside the Sweatshop," added Jimmy Kinh.

Jake, the pharmacist, told them, "I'm back on pill-duty, but," he pointed to thick scabbed scrapes across one cheek and over an eyebrow, "I went to a straight co-worker's wedding at Bromsberrow State Park and made the mistake of using the men's room."

Dusty pointed out, "These things have always happened in the Valley."

Pacing, Maddy cried, "Piled up like this in a month? You think it's coincidence?"

"What's happening at the Farm, Heaphy?" asked Paris

Collins. "Are you ready for our ACLU friend?"

Still numb from the sight of Cece's bike, she told them about the offer of reinstatement, her inability to reach Judy and the flak the Farm was getting because of its stand. Her sadness had passed. Now, like trapped electricity, so much anger hummed within her that she was ready to leap into whatever crazy fray Maddy might dream up. "What bugs me is how out of control it's all gotten. Jo tried to keep a lid on it, but couldn't."

"Jennifer Jacob's a journalism major," Maddy volunteered. "She can get all this into the paper."

"Can you?" Annie asked Jennifer.

Jo Barker broke in, "You know we need to do this diplomatically," she advised. "The people who started this can learn how wrong they are, the harm they're doing to Morton River."

"It's not up to you anymore, paisan!" Maddy told Jo with firm seventeen-year-old conviction. "Maybe Annie's getting her job back, but if you think that's the end of this, you're demented. What's your problem anyway?"

Again, there was silence, but this time, Annie realized, Jo was expected to answer Maddy. "Don't jump all over the mediator," Annie objected with automatic chivalry. "Jo's not the enemy. It was the whole lot of us, not just Cece's bike, that got stomped. All I can see are those old World War II newsreels of Nazi storm troopers marching, kicking in doors, kicking fallen people. When I was bad, my dad would say the Nazis were coming—made me go to my room to hide." She gave a bitter little laugh. "I was so scared that when my Brownie leader wanted me to apply for a campership, I dropped out of the troop. No way they were putting me in a concentration camp." The utter silence in the room made her stutter with self-consciousness. "W-we can't expect Jo to stop this war all by herself. My D dad was right. The Nazis are here!"

Paris came over and put an arm around her shoulder, saying, "The immoral majority has this hysterical anti-gay employment statute as a rallying cry. If the Selectmen pass it, nobody's going to challenge it unless all of us do!"

Annie sat down hard. She wished it had been Chantal beside her, but Chantal had stayed with Cece Green and Hope Valerie to deal with the police and the motorcycle. She smiled thanks at Paris.

Dusty said quietly, "Jo Barker, you're not going to find a way around this one. Look where keeping it quiet got Cece. Might as well face up to it—it's time to mount an attack here."

Jo nodded. "I tried to hold back the flood, but I'm just one woman."

"You did good," Elly said. "Now we all have to back you up."

Maddy whined, "If we'd stood up to them in the first place, they'd know they couldn't get away with this shit!"

"We made the best decision we could!" said America.

"This is exactly what they do—set allies against one another," said Gussie.

Jennifer cried, "You can all stand up and shout 'til you're hoarse. What are we going to do?"

Annie felt as if everyone was waiting for her to start the stampede which would set them in motion. She drummed fists onto her knees in excitement and anticipation.

A non-gay she'd never seen before stood. "There's more to it than the gay issue. I teach special education and I volunteer weekends at the Farm. I get sick of being told to honor the rights of my students and then told to treat them as if they're asexual. Darn it, we give animals more credit than that!" He looked around the room. "You know who I miss most from this meeting? Lorelei Simski. Where's her voice?"

More people spoke, but all she heard were the words of the special ed teacher. Chantal had said the same thing, hadn't she?

The hum inside her became an extension of the hum in the whole room. She could feel the mood shift from expectancy to strength. When she closed her eyes to calm herself, lezzie was scratched onto her very soul, right next to Lorelei cheering for the softball team.

"Who *does* Lorelei have to defend her?" She cried out into the hum. "Who does Cece have? And how many careers have I not even dared dream about because I'm gay? I want my damn job back. I will go to school. I've had it with giving up before I get started. It's just like Elly told me once. She said, this is my little dream, and it'll stand up to time and this Valley if I will."

"YES!" cried Maddy, leaping from her seat. She started her pacing again, looking like a precocious tactician. "Let's talk to the press. The other side's got their version plastered all over the *Sentinel*. Tell the paper your story."

"Me? Are you kidding? Get some other hero. I don't want to be chewed up and spit out by the right wing or the fundamentalists or the press. You want a march? I'll march with you. You want to have meetings? I'll come to your meetings."

Jennifer shouted, "Let's do a triple profile—Annie, Lorelei and Cece."

Maddy responded, "That kicks! Do it!"

Their passion was scary. She felt as much a pawn in their wannabe revolution as in the fundamentalists' reign of terror. At the same time she wanted to snatch a red flag and lead a parade singing, "Here come the les-bee-uns!"

"We'll picket all the churches!" said a non-gay.

To Annie's relief, Cece Green slunk in the door then, head down. Chantal Zak and Hope Valerie followed. Everyone in the room fell silent, waiting.

Chantal told them, "The cops said they'd never seen such violence against a vehicle. They kept asking if Cece has any enemies."

"What did they say about lezzies scratched into the bike? That makes it a hate crime," Paris asked.

Chantal, lips in a tense closed line, cast a quick glance at Cece.

"I couldn't afford to let them see it," Cece muttered. "I—" She drew a red bandanna from a back pocket and blew her nose, obviously trying to compose herself.

"We gouged the paint off that spot so you couldn't read what they wrote." Chantal glanced quickly at Annie. "One employment problem is enough, thank you very much."

Annie checked the faces in the room. She would have erased Lorelei's kiss too if she could have. She motioned Cece, Chantal and silent Hope to sit with her.

The larger group shifted and talked, as if to digest—what? Cece's survival instinct? Feelings of betrayal? She noticed Verne Prinz take a seat on a window sill behind America. Who had invited her?

Maddy spoke tentatively. "So what about that profile?"

Jennifer explained her brainstorm to the newcomers.

Cece looked up, "Are you out of your ever-loving gourd? Find some rich white boy to stick his neck out for you. Me, I'll have all I can do to find a way to get to work—and I don't hear anybody offering a ride. Leave *this* woman out of this mess."

No one said a word. Annie whispered to Cece, "Don't get tweaked. I'll drive you into work."

"Deal," said Cece, offering a limp high five.

"You beat me to it," Chantal said.

"And I'll find these dudes," Cece muttered. "Don't think me and my Rafferty Street bike buddies won't take care of business."

"We don't want violence, young woman," Venita Valerie said.

Cece gave her a resentful look. "Like you said, Miss Valerie, we're a long way from third grade. Those f—. Excuse me, those dudes'll never get punished unless I take care of them."

"She's right," said Jimmy Kinh. "Sometimes you can't fight with words or you lose everything."

"You said it, bro'. And if you want in when we find them, I'll give you the high sign."

Dusty stood up and got the meeting under control. "We have to do something, but most of us don't want to use violence. Although if I were younger—"

Elly looked sharply at her.

"But I'm not younger. On the other hand we're no big city radicals—"

With a coy glance at Jennifer Jacob next to her, Maddy grumbled, "No shit, Sherlock."

Dusty scowled. "We're respectable citizens. We need to start off on the right foot and picketing just makes us look like flower children. We have a legitimate gripe that can bring us sympathy. There is no earthly reason the conservatives should keep their foothold here except that everybody's scared of everybody else and ready to blame their next door neighbor."

Elly rested her hands on Dusty's shoulders. "But we worked damn hard for the position we have," Elly said. Elly's eyes slid toward Verne, then quickly away.

"You're fooling yourselves if you think you'll ever be fully respected," Paris cautioned them. "A queer businessperson is queer first, the enemy to people who hate us."

Jennifer agreed. "Do you think they spared the respectable Jews in Germany? Did 'good' people of color get to sit in the front of the bus? Did Colorado voters make exceptions for celibate homosexuals?"

"When I was growing up in the Valley," ventured Dusty, "the unions were strong. The Poles and the Italians and the Irish fought like mad, but they were all working people and voted Democratic, hated the bosses and the Klan. Now we've got Asians and blacks and Hispanics added into that melting pot, not to mention the yuppie commuters. There's got to be a way to show all of them that this is their fight too without irresponsible..."

A train came along and covered Dusty's words. Across the room, Verne, with a bemused look, half-turned and closed the window.

Chantal ah-hemmed and Annie teased her, "Still think you'd be interested in Verne?" She got a gentle slap on the knee in response.

Increasingly flushed, Maddy straddled a backwards kitchen chair and cried, "Listen, guys, I'm only a kid, but even I know if we water down what happened to Annie and Lorelei—and Cece—we'll drown ourselves. We've got the fire hot over this right now. Being responsible means taking back the power. No one takes a movement seriously until it gets headlines. If Annie and Cece won't turn their stories into headlines, we have to do something else to get noticed!"

"Why are we arguing?" Gussie pleaded.

"Because there's no center to hold us all," came a strong voice from the doorway. It was Thor Valerie. "I've been pushing all you liberals away from Valley Opportunity Watch's door for the longest time, wanting the black people to do for ourselves. But this is a beautiful sight here, this rainbow of humanity."

Someone began to applaud and quickly everyone joined in.

Thor continued, "I have to tell you, though, that good intentions and sit-ins, sit-downs and walk-outs and running to the press don't cut it anymore. You need a board of directors and a strategy, accountability and coalition building. I'll be the first volunteer for the Board. We're facing fascism and it's going to take every one of us to stop it. Jesse Jackson's Rainbow Coalition has finally come to town and we are it."

Gussie's voice was hoarse, her face red, her white hair all cowlicks. It was plain that she was both primed for battle and exhausted. "You're *all* right," she rasped. "We need to do a little of everything. For everybody. And the last thing we want to do

143

is run off Annie and Cece asking them to represent all the rest of us. We need every solitary soul to hold back the forces of evil. It's time I faced the music myself. Let them see who they're so frightened of. Little old me. Write a profile of Augusta Brennan in your newspaper." There was deafening applause and cheering. "Now stop this bickering and let's have positive ideas about how we're going to get this show on the road."

"Before all this," Annie said, laughing and making a sweeping gesture that included everyone in the room, "I thought politics was a boys' game, what they did when they got too old to fight in wars and had to find a new way to flex their muscles. Now I see that politics can be narrow and abusive, but it's really about the people. When you care what happens to a community, a law, a party, zap—you're a political being. Gussie, if you're dyke enough to be in the paper, then I want to be, too."

"Right on!" Thor called out when the new round of applause died down. He laughed. "You've been co-opted by the democratic system when you discover you can make a difference."

Annie said, "It makes me feel powerful. But I've never sat on a board."

"Board's are for some people, getting your name in the paper is for others," said Thor. "There's a place for you in this."

She laughed. "That's what I'm afraid of!"

Paris was nodding and smiling. Maddy looked close to levitating with excitement.

"I'm only a bookkeeper and a mother," Chantal said, "and I don't know a thing about revolutions or coalitions or politics, but I'll volunteer to get our side sending letters to the editor."

America Velasquez announced another meeting of Parents and Friends of Lesbians and Gays. "Sign up before you leave!"

"You see?" said Thor. "This is what we need—action, first one, then the next and the next."

Finally, as if suddenly filled with ideas, the crowd split into small groups to draft details. Jo, who had joined Verne at the window, said she'd get them a list of businesses that were pressuring United Way. Paris would write press releases. The teachers promised an educational series. Maddy would expand the action at her evening graduation with the help of the Yale group. Thor would talk to V.O.W.'s board about coalition building. Peg passed a softball cap to collect money.

"I still want to be more than a poster girl," Annie complained.

"Help me on the letter writing committee?" Chantal asked, her manner flirting. "You have some college, you can be in charge of grammar and spelling."

"I can do that," she replied.

"And writing sample letters."

"Uh—"

"And," Jennifer said, sidling up to Annie, "coming with me to talk to the editor so he can meet one of the main players."

Buoyed by the power of the group, she assented. "Sure. I can do that too. Who knows? Maybe the more public I am, the less likely it is that employers will hassle me because of my big mouth."

"Now you're talking," Jennifer told her. "Letterman here we come."

"That might be a little too prime time for me. What if my family was watching?"

"Don't they know you're gay?"

Her coward's secret. "I never told them."

"That's too weird for words."

"Hey, I came out twenty-five years ago. You told no one back then. Why do you think it's so hard for me to be showcased now? Old habits die hard."

Jennifer looked pensive. "The behaviors of oppression die hard."

Her arm on Cece's, Chantal said, "I'll bet I can persuade Cece to help with the mailings. We'll need a good licker."

Cece gave Hope a broad wink. "I've got a flair for that."

Hope grinned at the floor, then surprised everyone. "I think we should have a speakers group. You know, go round to the schools, be on the radio and the local TV, talk to churches and ladies auxiliaries. Like that. I'm no speaker, but I'm okay at getting people to say yes."

Jennifer lurched forward with a hug. "This is awesome. You women are so cool. I love you all."

The cookies Gussie had baked were long gone and the coffee pot empty. Toothpick had worn herself out attacking feet and now slept, despite the clamor in the kitchen, curled on Annie's lap, a furry oasis of peace.

Chantal's eyes shimmered with excitement as she patted the kitten. "Want to come over to my place after?" she asked.

Annie's palms were sweaty. She hadn't made a decision about Chantal yet, but they couldn't seem to say anything to each other without half-serious simmering looks. She imagined that Chantal would be as forceful in bed as she'd been at the meeting. "I'll have to check *my* calendar this time," she teased.

Toothpick looked up, moved to Chantal's lap and began to knead with desperate speed.

"Maybe," said Annie, "you should be one of the speakers at the rally. You're good at it. And you're a respectable mother of two."

"Respectable! I don't know if I've ever been accused of being respectable before."

Dusty slowly strolled past the window where Verne still lounged, did a menacing half-step in front of her and moved on with a laugh. Verne hadn't moved a muscle, but her face had gone pale. Annie, Cece, Hope and Chantal giggled together.

Maddy Scala was talking to Jennifer Jacob, using her arms and hands, bouncing on the balls of her feet as if she might spring through the roof at any moment. Annie nudged Chantal. "Are those two a number?"

"The kids? Isn't that sweet! I give them twenty-four hours if they're not."

Over Chantal's head Annie's eyes met Jo's. "Hi!" she called across the noisy kitchen, then softly asked Chantal, "Do you want to meet her?"

"I don't know. Should I, Sugar?" Chantal taunted.

She looked sharply at Chantal. "You're not exactly rivals," she assured her.

Chantal just raised an eyebrow.

Jo left Gussie's side and crossed the room. "You were great," Jo told Annie. Her eyes looked glazed when she turned to Chantal, as if she'd caught Elly's fever. "You've done political organizing before."

"Not me!" said Chantal with a meaningful look at Annie. "I'm a respectable mother of two."

"Do you think you can get some of your closeted business cronies involved?" Annie asked Jo.

"I just talked to Peg about that. She's thinking of inviting a bunch of likelies to her place for a barbecue and conscripting them. They'll be politely sloshed, feeling frisky. Maybe they'll make promises they'll be ashamed to back out of later. I'll help her. She'll probably ask you to be there so they can see you're not some relic of the olden days."

"Oh, but I am," answered Annie, not hiding her annoyance.

Jo colored. "I could lend you dressy slacks."

"No thanks, Jo, but if it'll ease your mind I won't smoke cigars while I'm there."

"Annie, I didn't mean you don't look fine the way you are. I just don't want to intimidate these women."

Annie winced, opened her mouth to speak, then gave up with a smile and a shake of her head. "Traumatizing the closet brigade might be fun," she said. She stiffened her fingers until they looked claw-like and advanced menacingly on Jo. If she was going to be a symbol, she might as well have a good time.

Chantal, as if to bridge unbridgeable chasms, held her back and changed the subject. "I'll get my kids and Merry's husband's family and my best friend and her family to write letters to the editor. I wonder about Giulia's fiance. We were talking at the game and he owns property all over town. We could use people like that on our side."

"Just think," Annie said, afraid to be utopian, but unable not to, spreading her arms as if to encompass a universe, "if they all got their friends and families to speak up—"

Jo said with a bitter laugh, "Most families won't say anything. Deep inside, a lot of them are ashamed of us."

"It's true," Annie admitted.

They all looked at one another for several seconds. Then Annie ventured, "Well—" and Jo said, "Well—" Chantal saved them by excusing herself to use the bathroom. Toothpick sniffed Jo's shoes, raising her little face with a grimace.

"Toothpick, be polite. You've smelled Rex before." Jo didn't seem to see the humor. Annie got serious. "I can't believe you came," she told Jo.

"I can't either. Or that so many people want Morton River to be a better place for us to live. It makes me think about staying."

Too late now, Annie thought.

"I remembered," Jo went on, "that you'd expressed some concerns about whether you'd acted appropriately with Lorelei.

When Judy went in to work for a little while last week, Lorelei begged her to start a ball team at the farm. Once a week at lunch there's a game with mixed teams of workers and employees. Lorelei plays shortstop."

Annie's position. She tossed an imaginary ball up and caught it, grinning. "So she's okay."

"Unscathed by being crushed out on you," Jo said with her smile. "Speaking of crushes, I talked to Verne about Elly. Verne admits to liking the groupie phenomenon that happens when she does residencies in the sticks, but she agreed to keep it professional around Elly. It was never more than a flirtation."

The bite of anger she felt was at Jo as well as Verne. The two flirts deserved each other. She hoped Jo would follow Verne to Siberia. Aloud, she suggested, "Maybe you need to talk to Hope about getting a speaker for Peg's barbeque. She's taken that chore on."

"I'm impressed. Let me see if I can catch her."

With the announcement, "Sweatshop's open in five minutes!" the Jimmies led a noisy exodus. People hugged, shook hands, flowed out of the house so full of enthusiasm Annie imagined Rafferty Street lit like a Christmas tree. At least, she thought, hands on her hips as she stood defiantly at the top of the porch steps, the neighbors would see their show of strength.

CHAPTER 15

Annie's head was foggy with too many emotions. She followed Chantal along Main in the Grape, so jittery she stalled at a light. She couldn't decide if she was more nervous about committing herself politically or romantically. Chantal led her up Bank into the tangled streets of the low hills behind downtown, in the general direction of Puddle Street. This neighborhood was better than Rafferty Street, but wasn't Park Avenue.

"I'll never find this place again," she told Chantal as she climbed out of the Saab, not surprised to find her mouth dry.

"I'll top it with a pink neon triangle to make sure you can, Sugar."

There was no sidewalk, no driveway, only a shallow stretch of grass. "Look at this street!" Annie exclaimed. "Two-stories, duplexes, that row of boxy brown Colonials! Steep roofs, flat roofs, bay windows, plate-glass windows, dormers." Most of the windows were already darkened for the night. Brightly colored plastic tricycles and other toys littered driveways and front yards.

"Does that mean you like our funny little valley?"

"It might," she agreed, smiling into Chantal's eyes. "It just might." Chantal held her gaze, and Annie felt a steamy warmth. Simultaneously, they looked away.

Chantal's place was a white wooden bungalow. Though the night was still cloudy, the rain held off until they got to the glassed-in porch. Inside, the living room was big enough for its blue couch, two patterned chairs, a console television and little else. There was a long mirror above the couch, though, which reflected the porch and suggested a room double the size. Annie sank into the protection of a wing chair.

"That wore me out," she said.

"What, finding my house?" Chantal was obviously still revved up.

She laughed."That meeting. The labyrinth was fun. Where are we anyway?"

"This is Violet Street. If you climbed the hill behind the house you'd be on Main again, where it turns north."

"So no neighbors in back of you."

"And a deep yard. My ex-husband always wanted to expand into it, but I was stubborn. I have a huge old weeping willow and an enormous cherry tree. I got him to dig us a pond in the shade, four feet across, just deep enough for the kids to splash in when they were small. Right now it's overflowing from all the rain, but usually it's hard to keep full because the willow drinks everything in sight. In the summer there isn't a cooler place in the Valley. This is the reason I'm in the closet at work, to pay the mortgage on my little bit of heaven. Come on, I'll give you the nickel tour. It takes about a minute and a half." Chantal was a dynamo, chattering and demonstrating all her gadgets.

"It's like a travel trailer, Chantal. Everything's built to maximize space." Annie kept her elbows against her ribs. "Did the house come like this?"

"No. I planned every detail."

Chantal pulled out drawers from the wall under the staircase. "My hutch," she explained with a dainty shrug, her futile attempt to mask her pride. Cutting boards slid out of the counters in the kitchen. Pots and pans hung on a rack that had to be pulled down from the ceiling. She pointed upward with a fingernail neatly painted pink. "The one place we had space was in height, so we have a lot of hanging lamps too." The kitchen table folded out, panel by panel, to seat four, six and eight.

"Just imagining all those people in this house could give you claustrophobia," she told Chantal.

Upstairs Chantal said, "I pored over the cute kid room designs in the women's magazines. My ex-husband was good at do-it-yourself projects." There were two tiny rooms with single beds that folded down from walls. "Merry and Ralph loved opening up their beds at night. This bathroom used to be a closet."

Annie felt jittery as she did every time the kids came up. She hadn't met Ralph, the soldier, yet, though he was due home on leave soon.

"Come on back down. You single butches are about as interested in homemaking as deadbeat dads."

The bedroom downstairs was the last stop. "I had single beds jammed in here by the time I threw Ed out, but I always wanted a bedroom that was designed to spoil Chantal. I did it bit by bit."

"Everything's built in except the waterbed and vanity?"

"The queen-sized waterbed, I'll have you notice."

The walking space was tight on a plush lavender rug, the drapes were a textured velour, the waterbed was covered with purple sateen that Chantal touched to make waves. Redone or not, the room felt crowded with Chantal's old heterosexual life. "I've never been with a woman who's been with a guy through marriage and child-rearing,...that I know of."

Chantal looked worried. "Not your style?"

"I don't even know what my style is anymore, to tell you the truth. It's just that there's nowhere on earth we can go to get away from heterosexuality, not even our bedrooms."

Chantal smiled. "Lighten up, Sugar. Give me a night with you in this room and I guarantee you'll feel different by morning."

Annie tried not to stare at the bed. To change the subject, she said, "I didn't realize you were so practical."

"Practical?"

"Beyond practical," she explained, her arms flung wide to indicate the whole house. "Like if you were formulating your philosophy of life, would it look like your house?" Here it came—her relationship-phobia exploded inside her. She felt sweaty and faint. Why was she here? She barely knew this woman with her children, and the imprint of a male on her home and life. Maybe single life wouldn't be so bad after all.

They were standing in the narrow space between the bed and the vanity. Chantal walked her index and middle fingers up and down the buttons on Annie's shirt. Annie made herself stay put. "Can a philosophy be practical on the outside and wild inside? That's why I wanted everything in the house to be as useful as I could make it, so I could fit in the good stuff too. The yard, the bed."

"We're so different," Annie observed.

"You know what would help your room?"

"An interior decorator?"

"A big old beautiful wardrobe and shelving, like this."

Chantal opened the door to a deep walk-in closet.

"Then I couldn't see any of my stuff!" Annie objected.

"That's the idea," said Chantal, returning to lay her head on Annie's chest, rubbing against her. "Less clutter."

"But I like reading in the easy chair and remembering the moments I bought my toy taxis, the little stories of my life."

"How I'd hate that! If I'm in bed I don't want stuff interfering with my dreams."

The room seemed to grow even smaller. Sweat trickled between Annie's breasts. "I'm so confused. Jo wanted to dress me up, you want to dress up my room. Maddy wants me to be an Amazon warrior, Gussie thinks I should be a dyke Gandhi." She was so tired and so worried about everything, she was almost ready to follow any woman's lead. "My stuff is part of my dreams," she challenged. "From souvenirs to old textbooks to memories of corner spas and cobblestones. I don't expect anyone to understand that, but it'd be great if *some*body would respect it."

It was true. She loved her life and all the trappings of it despite its recent vicissitudes. Didn't Chantal love hers? Or had she gotten in the habit years ago of locking it up—behind closet doors, inside a complex order—to keep it safe from all those people who were so foreign to the real, lesbian her? Hets don't capich anything, Maddy had said.

She edged out of the narrow space, but Chantal pulled her gently back, holding her forearms.

"I'm sorry," said Chantal. "I like you just the way you are. I'm one of those people who ought to start a consulting business organizing other people's lives, if only to keep me from volunteering myself unasked on friends."

"Oh, Chantal," she said. "You are such a nice woman." Swallowing hard, she leaned forward with closed eyes. These were neither Jo's cool closed lips nor Marie-Christine's conquering kisses. Chantal, at least in this, invited without directing. She pulled Chantal closer. What a wealth of softness. She felt Chantal's little hands at the small of her back, patting, smoothing, roaming onto her buttocks. Her blood seemed to swell its channels, her body to sigh a long while.

She stopped kissing Chantal, and looked into her light eyes, which appeared even sleepier than usual. Chantal's fingertips were on the back of her neck. Chantal's mouth drew her. Chantal seemed to expand and her house's boundaries to fall away. Annie straightened. Their breasts brushed together and she felt a faint hit of pleasure below. Their lips opened.

Her fingers barely touched the sides of Chantal's breasts. Chantal made a squeaky little sound and pulled away. She cleared her throat. "Why don't you go use the upstairs powder room? It'll be faster than taking turns down here, especially if you want a shower."

"The powder room?" she teased.

She climbed the stairs slowly, wiping the sweat at her hairline with her sleeve. Inside the stall shower, washing off the dirt of softball and the stress of the meeting, she took deep breaths. She dropped the soap twice, a third time. Why this fear? Was it Chantal's total neatness? Her kids? The uncharted waters of her, of a woman like her? At that moment Annie felt like she had nothing left to give anyone.

What's your problem? Nobody's perfect. You're all grown up. What do you want, some unformed pretty-girl? Someone life hasn't clawed at yet? So Chantal's a grandma with an order thing. So she's not going to be able to take you under her sophisticated wing and tell you what to choose in the fancy restaurants you'll never go to with her. You could've fought for Jo or stayed with Marie-Christine, dancing on the edge of relationships. You've got your own quirks. What are you going to do, fly out of here with apologies and steal Peg's niece away from Maddy?

Or was she still bruised by Marie-Christine's faithlessness? She'd be more careful in her forties than she had been in her thirties. A lover simply wouldn't get as much of her.

Part of her yearned for that old sneaking around, for the hungry one-night women she used to find back before AIDS, back before Vicky moved into her toothpick house. She'd spend the night at some woman's place and slink out at dawn, then hole up, anonymous, in a greasy spoon to eat breakfast with the truckers and night owls, a midnight to five DJ on the next stool, still hyped by his all-night patter. Then she'd drive home in her noisy VW feeling cleansed, relishing her lonely space by the beach. She'd felt comfortable then with those out-of-sync people who lived among strangers, meeting at counters and pining for company at home. But was that how she wanted to live now?

Another part of her still worried that Chelsea was where she ought to be. She'd visited for a week to see if she needed to move closer to her folks. She'd trodden the streets where the trolleys used to run, the tracks sunken between cobblestones, just like in Morton River. The house had always trembled when the trains ran by Carroll Street, but now it seemed to shake.

Her mom looked so tiny. Her dad was more silent than ever, more disagreeable, but not as scary. She kept noticing his white hair, and his scalp, pink like a baby's. He didn't look a thing like the burly veteran of her childhood, always exaggerating about the roads he'd built, like he was some sort of Hercules, doing it single-handed. Chelsea had never exactly been upscale, but now she didn't think her mom should be walking the streets even in daylight. With the city in receivership after all those years of corruption she worried about what would happen to services for the Chelsea seniors.

But that was guilt working on her. Her parents were still very active and her aunts, Dad's younger sisters, lived upstairs with their families in the second and third floor flats. In Morton River Annie was closer than she had been in New York, and now she had a car. That was enough. The thought of moving back to that cold, silent Chelsea house made Morton River look like paradise.

Chantal was here and now. Chantal was big. Chantal was the unknown. At the same time, Chantal was a return to her own Chelsea roots. Going to bed with Chantal was like going to bed with Morton River Valley itself. No wonder she was scared. Chantal, like moving to the Valley, might be a mistake, might be wonderful. If Marie-Christine and the New York years had been adventure and no-strings romance, Chantal was comfort and strings galore behind that adventurous seductive manner.

Whatever happened, she reassured herself, she had a home on Rafferty Street. She stuffed her sweaty underwear in a back pocket, opened the bathroom door and, trying to ignore the ghosts of Chantal's marriage, clattered back down to the bedroom built to spoil Chantal.

Chantal sat on a low stool before her vanity. The only light was a small lamp with a frilly shade. Chantal's reflection in the vanity mirror glowed like a pulsating spirit. Annie hesitated in the doorway.

"You asked once why I took philosophy courses in New York," she said. Chantal met her eyes in the vanity mirror. "Moving from idea to action is a major feat for me. Since I was a kid I've been paralyzed at times like this by the chasm between thought and act. Sometimes I throw myself into action to avoid decisions. I thought philosophy would explore that."

Chantal watched her.

"Instead, to tell you the truth, the classes were driving me nuts. Life's weird enough with its infinite options and Do-Not-Pass-Go-Do-Not-Collect-Two-Hundred-Dollars consequences."

"You think too much," Chantal said.

Annie stepped to the foot of Chantal's bed, fingering her cap.

"Go ahead and hang it on the bedpost," Chantal said, with a suggestive tone. She wore a long light blue silky nightgown and matching robe, both of which emphasized her eyes even more.

Annie reached for the post and stopped. Her team cap on Chantal's bedpost—why did that sound like an irrevocable commitment? Next stop, twin rockers on the sun porch. They looked at each other. "Uh, Chantal," Annie finally said.

"You've been trying to tell me you've got cold feet."

She looked at her feet as if to confirm it. "I guess I kind of do."

Chantal said nothing.

Annie looked up. Chantal's eyebrows were raised. "It's not you," she told Chantal. "I mean, you look great. You're sexy as hell. It's just—" She couldn't name the feeling she had.

"Fear," Chantal supplied.

"No. No, it's not that. It's like my sex drive disappeared. Crap, Chantal, I want you, you know I do, and I'm frozen."

"Is that a challenge, Sugar? Because if it is, I think I could find your defrost cycle."

"If anyone could do it, you could." They were silent again. Then Annie suggested, "Maybe it's having two failures in a row."

"Damn that Barker woman. I hear Verne may give her the royal heave-ho before they even get out of town."

"How did you hear—?"

"This is a smaller burg than you think, Annie. Ghost stories get around."

"Ghost stories." That's just what she'd been telling herself, ghost stories. "I guess I don't really think my ghosts are to blame, Chantal." She was still standing, still playing with her hat. She sat, forgetting it was a water bed, and almost toppled over. Chantal reached to steady her. "I never quite got the hang of these things," Annie admitted with a nervous laugh at her own clumsiness.

Somehow Chantal's hand had found a home in hers. "Too bad it's not ghosts," Chantal offered, squeezing her hand. "I could get into an exorcism."

Her regret was so obvious, her smile so brave, that Annie reached to hug her. "It wouldn't be fair to ask you to get rid of my ghosts. They're my problem." Then she stood. "I like you so much, Chantal. I'm really, really sorry about this. I'm going to go before I start something I can't finish."

"I like you too, Annie. And as happy as I would have been to get into your chinos, it hurts a lot less now than if you'd let me lead us down the wrong path."

"It may not be the wrong path, Chantal. I just don't know yet." She was in the doorway again, but couldn't leave. "I feel like I can almost say it, like if you're about to get a cold you start tasting a certain taste and eventually you recognize it's how you tasted last time you got sick?"

"Love-sick, maybe?"

"Love-shy, would be more like it."

"Sounds like a danger signal. I hope I didn't set it off."

"No. It's really not you, Chantal. I have the same taste, like a sour stomach, when I think about what's happening, about those people who think being gay should be punishable by death."

They just looked at each other.

"Oh, no. That's it, isn't it?" Annie flung her team hat to the floor. "Damn it, Chantal. First these hateful people cost me my job, then my peace of mind—now they're ruining my love life?"

"Annie, don't let them."

"Like I have a big choice. I wake up in the morning wondering how long I can stick to it, standing up to all these people who know who I am, know I own the Grape—just like they knew about Cece's bike."

Chantal glanced at the window. The Saab was outside.

Then Annie realized what she'd done. "Oh, my gosh. I never thought. As much as I worry, I never put it together that if it gets around that you and I—Chantal, I'm sorry. I was looking for comfort and I'm infecting your home with danger."

Chantal, in her silken finery, looked uncertain.

"You said it yourself, this is a small burg. Too small." Annie swept her cap up from the floor, urgency pushing her out of the house. "I'd better get the Saab off Violet Street."

Chantal didn't stop her as she exploded out the door.

CHAPTER 16

Two days later *The Sentinel* started its series on the "Gay Scare." Annie's story ran first. Jennifer had tried to avoid using her name, but the editor had insisted on specifics about employers and sports and churches. Without some anchoring facts, the piece wasn't newsworthy to him.

Every customer in the diner seemed to have a copy when she stopped on her way home to pick up dessert. She was out, in black and white. She'd promised herself a long quiet evening tinkering in the garden, playing with Toothpick, not worrying about the consequences.

The customers stared at her as Giulia wrapped her cream puffs. Annie would never understand how the same people who ate the food Dusty cooked, and drank the coffee Elly poured, could claim gay people were envoys of the devil.

Elly scurried out of the kitchen, pink baseball jacket, neatly repaired, over her shoulders.

"Let's go over to see Gramma Gus," Elly said, her voice tight, her eyes oddly worried-looking.

"I came over for—"

Dusty appeared behind Elly. "Come on, you two. In the car."

"What—"

"Didn't you tell her?"

"No," Elly said quickly. "I thought we could on the way over."

"What in hell is happening now?" Annie cried, then, seeing customers look up, shut up.

"There's something going on over on Rafferty Street."

"What?"

Dusty herded them both out the back door toward her old Dodge Swinger. "Hoodlums. Skinheads. Motorcycle types running wild. Gussie didn't say, just that she was ready to shoot back."

"Gussie wants to shoot back?"

"They're shooting paint balls. Yelling about witches and queers. Come on."

"I knew I should have moved out. This is all my fault."

"Just get in the car."

When they turned the corner onto Rafferty Street, Elly exclaimed, "This can't happen here!"

The clumps of young men in jeans and sleeveless t-shirts were not at their usual hang-out at the end of Rafferty Street, but stood in front of Gussie's house chanting words Annie couldn't make out. The sidewalk was splattered with yellow paint, but the front stoop had the worst of it. One of them had sprayed LEZ in black across the sidewalk. Crap, she thought with dread. They've run down the queer and I led them.

When several men started along the street toward them, she felt rage, not fear. A siren grew louder. "This," she told Elly and Dusty, "is what I've been scared of all my life. Nazis saluting Hitler. Neo-Nazis burning out the Gypsies in Germany. I can see Kurt in a Nazi uniform, his congregation goose-stepping along Rafferty Street. Those sirens better be for us."

"John was calling as we left," Elly said, her voice cracking.

Dusty declared, "We'll wait here until the cops come."

"And leave Gussie in there alone, at their mercy?" Annie protested from the back seat. "Let me out." The boys stopped in front of the house, shouted, made obscene gestures. They looked like the same ones who'd sat in the bleachers the day Cece's Suzuki was destroyed.

"Heaphy, you can't get to her," Dusty warned, voice commanding. Elly's fingers tapped incessantly on her cloth purse.

"They're not going to hurt me in front of the whole neighborhood." Some of the boys were peering toward the car.

"We're not going to give them the chance." The car had only two doors. She was trapped. Annie rolled down the window. "Heaphy, don't even think about it." It only went half way. "Roll it up or they'll pull you out, glass or not."

"But it's me they're after, not Gussie."

"Mobs don't listen," Dusty advised. "Who spilled the beans anyway? How did they know your address?"

A freight train passing the back of the houses let out a dispirited whistle, as if laden with troubles. Fleetingly, she wondered if Elly and Dusty were still at loggerheads.

"All they needed was one queer-hater at *The Sentinel* and a city directory."

Elly took her knuckles from her mouth. "Testosterone-crazed teenagers have antennae, like giant mutated cockroaches."

As they waited for the first patrol car pictures came into her head. "Do you guys remember *Victory At Sea*, that fifties TV series that showed film clips of World War II?" Annie asked. "My dad never missed an episode. These Rafferty Street good old boys are in uniform too—look at them—sleeveless t-shirts, jeans, the heavy boots.

"I knew I was right to be scared of walking alone around here, right to be afraid in America." She was aware of Elly turning and watching her face and equally aware that Dusty wasn't missing anything on the street.

"There's a black and white now," Dusty said. "El, honey, you've got to stop sniffling when we go in there. You don't want to upset Gussie more."

"Crap." Annie exclaimed. "If these barbarians give Gus a heart attack..." Even from here she could see that one of them had a swastika tattooed on his upper arm. What word had Thor used? Fascism.

She suddenly felt small. "All of this—the trouble at work, the bad news from Colorado and D.C., the rough time Vicky's having out in Oregon, the black civil rights struggle, apartheid, the riots and killings in Europe—these, these storm troopers—they're all faces of an evil I couldn't imagine except I watched their predecessors right there on TV."

"There's bad people in this world, all right," Elly agreed.

"But that's supposed to be over," Annie protested. "My Dad may have been mean, but he was supposed to have made the world safe for democracy once and for all. Our whole generation of baby-boomers was taught that. Was it a lie?"

"It's crazy, Heaphy, but you're right."

She hadn't even known she believed so strongly in democracy until now. Today, this minute, it was clear to her that the monster called fascism wasn't just a threat from the past.

"The bad guys never were busted, were they?" Annie asked. "And this time we're the chosen people, we get to see it first. We're the ones who have to confront it head on and stop it like our soldier dads were supposed to. What the world REALLY needs is superheroes."

Dusty pulled up in front of the house.

"Hold it!" an officer commanded as Annie rushed the front door.

"I live here."

A look of recognition, then a frown came to the man's face. Had the Norwood flock been passing her picture around? He let her pass without a word.

"It's me!" she called to Gussie as she unlocked the front door.

Gussie had pulled a chair into the doorway between her room and the kitchen and sat on it, her face waxen white, a little twenty-two rifle pointed at the door.

"Gussie! I didn't know you had one of those."

"It's my last resort, Socrates. I've been through these times before. If they come for me they'll never forget me."

"The police are out there, Gussie," cautioned Dusty.

Gussie rose. "I'll hide it," she said, turning toward her room. She swayed briefly, then slumped against the door frame.

Dusty and Elly reached her first. "Got her," said Dusty.

"Do you need your pills?" Annie asked, gingerly taking the rifle and gently placing it under the bed.

"Don't fuss over me," Gussie replied as Elly and Dusty supported her across the small room. Gussie lay on her bed with an air of great weariness.

Annie went to her side, inspired at the old woman's tenacious irritability.

Dusty brought in a uniformed woman. "EMT," she announced.

The cop had followed them.

"I want to press every charge in the book," Annie said, holding Gussie's hand.

The cop reached to a pocket for a pad and she led him to the kitchen. As she answered questions she looked out the window.

She said, "The kids—some of them aren't even kids—are still over there, smirking, smart-talking you guys." She needed a bathroom, or a year off from this craziness. "Is the paint water-soluble?" she asked.

"Usually," the cop answered. "What's the matter with your—"

"With Gramma Gussie?" she found herself saying, as if she called her that all the time. Then she raged, "She's eighty-three, and her home was just surrounded by thugs threatening her life."

"Okay, okay," he said. "I'm on your side." Outside an ambulance bleated as it pressed through the crowd of neighbors.

When Annie finished her statement, she stayed in the kitchen while the ambulance attendants readied Gussie. "This really *is* bigger than one dyke losing her job or Cece losing her bike. It's even bigger than a gay rights backlash, isn't it?" she asked no one in particular. "It's not about us at all. It's about scared little men realizing that they can't take our power away anymore."

"The good news is, we won't all fit in the closet," Elly agreed.

Annie, remembering the film clips, thought glumly, the Nazis put an awful lot of people in their cattle cars.

Dusty joined them. "Heaphy, you'd better stay here and make sure there's a house for Gussie to come back to. We'll go to the hospital with her."

"Is she bad?"

"In a pig's eye!" called Gussie in a quavering voice as she passed, lying on the gurney. She stretched an arm up to smooth her cowlicks. "Why won't they let me stay home? Because I'm old, that's why. It's discrimination. Anyone would be weak at the knees after that onslaught."

Annie walked beside her to the door, laughing. "Hey," Annie told her, controlling her own voice as best she could. "you're better off away from these creeps. We'll get this straightened out."

While one attendant adjusted a wheel on the gurney, Gussie complained, "The time I was the last one out of the ladies' room window at Punchy's bar in Toledo I never even saw a doctor. A cop," she said, poking a finger at the officer who had taken Annie's statement, "took a swipe at my head. The girls carried me around the block to somebody's apartment and somehow got me up two flights of stairs. When I came to we toasted our escape with a quart of ale, me with an ice pack on my bloody noggin." She swivelled her head around as they began to move her. "Do you think you can change the world by the time they spring me?"

Annie squeezed Gussie's cold hand. "I knew Jennifer's articles would make things worse. That's why I fought this profile idea."

Gussie squeezed back. "Don't let this get you down, Socrates.

162

Things always get worse before they get better."

"I love you, Gus."

Dusty and Elly paused at the door, watching as Gussie was wheeled toward the ambulance. "Gutsy lady," said Dusty. "Irregular heartbeat, blood pressure through the ceiling." She looked over her shoulder, then whispered, "The cop on the door? He's a member of our club."

She grinned over at him. "Tell Gussie I may not change the world, but Toothpick and I'll keep her house standing." She went cold. "Toothpick!" There'd been no sign of the cat since she'd arrived. She barreled up the stairs, raced into her room, Nan's room, the bathroom, her room again.

"There you are!"

The cat had stuffed herself against the back wall under the bed, but now came tentatively out. Annie hugged her until she struggled away. "I may send you to live with your aunts Peg and Paris for the duration, little cat. You shouldn't have to fight my war."

Was it then that she felt something shift inside? It was one of those once-in-a-lifetime moments she knew she'd remember always. Her eyes sought the sky beyond the window. She drew air into her tension-sore chest. Her whole body straightened, as if pulled by a force larger than herself. "You know, I think I'm glad Jennifer published her piece. We've drawn the line." She closed the cat in her room.

Toothpick was scratching at the door before Annie was halfway downstairs. "Count your blessings, kitten. Who's going to protect the rest of us?" she called over her shoulder.

She could see through the front window that the ambulance had left. There were fewer people on the street and those who loitered did not seem threatening. Apparently the police had arrested most of them. She closed her eyes, fatigued. Her body was just beginning to let go, shoulders slowly lowering, when the back door flew open. She spun around, wishing for the rifle.

"It's okay! It's only us!" Maddy and Chantal rushed in.

"You shouldn't be here," Annie said, reaching for a chair to lean against. Her legs felt liquid from the shock. "It's too dangerous."

Chantal nevertheless came to her and pulled her close. "Do you think I care?"

"You should."

"Why? You're doing a pretty good job of protecting the whole world," Chantal accused her. "What are you doing, setting yourself up as resident pariah? Nobody's seen you at the Sweatshop, you won't talk to anyone at work, you're probably just too responsible to quit the softball team 'til the end of the season. And you haven't returned one of my messages."

Chantal didn't know that Annie'd even suggested to Gussie that she ought to move out. Too late now, she thought. But Gussie had held her also—at arm's length—while she delivered a vehement lecture about turning to, not away from, her friends. "What can they do to me at this age?" Gussie had asked. "You know there's been many a time I've been a hair's breadth from the hoosegow."

Now Chantal wouldn't let go. "You managed to shake me up enough over at my place that I've been thinking about retiring from love for a while, but when Louie called me just now—well, I know right from wrong, Sugar."

"John called me," offered Maddy.

"You came here on your bike? With those Nazis outside?"

Maddy pushed up the sleeves of her enormous hooded flannel shirt. "You think I'm going to let some crude geeks stop me? Where's Gramma Gus?"

Annie filled them in. Chantal still held her arm and Annie clung hard. "They'll keep Gussie at least overnight because of her medical history."

"Should we bring her a few things?" asked Chantal.

Maddy offered her backpack. "Where's her stuff? We can use my excellent valise." She excavated a comb, newspaper clippings, grape gum wrappers.

"She's got an overnight bag downstairs. I'll get it," Annie said, trying not to smile as she and Chantal exchanged glances at Maddy's preparations.

"I'll keep an eye on the street then," Maddy offered.

"There's Cece with some biker-goons. I'd dig on giving those two flying lessons—to the nearest dying star."

Chantal nodded. "Her buddies. She'll get them to help."

Annie realized how much she'd missed Chantal's husky laugh. "Is Cece out to them?" she asked.

"Cece is out to everybody but the gang at Club Med,"

Chantal replied as she squeezed closer to Annie. "Maybe Cece is right, Sugar."

"You think tonight wouldn't have happened, Gussie wouldn't be on her last legs, if I stomped around town like Cece?"

"Well," Chantal said, her heavy eyelids lifting with roguish mirth, "there's stomping and then there's stomping. I mean, at your stompingest I don't think you're going strut like Cece when she's in her dotage."

Despite everything, Annie had to laugh. "Thanks," she said with the best scowl she could muster.

"So," Maddy reminded them, "this is all great, but what's the plan?"

"Do we have to have one?" asked Annie. "I'm ready for bed."

"Don't you want to be at the hospital with Gussie?" asked Chantal, not quite hiding an amused gleam in her eyes.

"Elly and Dusty are doing that. I'm staying home minding the store," said Annie. "Besides, Gussie needs some rest, not an audience." She looked pointedly at Maddy.

"You think I brought this attack on," Maddy asked, "pushing for action?"

"No. I just think we're not all capable of operating at your speed."

Maddy kicked at a chair. "I don't want anybody else to get hurt, paisan. I'll give it a try your way, but if this community's little surge of energy dies a slow death, be watching for me and Jennifer on your local yokel five o'clock news. Meanwhile, you want company watching the house?"

"Company? Let's have a damn party. You're still alive!" said Chantal.

"Compromise," Annie said. "When we get the paint cleaned up and good news about Gussie, then we party 'til the pop runs out." Chantal laughed again and let her arm go. For a moment Annie didn't move, didn't even breathe, just looked at Chantal. In this evening of quiet revelations there was something else calling her attention. The thoughts came slowly, while Chantal bantered with Maddy.

She expected to feel safer in the world when she was with a Vicky, a Jo, a Marie-Christine. Something deep in her yearned for them as guides, these women who seemed born to navigate what to Annie were uncharted seas. Their families were successful. She'd tried to stow away with the daughters of captains. Had she learned from them to navigate? Hell, no. To this day she steered straight into every ten-foot wave.

Now she'd chosen to take her stand in a place even native Jo planned to flee. There would be no free ride in Morton River, not with Chantal. If she made the trip, it would be steerage from port to harbor. Looked like, she smiled to herself, what she needed was a scrappy sailor by her side, not some captain's daughter. Maybe water was too unpredictable for her. Give her the Soo Line, the Burlington Northern, the Erie-Lackawanna, and a little home in the hills of Morton River.

Annie turned to Chantal. "Want to come down to the basement with me to get Gussie's bag?"

"Sounds adventurous."

"No, basements give me the creeps."

"Sugar, I love adventure."

"Mind the store just for a few minutes, Mad?"

"Primo!"

Chantal took her arm again. They squeezed through the door together. At the bottom of the steps Annie reached for the lightbulb string but Chantal stopped her.

"No," said Chantal, turning to her and pressing close. "Annie, I missed you. Why didn't you answer my calls?"

She hung her head, remembering that Chantal had felt safer outside Verne's apartment because she'd been with Annie. "So you wouldn't get wounded in my war."

"It's not your war. You have to share, you dope."

Annie looked off into a dark corner, spooky with spider webs and relics. For the moment, her fear had left her. It was perfectly clear that she wasn't backing off into any closet. "Yeah, I'll just lose it for us, won't I, all by myself."

"And make it worse for the survivors when you run off somewhere safer where we can't go."

"I'm sorry."

Chantal forced Annie's chin up.

"You'll let me help?"

"I need your help. Especially when I go back to the Farm outed, with the whole town waiting for me to abuse a client."

There was a thump, then a scrabbling sound. Annie whispered, "What was that?"

"Poor Sugar. Ralph has basement phobia too. Go ahead and turn the light on."

She started to reach for the light, but didn't want to let go of Chantal. She kissed her instead.

"What is this, desire therapy?" Chantal whispered.

"You do want to cure me of basement phobia, don't you?"

"Kiss me again, so I can make an informed decision." The kiss went on and on. A scrabbling sound interrupted it. Annie tried not to jump.

"Okay, Sugar. Stand aside." Chantal pulled the light cord and headed off toward the noise. "Who's making all this racket down here?" she called, noisily lifting cartons. "Yuck. A rodent porta-potty. Looks like you have a mouse problem. Got a trap?"

"Gross. You mean kill them?"

"It's the only solution, believe me. Though if you want to get one of those have-a-heart traps so you can relocate them to Pastor Norwood's church, that's fine with me."

"I should have come down here and cleaned up for Gussie." Annie was trying to be unobtrusive about it, but she'd backed up onto a step. She'd faced enough fears tonight. She'd hire an exterminator. "The suitcase should be right on top of that table. And we probably ought to bring some rags and thinner to clean off the paint."

Chantal, with only a small smile as comment, retrieved what they needed and followed as Annie bounded up the steps two at a time.

At the top, heart thumping, she breathed again. "Thanks," she told Chantal.

"Sure, Sugar."

She teetered, wanting to ask Chantal to stay, but terrified she'd back out again. "Chantal—"

"There's no hurry, Sugar," Chantal said, moving toward the others. "I'm not going far."

CHAPTER 17

As she drove home from work the next day, Vicky's words filled her mind, filled the Grape, filled the world. She'd called Oregon to tell Vicky about the Rafferty Street attack.

Vicky had been horrified. "I feel like I pushed you into this level of involvement," she confessed. "Out here we're trying to put human faces on prejudice. You know, the concept that the queer next door is no one's enemy? You've gone and done it, Annie."

"Right," she teased, "It's all your fault, Vicky. You know what I think got to the Rafferty Street toughs, besides finding the dyke-monster who molested Lorelei? A house that no men go in and out of. Except for one meeting, all they've seen is women perfectly happy without men. They are so scared of anything that messes with their power trip they have to flex their kill-it-if-it-thinks muscles."

"Still," said Vicky. "It makes me want to take care of you, as if I could."

"Yeah," Annie acknowledged. "I wish you could. I wish some-body could."

She'd been keeping Vicky updated about Chantal and now heard her silent query, Can Chantal? Instead, Vicky had said, "If you need a rest, you know you're welcome here."

"Maybe when it's all over, when you beat your bigots back, when I'm doing my real work and have some school behind me, when things settle down on Rafferty Street."

Vicky's voice was pained, as if she were breaking bad news. "Annie, this may not end for a very long time."

Annie pulled into her favorite train-watching spot and punched the tape button. Music sounded like so much noise to her these days that she turned it right off. "This may not end for a very long time."

A freight train came along, a loud commanding presence

that made life seem grand for a moment, larger than itself. She roared a great curse at the unperturbed Conrail cars as if they were to blame for every unfairness. By the time their simple clackety-clacking faded, her throat felt raw. Around the first bend the train threw back a come-hither call. A last rumble and then a profound silence fell before the mundane, irregular whisper of passing automobiles seeped back in. It was time to rejoin real life.

The rainy weather had disappeared for the moment. No flood heroics would save the gays of Morton River this time. She forced herself not to cringe as she bumped over the tracks and reluctantly rounded the corner onto Rafferty Street, her safe haven turned war zone. No one was in sight. She let out the breath she'd been holding. On this hot day, almost two weeks before the end of spring, music blasted out of a house down the street where a car, hood and trunk open, tools on the ground, sat in a driveway. The attackers weren't far.

The house was a mess from last night's confusion. She set about straightening it, imagining a new home for herself in San Francisco, or Kansas City, Ithaca, Northampton. Minnesota had just passed gay rights protections, but, darn it, Connecticut had them too, for all the good they did. How about Anchorage, everyone's end of the line? Amsterdam? Now there was a liberal city.

But Annie knew, as she handled Gussie's familiar objects, some reminding her of her own childhood, that she was an American right down to her toes, a Yankee who thrived on crisp falls, who enjoyed the odd snowball fight and had always been thankful to live in what she'd been brought up to believe was the greatest country in the world. Grump about life in the Valley as she might, she wasn't budging.

She walked up the street to buy some ice cream for Gussie. The shopkeeper seemed to start toward her, then shy away. Crap, she thought. Do I have to worry about where I spend money now? When he rang her out, he mumbled, "I'm sorry about those young punks. Is Gussie going to be all right?"

Overreaction or not, she wanted to smack his timid little face, but summoned up words she imagined Vicky might use. "Not unless the neighbors help take a stand against the punks."

He shook his head. "It's not right, but I can't afford to lose any customers."

Later, on the way to visit Gussie, she ran into Elly and Dusty in the hospital lobby.

"She's looking good, Heaphy," said Dusty.

Elly's face looked softer than Annie had seen it in a long while.

"You've got ice cream? She's been having erotic fantasies about peach ice cream, I swear," said Elly. "We brought her some real-world food too," Elly announced. "Wait 'til you hear her on hospital meals!"

Dusty looked better. She stood straighter, and there was a real smile on her face.

"Did Dusty tell you, Annie, that we're going to Ireland?" Elly's voice was hushed, as if she couldn't quite believe what she was saying. She wrapped her hands around the crook of Dusty's arm and squeezed herself close.

Innocently, Annie jingled the change in her pocket. "I might have heard a buzz somewhere."

Dusty propped herself against the back of a vinyl couch and folded her arms. "I've hired a guard service to make sure the Queen of Hearts is still standing when we get back."

"Don't forget my offer to help, Reilly." She lifted her chin at a man in white who stood outside the plate glass windows watching them, smoking a cigarette. "What's the breeder staring at?" she asked. "I thought Gussie would be safe here at least."

"Annie Heaphy, you've always worried too much. You don't have to fight the creeps twenty-four hours a day. For all we know he's gay."

"Tell me another one, El."

Elly grabbed Annie and danced her around. "Never mind that. I'm going to put Ireland on paper! Every green, mystical, impoverished inch of it."

"That's centimeters, I believe, lady."

Annie slipped an arm around Elly and flaunted their dance for the onlooker. "Bring me back a drawing of a gypsy wagon. I'd love to buy an original Hunnicutt."

"It'll be a true test," predicted Dusty. "We'll either kill each other or… Well, I'm hoping for the or."

"Dusty's worried that all we know how to do together is work."

"Vacationing may come more naturally than you think,"

advised Annie, bringing them to a halt. "Don't get too hooked, we need the diner."

She thought for a moment. "Tell you what," she said, visualizing a huge homecoming celebration. "You'll find a surprise when you get home."

"I don't know if I like that devilish grin," Elly said.

She'd noticed the wheelchair roll past, but was surprised when the tall bearded man maneuvered it around and back toward them. Then she recognized Judy Wald, the Director of the Herb Farm, in the chair. She looked shrunken, and leached of blood.

Judy smiled tremulously and held out a hand.

"What happened?" asked Dusty. Annie had forgotten that they knew each other through the Special Olympics.

Judy made a dismissive gesture with her hand. "It was a little more than gall bladder. I went back to work and got worse. Now they've taken out everything but the kitchen sink. And got it all, they tell me, though I'll be doing some other therapies to be sure."

Annie felt like the wind had been knocked out of her. "Geez, and here we were dancing. I had no idea."

"Neither did I. It explains a lot about my behavior recently, though. I was driven to distraction by the pain and scared because none of the doctors could find anything. When that horrible Mrs. Norwood called, I just couldn't deal with one more thing. I'm afraid you're the one who suffered—the whole town too, from what I'm hearing. It was a terrible decision on my part. Please let me apologize and encourage you to come back."

"You'll find a stack of massages on your desk—all from me."

"I'm so glad." Judy looked at Dusty. "She has a playfulness that's valuable with our client population." Judy faced Annie. "I like your ability to balance that with your staff responsibilities. You're so good with our workers."

"Not good enough," Annie grumbled. She could hear Elly, behind her, softly drumming her fingertips on her purse.

"It's true you're not experienced. You didn't get the support and information you needed. Lying in a hospital bed has given me a lot of time to plan. I'm going to increase the in-service training opportunities as well as supervision. If I get it approved, you'll get paid to take college level courses."

"You mean you don't think I screwed up?"

"As confused as I was it broke my heart to think I'd lose you from the staff, and that the workers would be without your obvious affection for them. They had a good time with you and were as productive as they've ever been."

Dusty smiled. "I'm glad you're going back, Judy. You *are* the Farm."

The bearded man, his glasses even thicker than Judy's, spoke. "That job's keeping her going."

"This is my husband, Matt. And he's right. I hope to be back at work two weeks from Monday, but I'll be missing a lot of time for therapy. Please come rejoin the team with me, Annie. I need you."

When Matt wheeled Judy away Annie looked at Elly and Dusty. "Holy moley," she said.

"She's right," Dusty said. "You can do some good at the Farm. And I want you as a Special Olympics coach this year. No guff. We'll take on every Mrs. Norwood in Morton River."

Elly gave her a hug. "This is a great place to live, Annie, except for the quicksand, the volcanoes and the snipers. You're going to love it here just like the rest of us peculiar folks."

Upstairs Chantal was holding Gussie's hand. Gussie spied the ice cream and elevated her bed. "Do you know they've been feeding me Jello? You'd think in this day and age dieticians would have more sense! Why give a sick person colored sugar? All the dieticians should get presented with a gallon of Jello on their death beds. See how they'd like it."

Annie said, "I can't believe I ever had the nerve to resent you. I should have known a whole community couldn't be wrong. You're a Valley jewel." She poked at Gussie's slippers under the bed with a toe. "There's something distrustful inside me that has to say no before it says yes."

Shyly, she let her eyes touch Chantal's over Gussie's bedding. Their hazy blueness got to her every time, making her insides shiver. "I didn't see your car in the visitor's lot."

"Ralph's home on leave. He's chauffeuring today. He needed the car."

Annie bit her lower lip, in conflict, but remembered Vicky's advice about letting her friends make up their own minds about taking risks. "You need a ride home?" she asked.

Without hesitation Chantal nodded. "I thought you'd never ask."

With all her misgivings, Annie was so pleased she gave Chantal a big sloppy grin. She turned to Gussie. "Things seem to have calmed down at home, Gus. The guy at the grocery store asked after you."

Gussie had managed to put on a little lipstick and face powder. "Yes? I'll give him a piece of my mind when I get sprung from this prison my doctor calls a hospital. Where was he last night? Where were all the neighbors? Haven't I almost single-handedly kept his ice cream stock fresh? Haven't I made chicken soup for half the people up and down the street when they've been ill? They come trooping up here to click their tongues, but don't want to talk about what happened or why. Boys will be boys! they say. They don't know what's come over kids these days. Well, I do," she went on between bites of mint chocolate chip. "I know exactly what's wrong. They're acting out their parents' prejudices. I told them I'll be at the window, Annie, twenty-two in hand, phone by my side. No more Miss Nice Guy."

"Do you have a permit for that thing?" Annie asked.

"You bet your boots I do. And I can shoot it too. It's probably time for us to find a place where I can teach you."

She was too afraid that the Hothead Paisan in her would be activated. "I don't think so, Gus."

Gussie paused to scrape the bowl. "Just as soon as I get out of here, Socrates, we're going to find a shooting range and do some target practice. What about you, Chantal, do you know how to defend yourself?"

"My ex-husband took us all out and gave us lessons when the kids hit their teens," Chantal answered. Then she gave her warm laugh. "I got so good I think that's why he didn't dispute my claims in the divorce." She looked at Annie. "But I agree. That's not the best way."

"Best, my arse," Gussie sputtered. "If you're up against it, you might not have a choice."

"What happened to Grandma Gandhi? If I'm up against it," Annie said, "I'd rather not have that option."

"What would you have had me do the other night? Last night—was it just last night? Ignore them? Peaceful negotiation? Run? With this body?"

Annie flushed. "You're right. I would count on my legs to get me away."

"There's a point when ideals are just not a strong enough self-defense," Gussie concluded.

"Okay, okay. I'll learn. No sense giving the enemy any advantage."

Chantal grew quiet but, Annie noticed, didn't seem in a hurry to leave. Annie was trying to keep the conversation going when Peg and Paris arrived with flowers and news.

Paris burst out, "Not one of them even had to spend the night in the city jail."

"Only the victim got locked up," complained Gussie.

"They were charged," added Peg, carefully rolling down her sleeves. "Our ACLU friend said if you want to try a civil suit against the boys she'll look into it."

"I like the gun idea better," Gussie muttered.

"But Heaphy, now that Judy offered to reinstate you, you have no legal recourse even though we know you've suffered as a result of her actions."

"It's okay. I'm going back to work in two weeks."

"Congratulations!" cried Paris, hugging her.

She told them about the exchange with Judy. "I just have to remember who it is I'm supposed to be fighting."

"I'm glad it's not Judy Wald," Peg ran her hands up and down her plum-colored silken sleeves. "They certainly keep this place air conditioned."

"It's so the Jello won't melt," Gussie interjected.

Chantal, laughing with Gussie, caught Annie's eye.

"What was the charge?" Annie wanted to know.

"Malicious mischief. Defacing private property. Disturbing the peace, that sort of thing. And I think they got that much only because they hassled the cops. They're probably cleaning the paint off your house right now. The parents were ordered to supervise that."

"A spanking," complained Paris.

"But," Peg added, "the headlines today will warn Morton River about the climate it's creating. They're running your profile tomorrow, Gussie. The editor wants to shame this damn town."

Gussie held up the paper. There was a two-column photograph of one of the swastikas the youths had sprayed on the sidewalk.

"That would be enough to scare me," said Annie. "As I recall, it did."

"Maybe you and Jennifer should cook up another article, about what last night was like."

"Don't you think Annie's been martyr enough?" asked Chantal a little sharply.

Paris looked at Chantal quickly, then nodded. "You're right. More of us will take our turns. How're you feeling, Gussie?"

As Gussie went through her litany, Annie's eyes met Chantal's again. She felt herself blush when they said their goodbyes together and she caught Paris' knowing look. She couldn't stop grinning.

"Come to my place, Sugar," Chantal suggested when they reached the parking lot. "I'll feed you some supper."

"I really need to be at the house tonight. If they come back...."

"Understood."

"But it's good to see you. I don't want to ask you over because it's dangerous for you."

Chantal actually stamped a foot. "Will you stop that, Annie Heaphy! Maybe it is and maybe it isn't, but don't you be telling me what to do. If I want to risk my snow white reputation keeping company with the most eligible bachelor in town, that's my right." She paused, as if to make certain that Annie wasn't going to try and cross her. Softening her tone, Chantal suggested, "Tell you what, we'll stop at my house and pick up a Jello mold or two, and eat at Rafferty Street. At least one of us will know how to use that rifle if we need to."

Annie laughed. "It might even be fun to fight this battle next to you. But I don't think I have any Cool Whip to go with moldy Jello."

"No problem. We'll melt Styrofoam packing peanuts. Same thing."

"I really want to spend the evening with you. Are you sure? They seem to be watching our place."

"Sugar—" warned Chantal.

At Violet Street she went in with Chantal to help carry the makings of dinner. A gust of spicy smells hit her.

"Ralph! Company!" Chantal chimed as they entered the little house.

Annie assumed Chantal was warning the boy to get dressed and be polite, but he came rushing out of the kitchen, apron over his giant-sized t-shirt and baggy knee-length shorts, asking, "Is it *her*?"

"Ralph!" Chantal scolded with a laugh. "This is Annie Heaphy."

"Hi!" said Ralph with warmth. He carried a steamy cloud of cooking smells with him when he came over to peck his mother's cheek and shake Annie's hand with both of his. "Am I glad to meet you!"

She'd expected Chantal's soldier son to be a gangly, muttering, embarrassed and oversized male reeking of hormones, but he was a plump duck-footed kid no taller than her five feet five inches, with a voice that sounded like it had never finished changing and nerves which seemed to keep him in constant motion. He talked incessantly and with surprising confidence for such a young man.

"I was just cooking up a batch of pierogies. You two want some?"

"To go, please, Ralph. We're worried about Gussie's house over there on Rafferty Street after what happened."

"Yeah. I don't blame you," Ralph said, twisting to study Annie. "I probably went to school with some of those guys. With this sissy out of town you can bet they've been looking for someone else to pick on. How about I'll make you plates to warm up? You have applesauce at your place?"

"Yes. Gussie eats it by the quart." Annie just watched the kid as he cooked the sausage, talking all the while, as if the stove were not generating insufferable heat on this warm June evening.

"I'm so glad Mom found a friend. She was working on being a pain. Me, I have the friends, it's a mate I want." He gently lay the pierogies on plates and dished out potatoes. "I could marry my pal Dora when I come home. She wants to settle down and have kids too, but I don't think that would be fair to either of us. You know what I really, really want? I want to be able to do all that with a man." He lovingly tucked foil over the plates. He was still talking when he handed his mom into the Saab.

"Drive careful," he warned Annie as she settled her glasses on her nose.

Once out of earshot she asked Chantal, "Why do I feel like I just got inspected by your mother?"

Chantal laughed. "Ralph's been like that since he could walk, leading me around by the hand, taking care of Mom. He's the reason I finally got the divorce before the kids were grown— he hated the way his dad treated me."

"Do you think he approves?"

"When you were getting in the car he gave me the thumbs up."

At a stoplight Annie said, "You tell Ralph for me that I said this about him." She held up two thumbs, grinned wide and said, "*Excellent*."

When they got to Rafferty Street they ate the spicy pierogies, called Gussie, played with Toothpick, watched "Murder, She Wrote" in Gussie's room and checked the windows now and then for trouble.

"Shall I call Ralph for a ride home yet?" Chantal asked from Gussie's easy chair.

Annie was on Gussie's bed. She bounced up and flung her arms out in despair. "You have to go already?"

"Monday morning is only a few hours away."

"You could stay here—in Nan's room," she hurriedly amended.

"Sugar, I didn't bring nightclothes or..."

"We could find some around."

"...makeup."

"Oh."

"What's the matter, you don't want to stay alone?"

"No. They're not going to bother us again so soon. It's—I don't know, Chantal. It feels so cozy, sitting here with you, watching the tube. Like normal life. I seldom feel like chasing excitement in Morton River, but I do get lonesome, even with Gussie around. She's so involved in her own schedule she really has very little time for me."

"And you know I have time for you."

"You seem willing to hang out, listen to me worry aloud about everything, make room for me in your life."

"That sounds pretty accurate."

"Even with all our clothes on."

"I like being with you even with all our clothes on."

So they wore clothes when they got into Annie's bed that night. Chantal, a much-laundered plain nightshirt from Gussie's drawer that smelled like Gussie's talcum powder. Annie hung her team cap on her hat tree and climbed in wearing the floppy men's paisley pajamas she'd bought now that she wasn't living alone. Toothpick attacked their feet for a while, then retired to the easy chair.

Plain or not, when Annie saw the drape of Chantal's nightshirt on her body she swallowed hard and looked away. What wonderful breasts, she thought. Then she reminded herself that she could do this without touching Chantal. She really, really could do this just for the company.

"Cuddle buddies, I think is what they'd call us in the personals," Annie tried to convince herself aloud, lying on her back with Chantal's head on her shoulder. She held herself stiffly away from the sweet willing body beside her.

Chantal squirmed. "Bunnies," she offered.

"Cuddle bunnies?"

"Mmm. Tell me a story."

"Shh. What was that?"

They both froze, intent on more sounds. Toothpick's ears were at full alert, her eyes staring at the window. "What did it sound like?" whispered Chantal.

"Thumpy-clashy, like somebody quietly bumping into the garbage can, if anyone can do that quietly."

"Do you have raccoons?"

"Now and then." They listened a while longer. "Sorry," said Annie. "I guess it was a false alarm." Chantal shifted, then turned on her side away from Annie. "Hey, where you going?" Annie protested, reaching out for her.

"Don't worry. I just need to change positions. This is how I sleep."

"Is it?" Annie asked, a little concerned about a flutter inside.

"What?" Chantal asked.

"Nothing."

"No. Something."

"It's just an intimate thing to know. How a woman sleeps."

"A good cuddle bunny would hold me now."

"Right." Annie slid an arm under Chantal. "Remember the day we met, at Medipak? It was another one of those moments, wasn't it, when life as we know it comes to an end? Not a moment of choice, but of chance. If Cece hadn't been at the meeting, if Judy hadn't laid me off, if Lorelei hadn't kissed me, if I hadn't gotten onto that plane and left Eugene, left New York, left Chelsea—"

"I still think," said Chantal sleepily, "you think too much."

"You're so warm," she said, encircling Chantal with the other arm. "And so soft."

"You like that?"

Under Gussie's talc she caught Chantal's scent. "I like that."

Chantal wiggled to fit into Annie's curve. Annie had been holding herself back to avoid pressing against Chantal's bottom. She relaxed and with the relaxation came a great wave of sadness. She heard it in the shuddering sigh that escaped her. Felt it in the tears that began to fall with no other warning.

"Hey!" said Chantal, trying to turn.

"I'm sorry."

"About what?"

"I don't know."

"You are so silly, Sugar. I won't look at you. Tell me what's the matter."

"Maybe nothing. I mean, maybe I'm just unwinding enough to feel what I'm feeling."

"You cry when you get in bed with a woman?"

Annie wiped her nose on the sleeve of her pajamas. "Crap. I feel so burnt. I think I'm finally getting a little taste of what it's like to be visibly different in this country. People hating me just for being me. No rhyme or reason. Just scared of me because I'm a queer."

"It's sure a different way of being in the world. Angel to devil. One day I'm a mom and A-okay, the next I'm something you scrape off your shoe."

Annie squeezed her. "It must be even harder coming on board later in life, after you know what you missed all those years."

"But I was missing so much more before."

She worked up her nerve. "Do you think trying to be straight all those years made you so, such, such a—planner?"

Chantal's body tensed. "What do you mean?"

Annie became aware of how warm she was. Her skin was damp. "Nothing bad. Just the way you planned your house. How you like everything just so. Lots of people are like that. I just was never friends with one."

"And it bothers you?"

"More like scares me a little. Like you'll want me to be just so. As a friend, I mean."

She could feel Chantal nod. "I thought there was something more than me having kids or this anti-gay business. I mean, you'll get used to the kids and I'm afraid we'll all have to get used to being leery around some straight people. About my fuddy-duddy ways—you're right, I've been accused of being a control-freak. I've never thought of it being because I'm gay, but it makes sense. I couldn't do what I really wanted—didn't even know what I wanted—so it was important to get my way in other things."

She rubbed her nose, now dry, affectionately against Chantal's back. "See why I like you? You didn't get all defensive."

Chantal reached around with a chilly foot to touch Annie's ankle. "I don't know that I'll ever change, though."

"Maybe I just needed to say that it worried me."

"I can see why!"

"Besides, there are times I need unscrambling."

"So you think I'll come in handy?"

"In a pinch." She moved a hand to Chantal's bottom.

"Don't you dare!"

"Just teasing."

"Don't I know it," Chantal said with an exaggerated sigh.

"Listen, Chantal," she said just as the idea came into her mind. "Will you come up to Chelsea with me one of these weekends?" She'd never taken a soul back to Boston since she'd left. Her heart accelerated. Maybe it would be a stupid move.

Chantal's voice was animated. She twisted her head toward Annie. "To see where you grew up?"

"Such as it is."

"I'd love to come."

"My family would be there. Not exactly a weekend on the Riviera."

Laying her cheek back against the pillow Chantal pulled Annie's other arm across her waist. "Tomorrow, on the way to work, we'll swing by the old firetrap where I grew up. But I'm not introducing you to the rest of my family yet."

"I'm not out to mine. My Dad's side is Catholic and already worried about me burning in hell." Annie was excited. "I can show you my old neighborhood, get your opinion about the shape my parents are in." For a brief moment she felt like she wasn't stranded in a strange world after all. She said nothing more until her heart slowed. "You know what?" she asked.

"What?" Chantal murmured.

"I don't want to go to sleep. You feel too good."

Chantal didn't say anything.

"You falling asleep?" Annie asked.

In answer, Chantal burrowed closer, kissing Annie's wrist in the process.

"Umm." She responded by letting her lips sweep the back of Chantal's neck. It was slightly damp from the heat. The blonde hairs were short and soft. She tightened her arms around Chantal, tasted her own moist minty breath, caught in her lips some of the fine blonde hairs beyond any scissors' reach. Chantal kissed her wrist again, nibbled her palm, warm raspberries falling into a bowl. Annie's lips drifted to Chantal's shoulder, nudged down a strap to explore the tender terrain.

She told herself that this was safe, just friendly, but then, with a slight movement closer, came the flush, starting at her rib cage and spreading up until her head was encased in an aura of heat and her every disciplined thought fizzled. The comfort of Chantal, the supreme seduction of her comfort was just too much. Lolling on the fringes of Chantal was like hovering between the instant before waking and an elaborately sensual dream.

Chantal lay perfectly still, lips against Annie's palm, but her breathing had quickened. She moved her hands up Chantal's arms. "You're so soft. I've never felt such a luxury of woman in my life." She'd never thought she'd like anything but the firm angular grace of her other lovers, but Chantal, Chantal was like a life-size down pillow, like heaped flower petals, like a celebration of womanly curves and recesses.

"You're like me." Not that she carried as much weight as

Chantal on that short a frame. "I always wished I'd gotten one of those tall thin bodies. It's humiliating, tiptoeing up to kiss a woman, being the one, now that I'm over forty, with the larger breasts, the padded hips. Tonight I finally understand why other women don't mind my padding."

Marie-Christine flashed like lightning into her mind. Hadn't she broken her spell playing with Jo? It was difficult not to regret the contrast. There had never been a hesitation with that one. She'd always been drunk with lust for Marie-Christine, a walking libido, wondrous at her every glance, willing at her every touch. She'd thrown herself at Marie-Christine, acting the classic fool, unknowing, uncaring that her wanton homage was to no goddess, but to a myth her desire kept alive.

"Sugar?" breathed Chantal into the heat of Annie's night.

"Sugar?" Chantal said more loudly. "There's such a thing as playing fair."

Chantal, Annie thought as her hands roamed the curves, a woman of substance, not a myth. A full whole woman, ripe with gifts and heavy with needs. An anchor, not a sail. They would fight the het wars together.

"Who's playing? I feel like sugar, warm pink spun sugar, cotton candy-headed, sweet on you, stuck to you, ready to be nibbled by your soft mouth. Turn over," she said, gruff because she spoke with the grit of sugar on her tongue. "No, don't," she said then and caught Chantal.

"Let up, then, Sugar."

"Stay where you are," Annie told her, as she loosed Chantal's arms and slipped her hands up to the vault of shoulders, down to the padding above the breasts, then to the lavish breasts themselves, at last. She cupped those abundant offerings, shaped smooth as warm water by the gown. She just held them, as if considering the essence of the physical Chantal, then sought the nipples, touched the tender little things lightly, lightly 'til they tiptoed to kiss her fingertips.

Chantal not saying a word, but rolling with her. Annie, finally, couldn't keep still, her whole body followed her tremulous arms, her lips insatiable on Chantal's neck. Her pubis brushed wantonly back and forth on Chantal's rounded bottom, every contact a spark. She wondered if she would, for the first time in memory, come like this, if she should let Chantal know, if it was all the tension of these months, or that Chantal was really so exciting, holding back like she was, obviously trying not to scare Annie off. "Chantal," she said. "Chantal."

"Annie. You feel so good. Touch me, touch me everywhere, don't take your body away."

Their words became mostly unintelligible, but Annie's hands knew what they wanted. She molded Chantal's hips, her belly. She returned to her breasts, lifted them, flattened them, teased the nipples until Chantal couldn't stay still.

She worked Chantal's gown, Chantal whose body followed her hands as if they were magnets, a degree right, left, forward, back, worked the gown up to Chantal's waist.

A woman's fragrance, Annie thought, the potent perfume of a woman wanting her. Goddess, it was delicious to be doing this again she thought, as she slipped her hand to Chantal's front and Chantal moved one leg to let her inside. There was nothing like this in the world, this woman opening for her and she slipped her fingers between Chantal's legs, like a waterslide Chantal was so moist. She found her lips, fingered them, then the avid little stem of her, with one finger and slithered lower to slip the finger inside, then quickly out, then in again, back to the stem of the woman, Chantal now wild with little movements, a long high sound from her throat, from her heart perhaps and pushing forward, down to Annie's fingers, two of them, up and down, hands scrabbling back to touch Annie anywhere, to hang onto her. With a great exhalation Chantal became for a moment still on Annie's fingers, her channel clenching inside, until she began a rocking back and forth and then a sharp inhale, exhale, inhale—"Sugar!" Chantal cried and collapsed.

Annie lay against Chantal's back, panting, like she'd seen animals pant, eyes shut, aware of Chantal's heat and pleasure and her own inner quivering.

Chantal twisted in her arms, pushed her by the shoulders down. "You've played so hard to get I feel like I'm flipping you, woman," Chantal breathed into her mouth.

"No," Annie tried to say. "I was scared."

"You scared now?"

"No. You feel so, so—familiar. Like we grew up together."

Chantal was rough with her, resolute, never giving her space to protest or waver. Heavier, Chantal used that to her advantage when Annie, with her first-time ambivalence, tried to change her mind. Chantal held her wrists while she kissed Annie everywhere she could reach, her demanding stubbornness sexy as heck. Annie, strung like wire now, her pajamas sopped, wanted Chantal between her legs, but couldn't say it.

"What do you want, Sugar?" Chantal asked.

"Chantal."

"I know that. Where, Sugar, tell me. I want you to tell me where. How."

Annie shook her head.

Chantal let her wrists go, kissed her some more, unbuttoned Annie's pajamas and lifted her own gown off. "Oh," said Annie at the sight of her. Chantal pressed herself down. "Geez," she said at the feel of the woman on her at last. She tried to reach between them, to touch Chantal again.

"No way, Sugar. I'm doing you." Chantal straddled her, a sight that stirred Annie's heart to doubletime. "Keep those magic hands to yourself," Chantal told her, "before you make me crazy again."

Annie smiled and reached. Chantal slapped her hands away.

"I mean it, Sugar, I want you to talk to me, tell me."

"I can't." Desire flooded out of her as if Chantal had opened a drain.

"Why?" Chantal asked, stopping.

"It's embarrassing."

"I'm not trying to be a perfectionist interior decorator."

Was that true? "It's not you. I've never talked about stuff like that."

"So you're shy in bed," Chantal said. "Your body will tell me, won't you, pretty body?" Chantal teased, dipping to touch her lips to a nipple.

Annie surprised herself with a sharp intake of breath. She imagined Chantal with some shadowy woman lover, and the explicit words between them.

Chantal was lying atop her, plush pelvis to pelvis. She began a rhythmic slide that pulled Annie's clitoris north, south, east and west. "Or *are* you shy? Maybe," she probed, "you don't want to own up to feeling good. I think you want to pretend that this might all be one big mistake so you can slink off into the shadows and worry that you've done the wrong thing." Opulent

Chantal kept riding her pelvis, rubbing against her clitoris, too hard for her to come, but tantalizing her. "Tell me, Sugar."

She shook her head, but Chantal kept on, their breasts grazing every time Chantal moved. The eloquence of Chantal's body above her own—round breasts to round breasts, curved belly brushing curved belly, Chantal's lavish white hips kissing hers—this was the stuff of a fantasy she'd never imagined. Annie shook her head again, a denial of pleasure. Chantal was right. No, I'm not feeling this, you're not giving me this, I owe you nothing. "Chantal!"

"What, Sugar? Stop? More? Harder? Lighter? I'm giving you the words, Sugar, tell me and you can have it."

It frightened her so much, this asking. What would happen to her now? "Chantal? Chantal?" She couldn't stand it. "Chantal, your hand now—"

"Yeah," Chantal breathed, smiling, eyes closed. Chantal lifted on untiring arms, never stopping her motion, lifted higher, lay beside her, fingers circling like sticky feathers, touching like butterfly lips. Did butterflies have lips? And it was happening, outside first, then deeper. Those short fingers danced on her with delicate, unremitting speed. She'd never let the feeling in so far before. When had she thrown her arms around Chantal? She was coming apart, her goddamn soul was coming, she thought as she crushed Chantal to herself, grinding against her, legs going every which way.

The next thing she knew, she was crying again, Chantal's hands caressing her head. She'd blanked out. Lost control? Never, never, even with the best. She looked at Chantal. "Oh, my god," she said as Chantal gathered her to her softness. The best. She'd never expected that of Chantal. She trembled and let herself be held, worrying that she was too old for ecstasy. Chantal would wear her out. She never heard the twelve-fifty six go by.

CHAPTER 18

Monday morning they got up early and stopped at Chantal's house so she could dress for work. Annie was banished to the kitchen where Ralph cooked them up a quick breakfast of eggs, Jones sausages, dollar-sized pancakes, real maple syrup, fresh juice and Oolong tea. The kitchen was cool, its heat swept away by a sudden shower that had fallen in the middle of the night, waking them both just long enough to murmur into each other's lips.

"Won't he make someone happy?" Chantal said when she came into the kitchen.

All morning at work Annie found herself whistling, pleased by Chantal and amused at the little fellow Chantal had managed to raise into a 1950s sort of housewife.

"You look like you got up on the right side of somebody's bed this morning," said Cece in the break room. "I wonder whose?"

"You're looking more chipper yourself, Cece."

"I pick up my car tonight."

"Car," Annie said, puzzled. "Car? Isn't that a little tame for your image?"

Cece brought her Thermos of coffee over to Annie's table. "I keep trying to tell you about it, girl, but since I switched to taking the bus to be with my Hope, the only times I see you, you've been, you know, out of it or something."

"I've been a little preoccupied."

"I hear you. It's this turning forty-five business that sold me on the car."

"When's your birthday?"

"Next month. Every winter it gets colder on the bike, you know? And Hope doesn't have wheels because of the epilepsy. So, well, Louie got me a great deal on this little Geo Tracker, like a midget Jeep? It is bad."

"Planning on keeping your job, then?"

Cece glanced sideways at her. "I'll fight those bigots for it. Things quiet down on Rafferty Street?"

"Paris and Venita are bringing Gussie home this morning before their classes." She hadn't talked with Chantal about announcing what had happened last night, but she had to struggle not to grin.

"Yeah?" Cece asked, inviting more.

"I feel like life's righting itself after another little spill. Let the fuckers try and knock me over again."

"Go for it, Heaphy."

"I'll be giving notice next week if you have someone else in mind for my job."

"I've got as many queers lined up to work for Kurt as he has homophobes."

Ralph came evenings and cooked them low-fat meals that kept even Gussie happy. Annie's sense of well-being became something akin to serenity. Chantal stayed over again. Things hadn't been quite as hot knowing Gussie was downstairs, but they'd managed to whisper and laugh well past the twelve-fifty-six train. She was groggy Friday morning when one of the pair of co-workers she'd met the first day, Mutt or Jeff—the tall thin one with the chipped tooth—approached, pushing a light green flyer at her.

"The Selectmen are voting next week," Amy told her. "We're going to let them know Morton River won't stand by for those militant homosexuals to worm their way in."

Annie came wide awake very quickly. "Militant? Worm?"

"Who wants homosexuals teaching our kids?"

The woman was acting perfectly pleasant. Could it be that the straights at Medipak really didn't know? "You mean you want them to grant licenses only to facilities that discriminate," she said.

"You have to discriminate against their kind. I don't want some pervert within a mile of my four kids. I'm sorry you don't have kids of your own, but you can add your voice to us who do. Especially for those poor retarded people who can't defend themselves."

She was paralyzed with anger. Her insides had turned to burning mush. She stared at the woman. Amy was the name on her velcro patch. "I don't get it. Just two nights ago there was this big deal in the paper about a priest getting caught for abusing a little girl. How come you're not storming the Catholic Church?"

"Because this is what's on my plate. The Lord wants these liberals and feminazis and homosexuals put in their places. When it's time to work against the priests, I'll do that too."

What was the look in Amy's eyes? It wasn't fear, not even hatred. It looked like a cold android blankness, all pleasantness programmed out now. Annie had a sudden rush of compassion for all the scared people like Amy.

"You really think there's a conspiracy between liberals and feminists and gays?"

"Can my husband get a promotion when there's a black working there? No. Are there girls in my boys' Scout troop? Yes. Can you trust that president?"

"You think the Selectmen can bring back the good old days?"

"I'll fight tooth and nail for my kids."

No one at the Farm talked like this. The prejudice at Medipak felt a lot more dangerous than Judy's clumsiness under pressure. As Annie entered the break room, many of the workers were reading the green flyers. Nicole had folded hers into a paper airplane and menaced Louie with it. Where was Chantal? The clerical staff took break right after the packers. If she could get rid of Amy and linger—

"Will you be there?" Amy asked.

"No," she answered, trying to keep defensiveness from her tone. "It's illegal, what you're trying to do."

"We'll change the laws then."

"Look, this doesn't make any sense," she started, but she knew she was just avoiding what she had to do. "Amy, do you actually know any gay people?"

Amy looked stern. "Of course not."

A-mazing. She tried to match Amy's sternness. "If someone you knew, not some stranger carrying a banner on TV, if it was a co-worker or neighbor who might lose a job because of screening, would you want that to happen?"

"Like who?" asked Amy, a sly look breaking through the blankness.

Crap, she thought. "You would, wouldn't you?" Over Amy's

head she caught sight of Chantal coming downstairs, flyer in hand. How could she quit and leave Chantal here alone? She couldn't come out. She'd expose Chantal too.

Amy tossed her flyers on a cafeteria table. "Take some for your family. I have to go upstairs for a planning meeting."

Then Annie saw Mrs. Kurt coming down the stairs from the offices, stopping to chat with Amy, a pleasant smile on her face. There was no place to hide. Mrs. Kurt looked directly at her, stumbled backwards and screamed, "Kurt!" She charged up the stairs. "Daddy!"

Fuck her, Annie thought, giving a jocular wave and silly smile.

She moved toward her lover. "I won't do this, Chantal. Just because I'm leaving doesn't mean I should choke to death on all my fear and anger. Maddy's right. Paris is right. People have always despised us. Now we're fund-raising fodder for power-hungry, soul-grabbing men. They give permission to the Amys to hate out loud. I want to talk to Kurt."

"Okay, Sugar." Chantal's forehead was wrinkled. "It's really like the AIDS activists say, silence equals death. Am I the sort of person who would have stood by and watched Nazis take away my Jewish friends and relatives? I don't like to think so. My great-grandmother was Jewish. Then why would I let this happen to myself? To Ralph? To you? I'll come with you."

"You sure? What about your mortgage?"

"Sugar, you weren't going to protect me anymore, right?"

"The stakes are a little higher, Chantal. Remember you said I couldn't hide from Mrs. Kurt forever?"

"I saw her organizing this whole screening push. Did she see you?" Annie nodded. "She recognized you?"

Annie had to laugh. "Went screeching up the stairs like I was a lesbian ax murderer."

"That's why she was screaming! But no, Annie, I'm not backing off. After all, you've spared my life so far, ax murderer or not."

She turned serious. "Whatever happens up there, Chantal, this has been a really great week for me," she said.

Chantal led her up the stairs. "For me too. And, you know what, Annie Heaphy?" Chantal stopped at midstairs and turned to her. "I'll stick with you wherever you work."

Annie managed a small smile. "That's just what I needed to hear, Chantal." They started up again. "Boy, do I hate this return to reality."

"It's all reality, Sugar. Even the good stuff."

"There you are!" Kurt said, suddenly emerging from his office. "I just got a call from the floor—"

"I know I'm late, but I have to talk to you, Kurt." Her stomach had never hurt so much.

Mrs. Kurt emerged from a room, saw Annie and tried to get her husband's attention.

"I told you, Paula, not now."

Mrs. Kurt said, "But Daddy."

"Five minutes, Paula. Let's make this snappy," Kurt said to Chantal and Annie.

He didn't ask them to sit. She felt like a grade-schooler called to the principal's office. When Chantal didn't speak first, Annie found her toughest cabbie voice and announced, "It's about the flyers being handed out by some of the crew."

"They have my permission," he snapped.

"That's part of the problem, Kurt. Some of us aren't exactly in favor of the city setting up discriminatory standards. As a matter of fact, I think it's really bad news, especially with the company taking sides like this."

Kurt continued to stand behind his desk. Now he leaned over it, supporting himself on his fists. His face had relaxed, as if he'd realized that a simple explanation would suffice to resolve this.

"I think you ladies know that I'm a Christian. I manage this company on Christian principles and assume that the rest of the businesses in the Valley uphold decent standards. There is no room in this country for the filthy behaviors we see being paraded in front of our youth. I don't advocate discrimination, but my job puts me in a position to help draw the line."

She looked at Chantal. "Tell him," Chantal said simply.

Despite the air conditioning she realized that she had broken out into a sweat. She'd never come out in the face of such immediate consequences before. He just didn't know, about her, about anyone gay.

She leaned toward him. "Kurt, I'm gay. And I'm the one your wife is accusing—wrongly—of touching that young woman at the softball game."

He paled, looked at Chantal. "And you? You've been with me over five years, Zak. You—your friends support this?"

"Don't talk like we're perverts, Kurt." He half fell, half sat in his desk chair. "Annie would no more touch Lorelei Simski than I would. You have a lot of gay employees, always have. If you dismiss all of us there'd be a definite personnel problem."

"You too?" Kurt said. "This has gone farther than I even thought." He looked stunned. "How many? How many of you are there?"

"That's not mine to tell you," Chantal said. "And Annie and I need to get back to work. Neither of us could stay silent, though, with our co-workers out on the floor waving those flyers around. We're not monsters any more than you are, Kurt. Most of us are good, some of us are bad, just like the straight employees."

"And," added Annie, "it's just no good, trying to hide any-more. I can't do it. If you fire all of us I won't go quietly."

Kurt stared up at them. "Is that a threat?" he asked, but there was no punch to the accusation. He simply looked like a man without a clue. With any luck, he had his clue now.

"No, no threat. Just something you should know. I couldn't protest at the Farm because I didn't want to hurt the workers, but here—a little publicity won't hurt the laxatives. Put yourself in my place, Kurt. I do good work. Would you stand by and just let it happen to you?"

Kurt held his head in his hands, eyes covered. When he looked up there was true puzzlement in his eyes. "How do I rec-oncile what the Bible teaches with what you're telling me? You're a mother, Zak. You're a model employee, Heaphy. Evil comes in all forms, but am I really prepared to recognize evil? Can I really tell my congregation that their neighbors and co-workers are abominations in the eyes of the Lord?"

"Do you really believe yourself that we're evil, Kurt?" Chantal asked quietly.

His eyes had become more clear. "I really believe you can be helped and forgiven."

"And I think," said Annie, "it's you who need to be forgiven— for judging us."

Kurt's face took on a pitying expression. Annie decided she'd had enough. She led Chantal to the door.

Outside Kurt's office they hugged hard. "He looked," Annie

said, "like we hit him over the head. Maybe—do you think he can learn?"

"I think he's going to have to. Fast. There's one thing most people don't know about Medipak that may make a difference, Sugar. As much as Kurt may strut around like the chief executive peacock, Medipak is part of a multi-national corporation."

"This is good news?"

"Remember the personnel manager at the Rafferty Street meeting who works for the surgical instrument company in Upton?"

"The black dyke? They have a sexual orientation clause."

"Same corporation, Sugar. I think ol' Kurt's hands are tied. Life may be hell for a while, but he's not going to get himself in hot water over a bunch of queers. The big bosses might even like to know who I saw in the conference room with Mrs. Kurt."

"Who?"

"Mutt and Jeff. They were folding these stupid flyers on company time and property."

Annie laughed. "It'd be pretty funny if Kurt was the one who got fired. Not that I wish it on him. It might backfire on us."

All afternoon Annie strutted through her routine, chest warm with pride, legs still a little shaky, waiting for her pink slip. But it didn't happen.

After work Chantal came over to the Grape with Nettie Wilson, the bookkeeper, by her side. Nettie, white haired, heavy, dark skin flushed even darker, was famous at Medipak for her snappish attitude and her capacity to sweat under stress, and today the men's white handkerchief she clutched was sodden.

"I just want to tell you, Annie Heaphy," Nettie said, taking one of Annie's hands in her own clammy one, "I'm so happy for the both of you that you found each other. Don't you worry either. If Kurt tries any funny business he'll have to give walking papers to more of us than the gays." She looked back at the building. "These people need to be leaving judgement to the Lord."

She swept away trailing a moist powder scent before Annie could think of anything to say. She finally called, "Thank you!" as Nettie rolled down the window of her battered old Impala.

Chantal took Annie's arm. "I came out to my whole department," she told Annie.

"You what?"

"It's the only way to show Kurt that we have some support. Even if he just thinks all of us are weird, maybe he'll talk to us before he acts."

She stared at Chantal. "You are some kind of woman."

"Your kind?"

"My kind," Annie answered. "Definitely my kind."

CHAPTER 19

Annie and Chantal spent more of the weekend by Gussie's side than in bed, and took some time that rainy Sunday afternoon to get together at the diner with Sheryl, Cece, Louie, Nicole and a few others to tell them what had happened with Kurt.

"Gawd," said Louie. "Kurt must have preached the sermon from hell this morning. Feel the flames, folks!"

Cece slammed her fist on the table so hard the silverware rattled. "I'm going to come out to that shit heel, too. What good does it do to keep my mouth shut? The insurance covered my bike—and my bike buddies wouldn't let me dirty my hands. They took care of the kids who did it."

Sheryl asked, "Who was it?"

"High school punks. You remember the kids who put the black runner in the hospital after that track meet last year?"

"The runner is our neighbor," Nicole said. "He'll never compete again."

"Tell him these creeps aren't going to pull anything else in this town soon."

On Monday, her last week at Medipak, Annie went to work filled with an expectant tension. She seemed to be working at doubletime, but couldn't slow down.

"Hold it!" cried Louie.

Annie couldn't stop. She slammed into him at full speed. Their bins went skidding across the floor, cards of aspirin tins, handfuls of combs, and dozens of bubble packs of lip balm scattering.

"Dizzy dame," said Louie. "You're in hyperdrive."

"You're right," she admitted. "I'm really sorry. You okay?"

Cece came to help them pick up and separate their orders. "What're you trying to do, Heaphy? Set a productivity record on your way out the door?"

"I'm just a nervous wreck."

"You'll make the rest of us look like we're on a work slow-down."

"Not likely. I'm probably making a million mistakes in my orders and I'll be pink-slipped even if Kurt doesn't find me morally unsuited to picking and packing. I probably ought to give notice early, before he beats me to it. If this is psychological warfare, I'm losing bad."

The rain lingered through Monday, but nothing happened at work. Tuesday nothing happened. All day Wednesday nothing happened. Annie stalked the railroad tracks behind Rafferty Street, silently ranting at Kurt as he terminated her. She was holding off giving notice until she saw what he did. She also had some vague idea that if Kurt canned Chantal she would quit in protest.

"Life's not like some TV show," she complained to Gussie. "I actually have to live through every tedious minute between crises and victories."

"Be patient. We've always survived the cycles before. This'll get sorted out."

"You're right. Now I know first hand about oppression. It's a long torturous process, isn't it? Being a despised minority means waiting around for the majority to pat me on the head or smack me."

"I wish all the kids could get out of Medipak, Socrates. It's going to make you crazy, watching them hatch their plots against us right in front of you."

"Don't I know it? But jobs don't exactly grow on trees around here."

Despite it all, the late May twilight was blue with promise at Maddy's graduation on Wednesday evening. Azaleas glowed like lanterns, leading the crowd into the vaulted auditorium of the high school. The excited adults chattered, the few children were quiet and big-eyed.

Maddy's dad had refused to travel out from Nebraska to watch his queer child graduate, but Giulia, more stern-faced than usual, and Mario, bowing and smiling to everyone, were back from their honeymoon. Teachers were encouraged to attend, so Venita, in a loosely woven straw hat whose brim made a radical dip down one side of her face, sat with Paris and Peg. They'd been able to get tickets for Annie and Gussie from other teachers. Chantal managed two tickets from an ex in-law whose sixth grandkid was graduating. She offered a seat to Jennifer Jacob. They flanked Maddy's mom, Sophia Scala, filling half a row.

"Only one man, Mario?" asked Sophia. "There should be more men. It doesn't look so good."

Annie looked at Peg who made a face, but whispered, "I'll try." She returned several minutes later with one of Maddy's gay Yalie friends. Peg introduced him to Sophia, who patted him into the seat next to her.

"How come you never come by the house?" Sophia asked him in a loud whisper. "I didn't know my Maddelena had any boyfriends."

The boy was saved by the first notes of the high school band. He grimaced. Gussie briefly covered her ears only to have a wrist playfully swatted by Venita. Annie and Chantal interlaced fingers. Annie was a sucker for "Pomp and Circumstance." She felt herself getting ready to cry.

As the graduates began their procession from the lobby to their seats, Chantal whispered, "I remember Merry and Ralph in their black gowns. Merry was absolutely solemn. Ralph kept twirling his tassel with an index finger, grinning like a kinder-garten graduate. And me, both times I used so many tissues the inside of my purse was damp for a month."

Annie rocked back and forth on her seat, craning her neck to watch for Maddy, but instead found herself meeting eyes with the guy in white who'd been smoking outside the hospital the day she'd stopped to talk with Dusty, Elly and Judy. She whis-pered to Chantal.

"There's nothing," Chantal said with a knowing grin, "like a little town for running into trouble. Where is he?"

Annie showed her.

"Oh! That's my ex-husband." Chantal waved. He gave her the thumbs up. "I told him all about you. He's just checking you out. He's a supervisor in the hospital cafeteria. His sister must have dragged him here to watch his niece graduate."

"You mean he's not the enemy?"

"No. Scowling is his natural expression. He's remarried, has two new babies and is glad I leave him alone. He's not above telling lesbian jokes, but really he could care less."

She hadn't quite sorted through the idea that there might be neutral non-liberal heterosexuals in the world when she saw the first triangle. "Chantal," she whispered, taking her hand, "look. I should have known Maddy would use buttons."

A good third of the kids wore oversized pink triangles, yellow stars, black triangles and other insignia for the Nazi condemned.

"Holy Navratilova," said Annie.

To be certain their meaning was lost on no one, each construction-paper cutout had been affixed with a swastika and a word: Gypsy, Disabled, Gay, Jew, Jehovah's Witness. Only twice was it obvious to Annie that the badge matched its wearer: the blind student and the young woman on Canadian canes.

Maddy, who was still fumbling to attach her black triangle—they must have put them on at the top of the aisle, just past the censorious eyes of teachers—also wore a Gay and Proud button.

Chantal was trying to save her eye makeup with a wet wad of tissues. Peg, on the other side of Annie, stood so erect she looked as if she'd burst her fancy vest buttons with pride. Jennifer was springing up and down on the balls of her feet, silently clapping her hands. When the last kid had filed in, the Yale boy started the real applause and, although much of the audience did not join, it took the national anthem, haltingly played by the band, to stop those who had. Annie's row sang the anthem with unbridled vigor. Look at me! she wanted to shout. Here she was at a small town graduation, singing the anthem, watching a political protest. She felt American in a way she never had before.

Later in the ceremony, as the principal introduced Maddy, Chantal leaned to whisper, "Has she heard if she's getting into Yale yet?"

"They'll take her, but she's waiting for the financial package."

Maddy bounded to the podium to give her speech. The legs of her jeans—no white dress for her—were obvious under the gown. The kid's curly black locks looked wilder than usual, spiraling out from under her cap. She punched the air as she spoke. She grinned. She mopped her eyes with a lavender bandanna as she told the audience what it felt like to have suddenly found out that she was going to be considered a freak the rest of her life.

"But it doesn't have to be like that!" she shouted into the

microphone. There was a smattering of applause. "I'm Maddy Scala, daughter of a junk-picker and a welfare mom. Two years ago I was one step away from a street corner and a dirty needle. I was a major drop-out, a teenage runaway. Like Janis Joplin sang, freedom was just another word for nothing left to lose."

"Right on!" shouted a student in the audience.

"Why?" Maddy continued. "Because of my packaging: I was different from most of you because I'm a gay kid. Do you know what it feels like to be despised because of who you are? There are small-minded people in every town and in Morton River some non-gays have decided to blame us for unemployment and crime and affirmative action and the fact that they can't understand or keep up with the changes in the world. These mean little people want our Selectmen to assume that gays molest while the real molesters—so many straight husbands and fathers—get away with murder in their own homes!"

Louder applause and a slew of yeses from female voices punctuated this remark. On the platform behind Maddy the school principal whipped the skirt of his robe closer around his knees. The valedictorian looked as if he were trying to swallow his delight. Annie was trying not to bounce in her seat. The kid was hot.

"I don't care who passed what gene on to me, or what any shrink or senator or colonel or preacher says about me, I have a lot to offer Morton River, and Morton River would be terrifically stupid to refuse the gifts of any of its kids." This got a resounding response, but one man stood and shook his fist toward the stage. A hand reached up to pull him back to his seat.

Venita whispered down the row, "I've never seen an audience so lively over a graduation speech!"

The deep breath Maddy took was visible. "And today I, Maddy Scala, daughter of a junk-picker and a welfare mom, teenage runaway and gay paisan, am also Maddy Scala, salutatorian of Morton River High School, and Maddy Scala, only the fifth kid from Morton River ever to be accepted to Yale on a full scholarship."

"She got it!" cried Chantal, jumping out of her seat.

The whole row leapt up to cheer and applaud, Sophia Scala wearing a wide smug smile to show that she'd been in on Maddy's secret. At least half of the audience had risen to give

Maddy a standing ovation. Annie shot up a fist and yelled, "Yes!"

Afterward, outside, a contingent of members of the gay group at Yale, V.O.W. activists and PFLAG members lined the sidewalk under lamp posts to reinforce Maddy's message, smiling pleasantly behind their posterboard signs: Separate Church and State—Don't Legislate Hate! No Screening—Discrimination Hurts Us All!

There were people who scurried by, but more who read the signs and even a few who stopped to talk and ask questions.

Annie and Gussie stopped by Elly and Dusty. Summer would arrive officially the next week and, as if to celebrate, the night was warm enough that almost no one wore jackets. Annie said, "I thought you two would be resting up before your flight. Isn't tomorrow the day you catch a five a.m. limo to JFK?"

"We were too thrilled to sit home when we could be part of the demonstration. It's like winning Revolutionary-For-A-Day," Elly said, a new brand of excitement in her eyes and voice. Verne might never have happened.

Dusty observed, "We should be home packing."

"You've been filling that suitcase for a month, you old pack-rat." Elly hugged Dusty's arm and explained, "Every two days she takes everything out and in goes an alternate wardrobe."

"The weather keeps changing over there. And it won't take a truck to get my things to the airport, like it will this one's," Dusty explained, pointing to Elly with a thumb. "If you hear we've gone down over the Atlantic, you know who's to blame."

"Come to Rafferty Street for cake and ice cream," Gussie ordered them, taking Elly's hand. "We'll make it a bon voyage as well as a graduation party."

"Can we bring Lorelei?" Dusty asked.

"Could you?" asked Annie. "I'd love to see her."

Elly answered. "The Simskis found the decency to let her go back into a group home. Lorelei was just pining away. And they're not total monsters."

"Can she keep quiet about visiting?" Gussie asked.

"We'll remind her what's at stake," Dusty said firmly. "We can only stay briefly anyway." She glanced at Elly. "Gotta finish packing."

Hope Valerie, Ralph Zak and Louie from Medipak had volunteered to set up the party. They'd cordoned off a parking space for the Grape.

"Where are all our ruffians?" Gussie asked.

Annie scanned Rafferty Street. "Cece put herself in charge of security. She's probably playing pool with the ringleaders right now, keeping them off Rafferty Street. Wait—there's some on the porch across the street, smoking. Maybe they'll just watch."

Gussie crowed. "Let them. I invited the next door neighbors and told them just how gay a celebration it would be. Oh, and the gay cop too. I think, from the hubbub out back, that we have enough bodies to defend ourselves tonight should any trouble-makers show up."

As they walked along the dark alleyway beside the house Gussie said, "Stop for a minute, would you, Socrates?"

From the alleyway they could see that the backyard was decorated with balloons, colored lights, Chinese lanterns and spot-lights of blue and red. Jake had outdone himself with the lights. There were dozens of people waiting for the graduate. Sheryl and Nicole from Medipak arrived with the bookkeeper Nettie Wilson in tow. Maybe, thought Annie, the long term battle in mind, just maybe, there are enough of us.

"You know," said Gussie, "Nan and Mr. Heimer were never party-givers. I wonder what she would have thought of all this." In a choked whisper she answered herself. "She would have delighted in it. Perhaps she's delighting in it, right here in our midst. Look at the flowers! She helped decorate for us."

Annie slipped a hand onto Gussie's shoulder.

"I want you to throw a party once I'm gone, Heaphy. You make sure to think of me then, won't you?"

"At every party I ever go to, Gus. But that won't be for a long while. We need you right here." She got on her knees. "You'll stick around a long time, won't you, Gus?"

"Get back up here. I'm not going anywhere just now. Still, there is a certain peace that comes with knowing my world is in good hands. A sense that I can let go and you and Paris, Hope, Cece, Peg and Dusty, Elly and young Maddy—and now Chantal—will take care of things and, when your time comes, pass on the work."

"You know, once upon a time I thought life was about having a good time."

"Oh, it is, Socrates, it is. But you're wise enough, or honorable enough, to know that our best times are the ones we work hard for."

Jo waylaid Annie once Gussie was installed at the head of the picnic table under a lantern gold as a harvest moon and swirling with moths.

"I'm so pleased you're going back to the Farm, Annie," said Jo with her wide elfin smile.

"Thanks to you," she answered, her heart a stew of feelings about Jo.

"Thanks to Judy. She's resting up for her return to work or she'd be here tonight."

"Good. I'll need her there Monday," Annie told her, unable to resist an unsuccessful scan for Verne. She saw Elly and Dusty arrive, a thinner but beaming Lorelei between them. When Lorelei spotted her she flung herself toward Annie, then stopped short.

"Can I hug you?"

"Yes." Annie tried to be less stiff, but it was still too hard.

"You need hugging lessons."

"It's true," she admitted, "I've never been as good as you at hugs, Lor."

"You still happy, Annie?"

"I'm happy to see my favorite passenger."

"Why don't you come back?"

"Don't you like your new driver?"

"Donald is Errol's brother! We sing! We sing, Hi ho, Hi ho, It's Off To Work We Go! And Whistle While You Work!" She tried to whistle the tune but ended sputtering with laughter.

"Lor!" said Dusty. "Let's get some eats."

Lorelei followed Dusty, but not without a last plea to Annie. "Donald has to go to his old job and in the rain all Kim's sorrel got drowned and she cried and you weren't there."

"How does next Monday sound?" Annie asked, her face flushing with pleasure.

Lorelei stopped short. "You mean it?"

"Don't be late!"

"Aw-right!" cried Lorelei, fist pumping the air.

Red and blue spotlights intersected on Jo, staining her white pants and light blue striped jersey a fluorescent lavender glow.

Jo's eyes were excited.

"I came out at the bank."

Annie felt her jaw drop in amazement. "You didn't."

Now the smile turned unexpectedly bashful. She found her anger at Jo was not very deep. "They were pretty shocked, but most of them are only fiscal, not social, conservatives, and a couple of them promised to put all the pressure they can on the Selectmen to laugh those rightwingers out of the meeting."

"Great!"

"They asked us to pack the room tomorrow night. Did you see that Giulia's new husband brought one of the new Selectmen tonight?"

"To the graduation?"

"No. Here. To the party." Jo indicated a smiling white-haired man whose picture was often in the paper.

"Geez. It's working. I didn't believe Gussie that this quiet sort of organizing she started would make a difference."

"Most people are decent. The loony radical right was just steamrolling over them."

"Will you make an announcement about the vote? We need to make sure we have that big turnout."

"I don't think so, Annie. Word of mouth might be best where there's an insider involved. Besides, I still have to survive at the bank."

"I thought you were on your way to bigger and better things."

The brown eyes seemed to fill with sorrow, as palpable as tears. "So did I."

Annie raised an eyebrow, guilt struggling with vindictive relish.

Jo shrugged fragile-looking shoulders. "Things didn't work out the way I—" She stopped, cleared her throat, shrugged again.

"She's seeing someone else?"

Eyes down, Jo nodded. "I seem to have a thing for cads."

She reached for Jo's hand, pleased beyond words. "You're made for better things," she counseled very seriously. "I'm glad you're sticking around."

Jo looked at the crowd, a smile returning to her lips.

Annie followed her eyes.

Maddy, gown and all, barreled around the yard with

Jennifer, to Louie's accordion rendition of the polka.

"I love seeing Maddy act like a kid!" Annie said. "Maybe she'll trust us grownups not to mess up too badly even if she takes a minute off once in a while."

Just then Gussie, looking like a dyke matriarch, bellowed with laughter under her golden lantern, patting down a cowlick.

Annie and Jo watched the Santiagos from next door peep through the hedge and find the widow who lived on the other side of Gussie's house. Paris herded all three under the blinking Christmas lights to the punch bowl, introducing them to everyone they passed. These three would not be silent if Gussie's home ever came under attack again.

"I'm glad Morton River's my home," Jo said, still lavender in the light. "Next time there's a party I'll bring someone from work."

Annie remembered something Vicky had said: Out here we're trying to put human faces on prejudice. "This really is how we'll win, isn't it, whatever the politicians, the ballots, and the courts say," Annie remarked, feeling a billowing majesty of emotion. When had she last felt that?

"Parties?" asked Jo.

"By coming out one by one. By introducing the widowed neighbors to the gay guy playing the polka, the bankers to the gym teachers, sending the kids out as emissaries into the big world, announcing who we are from podiums. It makes me feel powerful, like gay people have a mission, like we can, you know," she faltered for words, "try to save the world from fascism or something." She thought about her dad. Again.

"You have a hero complex, Annie."

She thought about that. "You're the hero—for coming out at work. I just kind of staggered out of my closet," she said, suiting action to words, eyes closed, and bumping into someone short and soft. "Sorry!" she cried, backing off.

It was Ralph, his mother on his arm.

"Is the punch that strong? Let me at it!" Ralph said.

Annie embraced Chantal, laughing, and wrapped her other arm around Jo.

Ralph rushed Maddy and lifted her with a cheer.

"That's my boy!" cried Chantal.

Giulia's husband Mario laughed as Ralph and Maddy spun

into him. Mario caught Annie's eye and came to where she stood with Chantal and Jo.

"I want you to know this. I am in the real estate business. It happens that I own some of these properties." He gestured with his hand toward the houses across the street. His Italian accent was strong. "And the unimproved lot at the end of Rafferty Street. For a long time I have wondered if I should sell, build, put up a fence to keep the hoodlums out. Now that I know what went on here while we were away I will build a home for Giulia. A big house, for Sophia and Maddy too. What do you call it? A showplace. This will chase out the children of Mussolini and maybe even improve property values for Augusta. I will get the city to replace those old cobblestones—"

"NO!" cried Annie.

"No?" He paused, looked into her eyes. "You're right. The cobblestones make this a special street. We will keep them. Repair them. Yes?"

He was gesturing toward the end of the street and, as if his hand could throw images against the dark, Annie saw a circular drive, if not cobbled, then brick, a two-story home in stained wood, the old trees still standing, azaleas, dogwood, rosebushes blooming in season, birds raiding bushes laden with berries. She saw peace too, the desire of an ordinary man to keep life decent for everyone. And the urge of strange Giulia trying, like all of them, to get through life the best she could. Of Maddy, who'd go through the tortures of the damned, living in comfort while she wanted to make changes more fundamental than a bandaid over a neighborhood.

"I feel so connected to everyone, Mario. Thank you for telling us." He bowed his way back into the crowd.

More dancers joined the first few. Chantal tugged at Annie's hand, startling her out of her amazement at Mario's plans.

"Dance with me?" Chantal's eyes, around the seductive blue-ness, were tinted with lavender light.

"How about after the Board of Selectmen votes?" But even as Annie said it she knew the vote would end nothing. She needed to celebrate every chance she got because they were in it for the long haul, all of them.

Louie quickened the song. Maddy escaped from Ralph and dragged Sophia into a dance. Dusty and Elly and Lorelei lurched by, a polkaing threesome, their laughter loud enough, Annie imagined, to be heard all along Rafferty Street. Annie looked at her watch, excited. "Ten-thirty-three," she said to Chantal, sweeping a hand toward the railroad tracks. "Listen."

The train gave its customary hoot as it approached the crossing at the end of Rafferty Street, and then added another long toot. Was there traffic at the crossing or had the engineer heard the music, seen the lights? Then the train was tearing through the night with a sound almost like bells under the roar—could they be the old train bells of her Chelsea childhood clanging, not a siren call, but a welcome home? Its groan became a background noise off and on, long, short, as it hit the curves going north along the Morton River, and still she heard that ghost of a bell growing more faint as the party sounds once again filled her ears.

Annie, laughing, took Chantal's hand and they danced into the passionate, widening circle.

MORE BOOKS FROM NEW VICTORIA PUBLISHERS
PO BOX 27, NORWICH, VERMONT 05055
OR CALL 1-800 326-5297   EMAIL   newvic@aol.com
Home page   http://www.opendoor.com/NewVic/

OFF THE RAG: Lesbians Writing on Menopause

Edited by Lee Lynch and Akia Woods An exciting collection, the experience of lesbians at this landmark change of life. Includes Sarah Dreher, Sally Gearhart, Karla Jay, Merrill Mushroom, Joan Nestle and Terri de la Peña. $12.95

SOLITAIRE AND BRAHMS Sarah Dreher

A gritty, painstaking look at the struggle for lesbian identity before Stonewall. Shelby Camden wonders why her impending marriage seem to constrict her to the point of depression and drink. Then she meets the independent Fran Jarvis, with whom she finds she can share her innermost thoughts. $12.95

BACKSTAGE PASS, Interviews with Women in Music by Laura Post

Foreword by Dar Williams Ani DiFranco, Alix Dobkin, June Millington, Margie Adam, Joan Osborne, Holly Near, Sweet Honey in the Rock, and Ferron, to name a few. An intimate glimpse into the personal and political lives of these rock, folk and jazz musicians. Includes great photos and discography. $16.95

EVERY WOMAN'S DREAM by Lesléa Newman.

Tales of sex, monogamy, fantasies, the future, and the possibility of lesbian motherhood. She's compassionate with her characters yet doesn't flinch from confronting hard issues faced by communities, gay and straight alike. "Sometimes Lesléa Newman gets the voice so good and so right that the rest of the prose shines in the afterglow." —Bay Windows $9.95

SECRETS by Lesléa Newman.

The surfaces and secrets, sensuality, and conflicts of lesbian relationships. $8.95

ICED   Judith Alguire

An action-packed novel of women's professional ice hockey. Alison jumps at the chance to coach the Toronto Teddies. It gets complicated when she falls in love with one of her players. $10.95

LADY GOD   Lesa Luders

Landy flees the mountains where she grew up. Claire befriends her helping Landy to untangle her sexuality, still bound up in an incestuous relationship with her mother. $9.95

DOG TAGS   Alexis Jude

Two female soldiers in Korea struggling to create a loving relationship in the face of harassment and homophobia. $9.95

LADY LOBO Kristen Garrett

Brash basketball jock Casey creates heat and sweat on and off the court. $9.95

WINDSWEPT Magdalena Zschokke

Women's sailing adventures. Mara, Olivia and Zoë come to an understanding of themselves and their goal of an all-women crew.$10.95